D1213820

The Bright Side
of Disaster

Ballantine Books

New York

The Bright Side of Disaster

A Novel

Katherine Center

This is a work of fiction. Names, characters, places, and incidents are the products of the author's imagination or are used fictitiously. Any resemblance to actual events, locales, or persons, living or dead, is entirely coincidental.

Published in the United States by Ballantine Books, an imprint of The Random House Publishing Group, a division of Random House, Inc., New York.

BALLANTINE and colophon are registered trademarks of Random House, Inc.

ISBN 978-1-4000-6637-7

LIBRARY OF CONGRESS CATALOGING-IN-PUBLICATION DATA

Center, Katherine.
The bright side of disaster: a novel / Katherine Center.
p. cm.
ISBN-13: 978-1-4000-6637-7
ISBN-10: 1-4000-6637-9
1. Unmarried mothers—Fiction. 2. Divorced parents—Fiction.
3. Chick lit. I. Title.
PS3603.E67B75 2007
813'6—dc22 2006051036

Printed in the United States of America on acid-free paper

www.ballantinebooks.com

2 4 6 8 9 7 5 3 1

FIRST EDITION

Book design by Dana Leigh Blanchette

For my mother,

Deborah Inez Detering,

who always loves me anyway

The Bright Side of Disaster

1

The end began with a plane crash. Just before midnight on a Tuesday in February. A girl I'd never met or even heard of died, along with her miniature dachshund (under the seat) and a planeload of passengers in the kind of commuter plane I'll never fly in again. I've pictured it a hundred times now: the quiet hum of the motor, the sleeping passengers, the sudden jolt, the cabin steward thrown sideways before he could finish his instructions. In my mind, it always looks like a movie, because I have nothing else to go on.

That night, I was asleep, safe on the ground, miles away in Texas in my hand-me-down bed, nestled under a patchwork quilt made out of ties from the seventies.

Since getting pregnant, I fell asleep before the double digits. It was something my not-quite-yet-husband, Dean, teased me about. He was a night owl. And I had been one, too. These days, a month before my due date, I was in bed with my swollen ankles up on pillows as soon as the dishes were done. He was out in the living room with his headphones on, likely playing air guitar.

In a slightly different situation, I would have heard about the crash on the news and thought no more about it. I am sure that girl meant many things to many people. And though I didn't know it at the time, and I would not have recognized her if she'd knocked on my door, she meant a lot to me as well—in a roundabout kind of way.

The day Dean came home from the office with the news, I'd been out in the garage for hours pricing things with little orange stickers. I'd quit my job at a fancy antiques store a few weeks back at the urging of the owner. She knew I was planning to quit after the baby came, but she decided it didn't make sense to wait. She took me aside one morning and said that I was, simply, too big. "When you can knock over a piece of Stickley with your belly," she said, "it's time to call it a day." She gave me some coupons for a mani-pedi, promised she'd always give me her dealer discount, and nudged me out the door.

So I was home. And planning our upcoming garage sale with checklists, spreadsheets, and a color-coded map of my yard. At thirty-six weeks and counting, what else was I going to do with myself?

When Dean walked in with a pizza, I was slumped over the aqua dinette in our kitchen, drinking orange juice and trying for an end-of-the-day rally. He popped open a beer and swigged down about half of it. His tie was wrinkled. Really wrinkled, like it'd been on the floor of his car for days before he'd discovered it. I wondered if it would be my job to see to such things when we were married.

He pulled two plates out of the cupboard, and just as I was thinking how much I loved it when Dean brought me pizza, they slid right out of his grip and shattered on the floor.

"Fuck!" he shouted. "Fuck!" He turned and slammed his palm against the cabinet.

I didn't say anything. After five years with him, I knew to lay low. My best friend, Meredith, and I called these moments "occasional eruptions of inappropriate rage." They were, you might say, a part of his charm.

He pressed his head against the cabinets, and I set about picking up. I had to bend over my belly to reach the shards, which made great clanks as they hit the metal bottom of the garbage can. When I went for the broom, he moved to his chair and sat down. Then he said, "A girl from work died last night."

"Died?" I said. "How?"

"Plane crash."

"Big plane or little plane?" I asked.

"Puddle jumper," he said.

I finished sweeping and leaned the broom against the counter. "Who was it?" I asked, sitting down.

"Just a girl. She worked in graphics." He lifted a slice of pizza and took a tentative bite, as if it might not go down well.

"Was she somebody you knew?" I asked.

"Yeah," he said, mouth full. "I definitely knew her." Her cubicle was around the corner from his, and she—her name was Tara—used to stop in and say hi. She had worked there for a year. She had been planning to come see his band.

We chewed for a while. Then, not sure what else to say, I shook my head and said, "I thought plane crashes only happened to people on the news."

"Well," he said. "She's on the news now."

After dinner, we sat out on the porch swing, as we did many nights. Our house was in one of the few historic neighborhoods in Houston that hadn't been bulldozed for townhomes or mini-malls. By some mystery, folks in our neighborhood were restoring their houses instead of replacing them. Living here was like living in another place in time.

On good nights, we'd go on talking after dinner. But tonight he kept quiet, nursing beer number three. He was holding the memo they'd passed out at work with details about the funeral and where to send donations. It had this girl Tara's picture on it.

She was Asian, with shiny straight hair and kissy lips. The picture was from her company ID photo, but even so, she was smiling as if the guy who'd taken the photo had been flirting with her. She certainly seemed very alive. And she was the kind of pretty that wasn't up for discussion.

"She's pretty," I said, looking over his arm.

"You think so?"

"Dean," I said, giving him a look that said, *Come on.* At the time, a little lie like that seemed sweet to me. I assumed he was trying to be a good fiancé by pretending not to know she was pretty. Like he only had eyes for me. "Yes," I said. "She's pretty."

"Was," he said.

"Was."

I tried to start up some other conversation after that. I told him that Meredith had bought a leash for her cat. I told him about a report I'd heard on a hurricane in the Gulf. I told him I'd heard a woman singing a version of "Hush Little Baby" on the gospel radio station that afternoon, and the sound had brought tears to my eyes. But the words came out of my mouth and fizzled like sparks before they hit the ground.

Some nights were like this, when Dean just couldn't rise to the conversational challenge. Meredith said he was moody, which was true. But we all had our shortcomings. Still, if we weren't going to talk, I wished he would rub my neck, or hold my hand. But he didn't.

Dean wanted to take a shower, so I followed him inside. I put on my DON'T MESS WITH TEXAS maternity nightshirt before I headed into the kitchen to clean up, and when I got there, I noticed the girl's picture was on the fridge. Dean had put it up with butterfly magnets, one placed in each corner. Very few things on our overloaded fridge merited more than one magnet. Not our list of frequently called numbers, not the picture of us at a wildflower garden on our road trip to Austin, not the liner notes for Dean's band's only album. But there she was, securely placed and there to stay. I wasn't sure I wanted her there, and I thought about taking her down and sticking her in a drawer with the take-out menus.

But I left her. She had the kind of eyes that followed you around the room. I'd thought that happened only with paintings in museums, but here she was, in my kitchen, watching me. While I did the dishes. While I took my prenatal vitamin. While I did a final sweep for pieces of broken plate. She even watched the door for my return while I took the pizza box outside to the trash. Back inside, I turned the dead bolt, started the dishwasher, and stood with my hand on the light switch. We held each other's gaze for a few minutes, and then I left her in the dark.

2

~

The next day, I adopted Meredith's cat.

Meredith had rescued the cat about six months earlier, when he was hit by a car. She took him to a nearby vet, who performed emergency surgery and removed one of the cat's eyes. The vet, who must have been a softy, did not charge Meredith for the surgery, or the office visit, or the kitty drugs, and Meredith was so grateful that she named the cat after him.

This was how Meredith came to own a cat named Dr. Blandon, despite her landlady's nonnegotiable no-pets policy. He had been hiding out in her one-bedroom apartment, which, according to the real Dr. Blandon, likely explained his recent weight gain—eight pounds in six months for a grand total of twenty. The real Dr.

Blandon even called him "obese," a term Meredith found "a little hostile."

She had defended her Dr. Blandon, saying, "He looks good. He wears it well. He's had a tough year." The real doctor warned her to put him on diet food, but Meredith refused. "I'm morally opposed to that stuff," she said.

Meredith, a size 12 herself, was exceptionally pretty, with a heart-shaped face and straight, wholesome blond hair. She was sensitive to issues of size. And she declared that the vet was a "fatist." "Too bad," she said. "Because he asked for my number."

Dr. Blandon the cat lived with Meredith until her landlady paid a surprise visit to discuss a late rent check and saw him snoozing in his tiger-striped kitty bed. She almost kicked Meredith out on the spot.

That was when Meredith arrived at my house. I'd already gone to bed. "I'm so sorry to wake you," she said at the door, tears on her face. Dean was out with the band, and I sat her on the sofa and made her give me the blow-by-blow. Even though she was a very close friend—the kind of friend I could call just to say I was bored—I had never seen her cry before.

"This pet really means a lot to you," I said.

"Some cats are just cats," she said. "And some cats are people."

"And your cat is a person."

She nodded.

"Do you need a place to stay?" I asked, looking at the little duffel bag she'd brought in.

"No," Meredith said, unzipping it, "but Dr. Blandon does."

She pulled him out and set him on the rug.

"Oh, no!" I said.

"Just try him on for size," she said.

"I can tell you already," I said. "He's too big." And as I said it, all twenty pounds of Dr. Blandon hopped up onto what was left of my lap and started kneading my belly.

I pushed him off. "I can't take him."

He jumped back up.

"He's indoor-outdoor!" Meredith said. "There's no litter box! He's not sick! He just needs love! If I take him to the pound, he'll be killed!"

Dr. Blandon was purring like a motorboat. I petted him and couldn't feel any bones.

"See how fluffy he is?" Meredith said.

"Fluffy?" I said. "Or fleshy?"

"Judge him if you want to," she said. "But you have to admit, he's a pleasure to pet."

He was.

I ran through a list of other people she could give the cat to, but she'd tried them all before and been turned down—which is how she wound up living her secret cat-life in the first place. "I never would have come here," Meredith said, "if you weren't my last hope."

Maybe it was the tears. Maybe it was all my mother-to-be hormones. But I agreed to take Dr. Blandon on a trial basis.

"I hate myself for asking you," Meredith said.

"Dean will have to go for it," I told her. "And he's not going to."

She nodded.

"But I'll tell him we're cat-sitting," I said, "and try to sneak him in that way."

Meredith didn't say much about Dean anymore. I had recently created a rule that she was not allowed to say anything about him that wasn't nice, and now her standard response to any mention of Dean was a closed-mouth silence.

Meredith and Dean had gotten off on the wrong foot when I'd first started dating him years back—mostly because he was desperately pursuing my friend Nadia for a while after we got together.

"That's pretty fucked up, don't you think?" Meredith had said one too many times.

My friend Nadia had been a project manager in a power job at

Shell Oil. She had a silk-and-leather wardrobe and rectangular glasses that made her look both smarter and cooler than anybody in the room. She was exfoliated, she was plucked, she had glossy black hair, and men were always hitting on her. Hitting on Nadia was a no-brainer.

And I was almost her opposite. I didn't own a hair dryer, mostly wore jeans, and had an affection for sneakers that Nadia didn't understand. In my good moments, I rated myself as "pretty cute," but I was no match for her. I got hit on myself, sometimes. But never, ever when I was with her. And Dean was no exception.

He spied us one night at a swanky after-hours restaurant, and when Nadia got up to go check out the bathroom, he sat himself down across from me in her chair.

"Hi," he said.

He was cute. Shaggy hair that had probably been blond when he was a kid. Blue eyes with lashes that sisters always envy on brothers. Teeth that were just crooked enough for character. At that moment, he had a love-struck look to him that made me think, in that instant, against all my self-deprecating instincts, that he was appearing out of nowhere to ask me out. And right then, before we'd even spoken to each other, I felt like the answer to any question he could ever ask me would be yes. Yes, yes—hell, yes.

"What can I say," he said then, leaning in, "to get your friend to fall in love with me?"

"Nadia?" I said.

"Oh, God, her name's Nadia," he said, collapsing backward against the chair like he'd been struck by an arrow. "That's such a cool name."

"Well," I said, sitting a bit straighter and arranging my spoon on my napkin, "I'm not sure that you're her type."

Her type, in fact, was businessmen. Tall, BMW-driving, occasionally married businessmen.

"Just give me some tips."

"Really, chief, my best tip is to find somebody else."

"Give me her number."

"I'm not going to do that."

"Then do this. Give me your number, let me convince you I'm not a psycho, and then give me her number."

"I don't think you're a psycho," I said. "I just don't think she's going to go out with you."

"Please," he said.

He had a pen out already. He reached his hand across the table and waited, looking at me. I could have rooted in my purse for a scrap of paper, but instead, I took his hand, turned it over, and wrote my number across the palm. Beneath the number, I wrote "Jenny." Not a name to make anyone fall back in a chair. A name that seven girls in my graduating class had. As he pulled his hand back, I wished like anything that I had written something else—"Jasmine" or "Vivian" or "Delilah."

He looked up. "Jenny," he said. "I'm Dean."

He called me the next morning and set about wooing me. Wooing me so that I would go to bat for him with Nadia. He opened the car door for me. He burned CDs for me. He gave me a potted orchid. He rubbed my neck in traffic. He took me to eat the best Vietnamese *pho* I had ever tasted. At a roadside carnival, he spent thirty dollars trying to win me a bear. And all the while, he asked me question after question about myself, listening to the answers like I was the only person in the world who mattered.

And I was wooed. I was so wooed that I forgot why he was wooing me. After two weeks of what felt like the beginning of a relationship between the two of us, as we finished dinner at an Indian restaurant and just as I was starting to think I might get a good-night kiss when we got to my house, he said, "So. Can I have it?"

"Have what?"

He looked at me like I was nuts. "Her number," he said.

What choice did I have? I gave it to him.

Here was the problem: I liked him. By then, I already liked him.

And even though it defied all logic, I knew that, whether he knew it or not, he liked me, too. I could just feel it. We had something.

What followed with Nadia was predictable. He called her, pursued her, was denied, pursued her harder, was denied and then mocked, and finally gave up. And I consoled him. And one night, after a six-pack of beer and our hundredth conversation in the series How Dean Had Blown It, he said, "You're kind of pretty, too." And then we slept together.

That was how it started. We fell into a relationship after that. Once Nadia was out of his sights, he found all sorts of things to appreciate about me. The scar on my elbow he liked to trace with his pinkie. My chocolate-chip cookies. My outie belly button. My dimple. The way I could braid my hair upside down. The way I slept with one foot out. The little humming noises I sometimes made when we kissed.

He still got moody about Nadia from time to time, and so it was a great relief to me when she moved to London for her job. She couldn't understand why I was dating Dean, and I never quite got the feeling that he was over her. And so Nadia and I fell out of touch.

Meredith had watched the whole scenario unfold with distaste, and even though she eventually got along pretty well with Dean, she remained "uncomfortable" with our "dynamic."

"He's a nice person," she said once, before we had enacted the Nice Things rule. "But he's a bad boyfriend."

"He is not!" I said.

"He should like you more," she said.

"He does like me," I protested.

"He should be more consistent," she said.

He was not, in fact, a bad boyfriend. But he was unpredictable. Meredith had been a psych major in college. She classified his behavior as "variable reinforcement," explaining it once this way: "If you always give a rat a treat, he loses interest in getting it. If you never give him the treat, he loses interest. But if you occasionally, from time to time, give him a treat, he's hooked."

"I'm the rat?" I asked.

"You're the rat," she said, as tenderly as she could.

Rat or not, she was right about one thing. I was hooked on Dean.

Meredith said, "I just want you to be with somebody who thanks his lucky stars for you every day."

Dean did not thank his lucky stars for me every day. Probably not even once a week. But when he did appreciate me, he did it well. Like the night we went bowling, and, after about ten gutter balls, I rolled a strike. The two of us hopped around in a little victory dance. It was Monday Nite Disco bowling, and the place had smoke machines and mirror balls. He picked me up to spin me around and, before I knew it, I felt like we were all alone. He put his mouth against my ear. "I'm in love with you," he said. "Did you know that already?"

I could have said something brassy, like "Join the club, baby." But instead, I got shy and put my head into his chest.

He burrowed his face down close to mine, pressing for an answer. "You know that, right? You knock me out."

Meredith was there that night with a fling of hers we'd nicknamed Fabio. She was just a few feet away, but she couldn't hear us talking. Meredith knew a lot about Dean, but she didn't know everything. It was easy for her to say mean things about him. She'd never been in love. And love always looks different from how it feels, anyway.

But on the night I took Meredith's cat, she was feeling too grateful to say anything mean about anybody.

"Where is Dean, anyway?" she asked.

I made an air-guitar motion.

And she nodded. Because the Nice Things rule applied to Dean's band as well, of which she had once said, "They're not a real band. They're a bar mitzvah band."

And that was exactly the kind of gig his band played. Weddings, school parties, high school reunions, and the occasional local club. They played mostly cover songs, though they had a few of their own that they were very proud of. I couldn't argue with Meredith on the facts. But to me, the band was cute. To her, it was just plain sad.

"They're too old to be playing covers," she said.

"They just do it for fun," I said. But that wasn't exactly the truth. Those guys really did think that they had something special, and they really did hold out hope that they might get famous someday. They practiced every Saturday from noon to six, and many Sundays as well. And even I could tell that they weren't going to make it. But that was Dean: entry-level retirement-plans analyst by day, rocker by night. He made pretty good money at his real job, and he paid half my mortgage—calling himself a "renter." But in his estimation, he was an artist. And the copying, stapling, and staring into the computer he did at work was an insult to his integrity.

"It's a waste of time," Meredith said. "How many hours a weekend does he spend practicing with those guys?"

Meredith, who loved all kinds of music, had thought he was kidding when he first played her a track of one of their songs. After he was gone, she said, "The worst thing about them is their name. But the music is also very bad." I couldn't argue. The band's name was so bad that when asked, I used to pretend to forget it. Or make something else up on the spot. When Dean gave me a band T-shirt, I "lost" it in an unfortunate laundry incident. But here it is. They called themselves the Hard Drives.

There were things Meredith liked about Dean. She freely admitted that he had a nice ass and good forearms. She liked his shaggy hair, his baggy corduroys, and the way he dressed in resale bowling shirts with names like "Hank" on the pocket. "He looks like a musician," she said. "He just doesn't sound like one." She was willing to admit that he had a genuine charm and a je ne sais quoi. "If only he could put that on a CD," she said.

And she even came with me to Dean's gigs sometimes. If I went alone, I usually sat at the bar. But if she came with me, she'd give me a "what the hell" look and start dancing, and I would, too. In that way, she was good for our relationship. But she made no secret about her bottom line: As a boyfriend and as a musician, he was subpar.

And that's why, the night I took Dr. Blandon, after a few questions about how I was feeling and what the baby was up to "in there," we talked about Meredith. As Dr. Blandon sniffed around the house, I made tea, and Meredith told me she was going to break up with her boyfriend.

I said, "You are really crazy."

"It's just not right," she said.

Meredith had been through five boyfriends in two years. She'd fall in love on the first date and then spend the rest of the relationship racked with disappointment. She left men for many reasons: too hairy, too quiet, bad breath, tattoos of teddy bears, bad flossing habits, video-game addiction, and mispronunciation of words like *espresso* and *et cetera.*

"I'm not superficial," she insisted. Her current boyfriend was a sweet waiter at an Italian restaurant who sneaked her free cannolis. She'd been with him for three months, but we were still calling him the Waiter. She was ending it for this reason: He did not like to read.

"He quit halfway through *The Catcher in the Rye,*" she said.

"In high school? We're talking about high school?"

"The point is, he started the book and then he lost interest. He made a choice to stop reading."

"Who cares?"

"I think J. D. Salinger would care."

"You're looking for a reason to leave."

"No," she said. "I'm looking for a reason to stay. And he can't give me one."

"You're a hard-hearted woman," I said.

And then we came to the part of the conversation that was so familiar to us we could have been reciting movie lines.

"You're too picky," I said.

"And you're not picky enough."

Before Meredith left, she got a box of Dr. Blandon's things from her car: A Snoopy food bowl that said THE DOCTOR IS IN, a cat toy that looked like a dead mouse, some hair-ball paste, a bag of food, a cable-knit cat sweater, and, of course, his new little leash.

"I'm not using this," I said.

"I snuck him out to the park last week," Meredith said. "He likes it."

I looked at Dr. Blandon. He looked at me.

"No, he doesn't," I said.

I left Dr. Blandon licking his belly fur on the sofa, hoping that Dean wouldn't notice him right away. But Dean did notice him—as soon as he came to bed. He woke me at around three in the morning, saying, "Why is there a raccoon sleeping on your face?"

"It's Meredith's," I said, shoving Dr. Blandon down to the floor. "We're cat-sitting."

"For how long?"

I yawned on purpose and said, "A few days."

Taking Dr. Blandon was, perhaps, a decision I did not think through very well. Dean hated cats. Hated them enough that he refused to pet one, even if it came over and started brushing against him. And my mother was so allergic that her eyes watered if she even had lunch with a cat owner. Across the table! And even I, in just about a month, was going to have more caretaking to do than I'd be able to handle. But, in my own defense, I didn't really know much about the future at the time.

3

I wasn't sleeping well. In between deep, comalike periods during which I drooled and snored with great abandon, I was awake and restless. Shifting positions in bed. Getting up for water. Standing at the window.

I was trying to keep a pregnancy journal—you know, collected wisdom for the baby. I had read about it in one of my many pregnancy books, and it'd seemed like a good enough idea that I went to an art supply store to buy a special acid-free notebook.

But when I actually started to write, it felt weird. For one, the baby didn't seem real at all to me. Even with seven ultrasound pictures on the fridge, I could not wrap my head around the fact that there was a person inside my body. The kicks that are supposed to be so thrilling felt more like muscle twitches than anything else. And I felt cheesy writing to a person I'd never met. We didn't know each other at all, really. We were strangers sharing a placenta.

Still, I tried anyway.

Dear Baby,

Even though I am a happy person in most ways, and my life has turned out far better than I thought it would, I still find myself worrying about you. My mother did the best she could with me, and I turned out fine. But I want to do better than that with you, so that you never have to feel sad or discouraged or worthless. I plan to give you a hundred kisses a day. I wonder if that will do the trick.

Love from your mama

Even *mama* felt strange. I wasn't anybody's mama yet. But I figured I should keep making myself say it. Eventually it would be true.

My acid-free notebook was green and gender-neutral, even though the baby was, in my mind, without question, a boy. It had been Dean's idea to wait to find out the baby's sex. He thought it would be "cool"—cooler than what everybody else did, which was to find out as soon as possible. "Do you really want to be just like everybody else, Jenny?" he'd said, as though he already knew the answer. "Don't you think it's better to find out with your own eyes than from some ultrasound technician?" And when he put it that way, finding out in advance didn't seem so necessary. I didn't mind waiting, anyway, because I knew, I just knew, this baby was a boy.

"How do you know that?" Dean had asked one night on the porch.

"A mother knows," I said, pulling rank.

I loved being pregnant, and I basked in the warmth of pregnant life. When you are pregnant and seem happy about it, people project their best dreams for the world on you. You epitomize hope and new beginnings, and people are drawn to talk to you about it and touch your belly.

When I started to show, I also started to use the word *husband* for Dean—even though he wasn't going to be my husband for several months yet, and even though it felt just as weird as calling myself someone's mama. I also worried that it might just be bad luck. But it simplified things, especially for old ladies and grocery checkers who wanted to believe that I was doing things properly, that everything would be taken care of for this baby I was making.

When a ninety-year-old woman leans in to you and says, "Your husband must be thrilled," you simply cannot raise a twenty-eight-year-old eyebrow at her and say, "Let's hope he makes it to the altar, lady." You have to say, "Yes," with a shy smile and a pat of the belly, "he sure is." It's like a community service. And so, in that spirit, long before our wedding date, Dean became my "husband."

After all, we were engaged before we got pregnant. We had a venue and a florist and everything. So we'd played a little fast and loose with the birth control. So the timing was a little off. Our intentions were good.

Now we had a big wedding, planned largely by my mother, set for a month after my due date. My mother was a decorator, and that's exactly what she'd call herself, despite the movement to say "interior designer." She was very good at what she did, and she didn't need a fancy label to prove it. For all the same reasons that she loved decorating, she loved planning our wedding. Flowers! Fabrics! Romance! The arranging of everyday things—chairs, food, guests—to make them look extraordinary was a challenge my mother loved.

And I didn't mind. I also took an interest in the aesthetics of things, but I was a dinette set to her Chippendale. I remember once asking my mother if I could work for her as an assistant and she said, with a squeeze to my arm, "Oh, honey. You're too funky for me." She claimed to have no memory of this moment.

My mother hardly ever called me by my name. I was—as were all the people in her life, from the lady at the post office to her best friend, Larry—always "honey," or "sugar," or "sweetheart," or if she was feeling sassy, "lady" (as in, "Where'd you get those cute shoes, lady?"). It was very Texas. And she was very Texas. And boy, could she decorate. With my wedding, as with other things in my life, it seemed wise to follow her lead.

She was petite, with dark brown hair ("I want mahogany," she told her colorist) that she pulled back in a sleek ponytail. She had lovely pale skin and wore red lipstick for a "splash of color." She was always pressed and put-together. She wore shiny alligator shoes and silk scarves tied just so around her neck. She had giant, cartoonish, light-adjusting glasses with lipstick-matching frames that she wore so devotedly it was hard for me to imagine her face without them. She was fancy and feminine but never stuck-up or prissy. All that silk and perfume was balanced by her big Texas personality. Five feet, one inch of feistiness, and I adored her.

We were not much alike. "You just take after your daddy," she once said to me, leaning in and pressing her nose to mine. "But you got all his good stuff."

For the wedding, we'd had to reserve everything a year in advance, and the very afternoon that we'd told our parents about the engagement, my mother was on the job. Weddings were big business. All the good places and caterers and florists went fast. We'd wanted to do it a little sooner, but my mother put her foot down. "I've waited for you two for a long time," she said. "We're doing this right."

And so: the standard yearlong engagement. Dean and I picked a weekend, and in under a month my mother had secured the sculpture garden near the museum, a florist who'd been in *House & Garden,* a cake lady with the unexpected name of Rosita Rosenstein, and the most expensive caterer in town.

My long-divorced parents, who did not speak to each other unless forced, came together in honor of the event-planning. We met for lunch near the medical center, and my mother sat frozen with her lips pursed in a pout the whole time. She did manage to argue with my father and to eat her entire salad, leaving only streaks of orange dressing on the plate, but she never lost that pout.

My father, who, at six-four, was over a foot taller than my mother, had the handsome gray hair and easy athletic movements of a man who was more comfortable in public than in private. In recent years, he'd become a regular "consulting physician" on a local morning TV show, and folks all over town now came up like old friends and called him "Doc." He'd whitened his teeth for the gig and done a little time at the tanning booth—though I was sworn to secrecy about those things.

My dad was late to lunch because he'd been in surgery. ("They don't have cell phones in the OR?" had been my mother's greeting to him.) He showed up in his scrubs, and people kept coming up to our table like he was a movie star, reintroducing themselves and waiting for recognition. He punched them on the arms and called them things like "buddy" or "sport" or "chief." He was affable and popular. And rowdy. My mother's attention to propriety brought out the devil in him.

It was hard to think of two people less suited for each other than my parents. When they met, in college in the late sixties, she wore her hair in a smooth ponytail. He was joyriding a motorcycle he'd just fixed up at his part-time job, and he smelled like motor oil. He pulled over at a crosswalk and asked my mother for her number. And in a moment of recklessness, she gave it to him.

"Why did you do that?" I asked her once.

"Oh," she said, closing her eyes just for a second, "he was so handsome."

It was strange to think that they had ever been together. And at the same time, it was easy to pretend that they had never been apart.

"Jenny," my father said, "we're thrilled. We never thought you'd do it."

"Don't speak for me," my mother hissed.

"Jenny," my father started over. "I, myself alone, never thought you'd do it."

"You didn't?"

"Being your mother's daughter, I figured you'd repel men like Deet on a mosquito."

My mother glared at him.

"Okay, kids." I said. "Just a friendly little lunch here. Let's not get vicious. Deep breaths." I took a gentle, illustrative breath, and I noticed with some tenderness that my father followed my lead and took one, too.

"I'm kidding," my father continued. "You're not repellent at all." He winked at my mother, who looked away as if he'd flashed her. "The way your mother is."

This was my dad being affectionate. He loved to piss people off. And the more over-the-top his insult was, the more you just had to realize he was messing with you. My mother, needless to say, no longer enjoyed being messed with.

"I don't know if you should invite Aunt Elsa," my mother finally said.

"Money is no object!" my father said, his arm flying up like a flare. Then he reached over to tousle my hair, and said in a conspiratorial voice, "Let's throw a shindig they'll never forget."

"If money is no object," my mother said, "I'd like some of Jenny's college tuition back."

"Hello!" I waved at her. "Let's keep it clean, folks."

After much wrangling, my father agreed that he'd put up a lump of wedding cash at the beginning and my mother would bill him afterward for whatever part of his half that didn't cover.

"Just don't spend it all in one place," he said, handing my mother a check.

She took it as if it were an old banana peel and dropped it in her purse.

Later, as she tipped the valet parker and called him "Sugar," my father ogled her a little and said, "That's a hell of a woman."

On the drive home, just my mother and me, she careened along, talking about my dad, using terms like "patronizing," "self-centered," and "obsessive narcissistic agenda." That last one she had picked up from the only self-help book she'd ever read.

I felt oddly removed from the whole thing. I would have been happy, I thought, doing something very small in someone's backyard or in a park. It wasn't that I didn't want a big fancy wedding. It was there for the taking, so I took it. But, truly, I was just pleased it was happening at all.

So it was an undeniably awkward moment when, two months or so later, I met my mother for coffee and told her—before I'd even told Dean—that I had some surprising news. As expected, she teetered for a moment between the "not married" part of the situation and the "grandbaby on the way" part. Happily, she decided to focus on the positive.

Quick calculations determined that I'd be finished with the pregnancy at least a month before the wedding. After making some dire predictions for my boobs and belly, she decided that the pregnancy would be only a minimal disruption, that the dress could be altered, and that she'd even be willing to hold the baby during the ceremony.

"You'll need pads for your bra," she said, making a note of it on her checklist. "When you were an infant, a baby could cry across the street and I'd be soaked."

"What if I'm too tired after the baby comes to even be there?" I said to my mother.

"You'll be there," she said. Then she said the timing could have been worse. "At least you don't have to walk down the aisle at nine months like an elephant in a maternity gown."

"That," I said, "is a heck of a silver lining."

"You'll still look pregnant even after the baby's out," she said. "Just not quite that pregnant." She looked back down at her list and adjusted her reading glasses. "Anyway," she said. "You know the rule about weddings: better fat than pregnant."

"That's the rule?"

She patted my hand. "Just the opposite of true life."

But I worried. "Maybe we should just get married in Vegas right now," I said, "and throw a party next spring instead."

My mother thought about it. I could see her thinking. About the twinkle lights we were going to hang in the sculpture garden. About my white-rose-and-wisteria bouquet. About the calligrapher my mother had stalked until she worked us in. About the scandal of canceling.

"Nobody's going to Vegas," she said. "You can have a baby before you're married. But you absolutely cannot have a shotgun wedding."

I was happy about the baby. Of course, there was the initial "not quite married" anxiety. And I did worry that my getting knocked up might freak Dean out. Though he never said it, I sensed he was taking things one step at a time, and I feared two steps at the same time might be one too many. But when he got home that night, I had cooked a yummy tomato-lime Mexican soup. As we sat at the dinette talking, I felt the pleasure of anticipation for all the good things that life was delivering to my door just bubble up out of me. In a funny way, though I never would have chosen to get pregnant out of wedlock, the situation felt exactly right to me. Things were really settled for us now.

I'd wanted to wait until he had a beer in him, so he'd be nice and relaxed when I said the words. But I could feel my face glowing, and I was failing to repress a whole series of smiles. And finally, Dean said, "What is up with you?"

And I just burst out, "I'm pregnant!"

His eyebrows went up. "Hey!" he said. "Hey!"

"Are you happy?" I asked.

He nodded, looking around the room like he'd never seen it before.

"I wondered if we'd have kids," he said.

I said, "Apparently, yes."

We curled up on the sofa that night and watched TV. Actually, he watched TV—an action show that involved an alien disguised as a stripper. My mind kept drifting. I thought back to myself in middle school, when my parents were getting divorced, to all the times I had tried to imagine what my grown-up life would be like.

I had wanted to believe that I would find someone to love who loved me back, but of course, as girls do, I had feared that I would wind up unlovable and alone. Nobody was in love with me then, with my braces and cowlick, so it was hard to imagine things would ever be any different. On the sofa with Dean, I found myself wishing that I could go back and visit that girl and show her a video of all the good things to look forward to. "It's all going to work out," I'd say.

Just a year before, when Dean was needing "space," and I was worrying that it was the beginning of the end, I never would have imagined this. This ending for us had not been certain. He had wavered between certainty and uncertainty and, in the end, wound up right here, on the sofa, with me. That moment really stands out in my memory: my head against his chest, my eyes closed, me pregnant and him happy about it, our future just curling up in front of us like a gentle dog.

The next morning, I went out and bought prenatal vitamins and a whole stash of organic fruit. And there, standing next to the B-complex bottles, I set out to become the best damned pregnant woman in the whole history of pregnant women.

Dean himself decided to quit smoking in honor of the baby. I had been planning to ask him to, but he beat me to it, and I was indescribably relieved. He'd been smoking off and on since he was eleven or so, thanks to his older brother, and I did not at all like the idea of becoming the parole officer who monitored his cigarette-free life. Now I wouldn't have to. Not twenty-four hours after he'd found out about the conception of our little one, he was dumping his Marlboros in the kitchen trash.

"Maybe you should go on the patch or something," I said.

"No, no, no," he said. "I'm good. I'll just quit. No big deal."

I was quiet. Too quiet, I guess.

"What?" he said.

"It's just that you've tried to quit before, you know, to no avail."

"That was different."

"What was different?"

"I didn't have a good reason to quit before." He grinned at me. "There's a baby coming. That's it. I'm done."

Two weeks later, he started up again. But only a little bit. And only out on the front porch. And only because his boss was "riding his ass" at work. The tension, the stress. I acted understanding, of course, but then later took the passive-aggressive approach, every time he lit up, of waving my arms wildly and leaving the area.

"We're outside!" he'd say. "There's more than enough air to go around."

"It's not good for the baby," I'd say, letting the screen door slam behind me.

Truly, we'd had this conversation so many times, after a while we could have just played recordings of it and then gone out to the movies. He wouldn't go on the patch because the patch was for wimps. But each time he tried to quit, he became cranky, jumpy, and totally irrational, and stayed that way for days, until he finally broke down and sneaked a cigarette. I could always tell when he'd done it, because he'd smell like spearmint, and he'd come up behind me and try to chew on my ears while I cooked supper.

Frankly, this time it was a relief. After a while, we took a break from the quitting project. But then he could smoke only on the porch. And not anywhere near me. And sometimes I'd even refuse to kiss him after a cigarette, calling his breath "secondhand smoke."

So I had become a fresh-vegetable–eating prig, and he had gone the other way, smoking, I thought, possibly even more than he had before, because his cigarettes now possessed the added allure of being a naughty pleasure. But I was happy. As long as he didn't smoke around me, or around the baby, or in the house, or in the car, or leave his cigarettes lying around where the baby could find, eat, or, God forbid, smoke them, we'd be fine. For a while, anyway.

4

~

The week before the garage sale, many months after he first started quitting, Dean must have gone through three packs of cigarettes. I found empty packs in crazy places: Dropped behind the toilet. In a flower pot by the back door. On a shelf in the baby's partly decorated, unisex room.

Time was getting short. I was due in three weeks. I'd been as laissez-faire about his smoking as possible, but here in Month Nine there was a discernible baby on the horizon. And despite all the research I'd done on how secondhand smoke related to fetal health, infant health, cancer, asthma, attention deficit disorder, grades in school, athletic ability, and future adult happiness, I also knew a fundamental relationship truth: I couldn't tell Dean what to do. If he couldn't quit (or wouldn't), then he couldn't quit (or wouldn't). But it seemed to me like it was worth one final try.

I gathered up his three ashtrays—one with a Houston Astros logo, one made of thick green marble, and one that he'd made himself out of tinfoil. I stood in the archway by the living room, holding them in my hands like a juggler.

He had his headphones on. It was evening, but he was still in his suit and loosened tie, slumped in his recliner. It was the only piece of furniture from his old house I'd allowed him to keep (and its days were numbered, because I'd already made a garage-sale sign for it that read FREE TO A GOOD HOME).

He saw me and obtusely pulled his headphones off one ear. "What?"

"What price should I put on these?"

"No price," he said.

I pushed on. "Free, then?"

"We're not selling them."

I had hoped that if I approached the whole thing with a mischievous twinkle, we could settle the smoking issue with wit and style.

"How about we set them out on the curb for needy neighbors?"

"It's not funny, Jen." He snapped the headphones back on and that was it. The conversation was over.

This is how he'd been all week.

"It's anxiety about the baby," Meredith said when we went for coffee after she got off work. "He's gone into his Cave."

"Well, how long does he have to stay in there?"

"There's no way to know. Just leave him be. And for God's sake, don't go in."

"I can't go in the Cave?"

Meredith closed her eyes for emphasis as she shook her head.

"Well, what am I supposed to do out here? Build a fire and roast marshmallows?"

Meredith got very Zen when she talked about self-help. "Do the garage sale. You'll see him when you see him."

Meredith and I had been meeting for decaf after work a few days a week ever since I quit my job. We had worked at the same antiques shop together for six years, laboring for a woman named Dahlia, who referred to us on the phone as her "minions," but who—and this is why we both kept staying—had fantastic taste in junk. She could find beauty in anything: broken yard ornaments, glass bottles shaped like matadors, wooden fishing lures, old dress patterns, hubcaps, boxes made out of seashells, furniture with crackled paint, lamp shades made out of baskets. She understood that beauty could be almost entirely about context. Dahlia brought her finds back in boxes, had Meredith and me arrange them in her clean, bright shop, and sold them for ten or twenty times what she'd paid. She kept us there late most nights, and she didn't smile much, but the thrill of watching the transformation from trash to treasure kept us glued to our jobs. But now that I was gone, Meredith was lonesome. She kept calling me to meet her after work.

Meredith was helping me with the garage sale. She loved challenges of display and presentation. She loved the psychology of getting people to want things. She'd been helping me price things, and she was going to come over Friday night to help get it all ready to go the next morning.

Dean had also promised to help.

"You're going to be nice to him, right?" I asked.

"I'm always nice to him," she said.

"Sure," I said. "To his face."

The sale had been a long time coming. I'd been trying to make it happen for months, despite Dean's lack of enthusiasm. But now there was an ad in the paper. The hordes were coming and would be assembled on our lawn before the break of dawn on Saturday.

Maybe it was the anticipation of adding a whole new person to our two-bedroom-one-bath, or maybe it was the fact that I myself had gotten larger, but the house had started to seem small. "It *is* small," my mother said when I mentioned it to her. "If it were any smaller, it would be a dollhouse." I needed to make some room. I'd tried to organize the kitchen cupboards and my closet to make my storage more efficient. But it was no use. I just felt like a hamster rearranging my shredded newspaper. What I needed was a cleaned-out cage.

And cleaning my cage entailed pricing everything I could get my hands on. In particular, things like the cracked bike helmet, mismatched free weights, and laminated NFL place mats that belonged to Dean. Not to mention a garage full of bachelor-pad furniture that had not been allowed to cross my threshold.

Understandably, Dean wasn't too enthused about the project. But he had promised me he'd help. I had squeezed his hand to underscore the importance of my words and said, "I really need to get this taken care of." He'd heard me, good man, and he'd canceled band practice for the weekend. It was his job to do the heavy lifting, since I was so rotund I could barely turn over in bed. He'd said he was up to the task.

That was weeks ago. Then he was helpful. Now he was in a mood. And apparently also in a Cave. And I still had heavy things that needed lifting.

That Friday afternoon, Dean got asked to help somebody from Retirement Plans move to a new apartment after work. Dean and some of "the guys." He told me about it as soon as he got home, lingering only long enough to change into jeans.

"What guys?" I said.

"The guys at work."

"You have guys at work?"

"Sure," he said, and shrugged.

"And they help each other move?"

"You weren't cooking tonight, anyway."

"But now I'll just be out in the garage, pricing things by myself."

"You've been out there by yourself every night this week."

"Yes, but now we're in the home stretch."

"I thought Meredith was coming over," he said as he stuck his wallet in his back pocket.

"She has a date with her veterinarian," I said.

Dean raised an imaginary glass to him. "Good luck, buddy."

"If you stay," I tried again, "I'll do the rest of my pricing topless."

He kissed me on the head, completely untitillated. "I won't be out late."

"Dean!" I said, in one last try. "There are cockroaches out in the garage."

"They're just as scared as you are," he said, and clicked the door closed behind him.

And so I pouted. This was not how I had pictured things. He was supposed to be helping, teasing me about my crazy knickknacks: a set of snowflake earrings, a mug in the shape of a cowboy boot, a wiener-dog paperweight. We were supposed to be in this together. The garage was full, stacked high with the things I'd been carting out all week.

I priced alone until my eyes were bleary and my butt ached. Then I hauled myself up and headed back inside, stumbling over a fallen branch in the yard on the way. Inside, I put on my nightgown and got into bed. It was twelve-thirty.

When Dean said he wouldn't be out late, what exactly did that mean? Was it possible that he was having such a good time with these guys that he could not tear himself away, even knowing that I was alone in our cobwebby garage? What kind of guys were these, anyway, rousing at the end of a long week to lift heavy furniture together like at some kind of Amish barn raising? Since when did they help out co-workers? As far I'd seen, it was just row after row of gray cubbies.

Maybe they were bonding. Maybe they'd gone out for a beer afterward. Maybe they were joking around about the guy with three paper shredders or the guy who always wore bow ties. Maybe this night out would make Dean's days at the office more meaningful.

Or, and this thought popped my eyes open, maybe, instead, his

Explorer had rolled over on the way home. He could be in a hospital, doctors leaning over him, working frantically to stop the bleeding, using words like "clamps!" and "stat!" It was too much to bear thinking about, and the thought of him calling out for me in the unearthly light of the ER kept me from sleeping for a good long while.

I tried to imagine life without him. No one to eat PB&Js and leave the crusts on paper towels all over the house. No one to rent disaster movies. No one to make Saturday-morning pancakes with chocolate chips and marshmallows. No gentle, obsessive guitar strumming as the background music to my life. No kisses. No arm across my stomach while I slept. No one coming home.

It was too much. I turned on the light and read movie-star magazines to turn my brain off until I finally dozed off, with a page full of "Stars Getting Parking Tickets" spread open on my belly.

I don't even remember him coming to bed. But by four-fifteen, when I had to shift position, get up to pee, walk around the house for a while, and bemoan the fact that I was not sleeping, there he was, passed out on his side, still wearing all his clothes, reeking of cigars and some kind of manly-man liquor.

I watched him for a while, then pulled the covers up over him and crawled into bed myself. Any way you sliced it, this behavior was not a good sign. But dammit, we were having a garage sale. Not to mention a baby. And I had to get some sleep.

5

Five o'clock came too soon after that. My alarm went off and I startled awake, leaping up and pulling my inner-thigh muscles for the thousandth time. The midwife had explained the inner-thigh situation to me very cheerfully: "Your body is relaxing and getting loosened up for the birth." That was me. Loose and relaxed. So much so that I could barely get in and out of bed without groaning. Another reason to poke Dean.

"Hey." I poked him.

Dean did not move.

"Hey. It's time to get up."

Dean had a pillow on top of his head. I took it off. "Hey!"

"No, no, no." He put his hand over his face. He was literally sweating alcohol.

"I'm going to make some coffee," I said. I maneuvered out of bed and flipped on all the lights as I left the room.

Teeth brushed and fanny pack fastened (I went with above-the-belly), I left the coffeepot brewing and headed to the garage to start bringing small things out. Dean would have to get the fold-out tables and the display shelves later. I'd just start moving the merchandise.

And so there I was, a lumbering shadow on the dark lawn, trudging up and down our cracked driveway and skimming my sneakers through the dewy grass. It was absolutely black outside. I carried a flashlight, which just made things seem blacker. It made me feel jumpy to be out there alone, unable to see. After I almost screamed when I snapped a stick in the grass, I decided to go check on my man.

Fast asleep. Now with my pillow over his head. I brought him some coffee and set it on the bedside table.

"Let's move," I said to him. "It's spooky out there alone."

But Dean didn't move. And when I tried to take the pillow, he was ready. He grabbed it and held it in place.

"Come on," I said.

Finally, the pillow moved a little. "I'm not getting up," Dean said.

"Here's your coffee, and I've got your jeans—"

"I'm not getting up."

"Yes, you are."

"No, I'm really not."

I didn't know what to say. This was really, truly something I couldn't do by myself.

"How am I supposed to move the tables and stuff?" I said. "How, exactly, am I supposed to do that, with my giant, pregnant, dinosaur belly?"

"I'll get them later."

"Yes," I said, feeling frantic, "but later, the garage sale will be over."

I waited for a response. Nothing. After a few minutes, he pulled the pillow back over his head.

I stood up. I couldn't move those tables without him. Or any of the furniture. Or the papier-mâché horse, or the potted banana tree. All the big-ticket items would remain piled in our one-bulb garage. Drive-bys wouldn't stop for a grassy yard strewn with knickknacks. People stop only for the big stuff. So the day would come and go, and I'd still be stuck with the navy-and-brown couch, the mold-speckled Persian rug, the rattan plant stand, and the particle-board bookshelf. Not to mention that after all these months of planning and waiting, I'd have made none of the money that was supposed to finance a changing table, a diaper pail, a stroller, and a crib, at the minimum. Instead, I'd have a life full of crap.

I grabbed the pillow off Dean's head, and he put his hand over his eyes, saying, "What is your problem?" He sounded like a teenager.

I threw the pillow back at him, and felt my voice rise up out of me. "I am not your mother asking you to mow the lawn! This is not a Saturday-morning chore! You fucking promised you'd fucking help me with this fucking garage sale, you fucking asshole!" I walked out, slamming the door so hard the knob fell out and hit the floor. I expected him to scramble out after me, but he didn't.

And then I was back in the yard, alone again, spreading sheets out on the grass for the knickknacks, figuring at least a blue chambray background was better than nothing. Whatever tears were coming, I was wiping away fast. I could figure this out. I could make this work. I waddled to the garage with my sights set on the potted banana tree. It dragged okay on the concrete, but the grass put a stop to any forward motion. I got down on my knees and pushed. Nothing. Then I tilted the pot over and began to roll it across the yard. It was working! The potting soil was spilling, but it was working! At the very least, the banana tree would be done.

And it was there, with pregnant me on my knees in the grass, that a voice came out of nowhere.

"Need some help?"

I looked up to see a man in his pajamas. Blue cotton bottoms, a white undershirt, and some Tevas. He had super-short brown hair that was starting to gray at the temples. He wore tortoiseshell spectacles. And he was waiting for a reply. I pushed myself up into a kind of kneeling squat.

But before I could even speak, he bent over, lifted this plant that must have weighed seventy-five pounds as if it were a kitchen herb, and set it down near the sidewalk. I want to say he lifted it one-handed, but I'm not sure that's true.

I worked my way up to standing.

"What else can I do?" he said.

"You're awfully chipper for this hour of the morning."

"You bet."

"Are you here for the garage sale?"

"No," he said. "I'm here for my dog."

I looked over and saw a golden retriever, unleashed, peeing in my bushes.

"I'm Gardner. I'm your neighbor," the man said.

"I'm Jenny." We shook hands. Mine was wet from dew, and I felt self-conscious about it.

"I've seen you before, waddling around."

"Thanks for the image."

"I live in that house," he said, pointing at one a few houses down that had been sold as a fixer-upper. I'd been watching its slow transformation: sanded and repainted, window screens restored, roof replaced, new driveway.

I had been so relieved to see the house being restored instead of stripped down and updated. Lots of people moved into this neighborhood and, for example, just ripped out the "old" windows in their historic houses and replaced them with flimsy aluminum things that were newer and far, far cheaper. The windows went, the wood siding got replaced with vinyl, the simple porch railings came off to make way for froofy, neo-Victorian spindles that did not at all match. And suddenly, the old house was gone, replaced by a bad imitation of its former self.

But the guy with this house, he knew what he was doing.

"Oh!" I said. "I was afraid that house would be a teardown."

"It probably was," he said, shrugging. "Sometimes I'm a sucker."

"Maybe you should work on that," I offered.

"Maybe I will. But probably not until I finish helping you haul stuff out of your garage."

"In your pajamas?"

"In my pajamas."

I looked around for his dog, who was now perched on my front porch like a lion.

"What's his name?" I asked.

"Herman," he said.

"Good name," I said. And with that, he followed me back to the garage.

He moved coffee table after file cabinet after moldy ottoman while I arranged the knickknacks properly on the tables he'd set up. He was like a superhero. He even dragged Dean's recliner out of the living room for me. I'm tempted to say he did it all one-handed, too, but I'm pretty sure he didn't.

My helpful, early-bird neighbor. I'd already forgotten his name.

When he returned from my garage with a cast-iron typewriter under one arm and a leopard-print beanbag chair under the other, I said, "You're a heck of a neighbor."

"That's what they tell me," he said.

I was still putting on price tags. Pricing in advance is the key to a good garage sale. If you get lazy and decide to just make something up when someone finds that Niagara Falls lamp in the cardboard box, you'll wind up charging twenty-five cents. It's hard to demand money from people. Especially from people shopping at your house, in your front yard, pawing through your things. It's not just your merchandise out there on the lawn. It's your life. You charge a quarter, your customer forks it over, and everybody's happy. And at the end of the day, you have fifty bucks to show for your labor.

You are in charge at a garage sale, but you are also vulnerable. And desperate for a sale. In that split second, as you make up the price, you know that they know that you're making up the price.

Judgments about your stuff—and, more important, you as a person—follow. Who doesn't want to be a good person?

Better to start with a price tag, even if you come way down off the price. Then you can feel like a good person for taking less, but still make some cash. Of course, some people don't need to feel good about themselves. The first garage sale I ever had, my mother made four hundred dollars for me off ten items. She drove a hard bargain.

This morning, I was using tricks of display to lure people: everything neat, easy to see, easy to pick up and look at. Clothes hung symmetrically on portable racks by numerical size. Furniture sat in prominent spots on the lawn. Big signs taped to the tree and front porch beckoned people over. Things were coming together.

And then Meredith arrived to act as a pretend shopper. She wanted to create bidding wars with people, but I insisted she hold back. It was early for her, and she had the puffy eyes of a girl who'd had a good date the night before.

"How was your date with Dr. Blandon?" I asked.

"Disaster," she said, leaning in and kissing me on the nose. "But I might be in love."

"You're always in love," I said.

She shrugged. "Always and never."

Meredith had been slouching a little, but as my neighbor walked over to us across the yard, she straightened.

"Nice pajamas," she said, and headed off to categorize my CDs by genre.

"You have a lot of stuff," he said to me.

"You have no idea," I said.

"I may come back later and shop," he said.

"Your money's no good here," I said. "Just come back and take things."

Then he said, "How were you planning on getting all that stuff out of your garage, anyway?"

"I was planning on having some help," I said.

"And that help—"

"Is fast asleep in our bed."

"Ah," he said. And then, almost under his breath, "Good help is hard to find."

He headed back to the garage. I stood next to Meredith as she watched him go. She gave an appreciative "Umphh!"

I looked at her.

"I thought you were in love," I said.

"Oh, that's right," she said, fingering a feather boa dangling from a rack. "I forgot."

The sky was lighter now. It was almost six-thirty and the die-hard garage-salers, the ones who knew that the best stuff can disappear before the sale even opens, were arriving. The yard started to fill up, people tromping across the grass like folks at a fairground, and my neighbor was up on my porch, just about to wake his dog and head home, when my mother sped up in her shiny black SUV and hit the brakes in the driveway.

It was always so funny to see my five-foot-one mother slide down out of that car. This morning, she zipped up to the porch with a red scarf around her neck, a tray of take-out coffee in one hand, and said, "I know, I know! I'm late! But I've got coffee. Decaf for you. Latte for Dean." She handed Dean's to my neighbor without noticing and turned to scan the crowd. "And pure plain black coffee for me, the only way my daddy ever let anybody have it."

She paused then and looked at my neighbor.

"You're not Dean," she said.

"No, ma'am," he said.

"He's my neighbor," I offered. "He's helping with the heavy stuff."

"In his pajamas!" Meredith shouted, walking over from the sweater box.

"In his pajamas," my mother said.

My neighbor handed back the coffee.

"And Dean is?" She looked at me.

"Indisposed," I said.

My mother nodded and handed the cup straight over to Meredith, saying, "Sweetie, you look like you could use it." She gave Meredith a kiss on the cheek and then wiped off her lipstick print with her thumb.

The yard was buzzing like a hive now. It was time for me to start watching for the shoplifters and the price-tag switchers. My mother led my neighbor off to help her carry the Exercycle she was contributing, and I stood guard on the porch steps, fanny pack atop my giant belly and Herman the sleeping dog at my feet.

When my neighbor was finally gone, after far too many thanks from me, my mother said, "He's adorable."

She refrained from making any comments about my sleeping fiancé. Instead, we chatted about her latest clients, a nouveau-riche couple who had no taste. None at all.

"That's where you come in," I said. "That's why they pay you the big bucks."

She agreed. But they were fighting her every step of the way. They wanted overstuffed furniture. They wanted every piece in the living room to match—"A living room suite!" she shrieked, as if they wanted a bed of nails. They had an unfortunate penchant for the color maroon, and they consistently picked the ugliest fabric from any group of swatches.

"It's no fun when you have to work so hard," she said.

"That can be said of many things."

She wasn't staying long, and as she headed back out to the car, I remembered something I'd been wanting to ask. "Are you and Dad fighting?" I shouted across the lawn.

"Me and who?"

"Dad."

She shook her head. "I haven't talked to him since—I don't know. Ages."

"He called and asked about you yesterday. How you were doing. I thought you must be fighting."

"Nope," she said, and she climbed up into her car.

By ten o'clock, the only remaining piece of furniture was Dean's recliner—which, at "free," was apparently priced too high—and my tables and the clothes racks were half empty. It was time to put up the EVERYTHING ½ OFF! sign. My fanny pack had gotten so full that I'd had to lock big handfuls of money inside the house two separate times. I was still carrying a feeling of uneasiness about Dean, but the day was pleasant—sunny, cool, a slight breeze—and I'd made at least a thousand dollars, so that was something.

Meredith and I sat on the porch swing and watched the stragglers paw through what was left. My ankles were swollen, and Meredith kept talking about them.

"You have no ankles!" she said. "They're like Coke cans."

"They're creepy, aren't they?"

She had haggled with people for me all morning. She had rearranged hats and sweaters to make them look pretty. She had insisted that I stay off my feet as much as possible. And, more than that, she was having a great time. I found myself feeling glad that Dean had slept in. He would only have been grouchy.

"There's something I need to tell you," Meredith said, stuffing the fanny pack with money after a lady had bought a plastic goose lamp. She paused in front of me on the swing.

"Okay," I said.

"I'm not quite sure how to phrase it."

"Just throw something out," I said, "and then we can revise."

She looked at me. She shifted her weight. Then she said, "I don't like babies."

"What do you mean?"

"I don't like them."

"You don't like them?"

"I don't like to be around them. I'm not interested in them. And everybody I've ever known who's had a baby has become a total moron."

I swung a little. "Those are some feelings."

She nodded.

6

~

I stayed mad at Dean all day. What I hadn't expected was that he—inexplicably and against all logic—was mad, too.

I planned to pout, and refuse to meet his gaze, and give him the silent treatment all day while he marinated in guilt for the way he'd let me down. I'd expected him to start groveling as soon as he woke up. I had been counting on him! Though he made a lot of mistakes with me, he usually followed them up with apologies, sucking up, gifts, or tender, thoughtful Ladies' Nite sex.

Not this time. No sex, no gifts, and absolutely no apologies.

He was polite and slightly cold as we finished up the garage sale. Then we piled everything that hadn't sold in the back of my Jeep to take to the Salvation Army. Meredith took off with an air kiss as

"So, you're thinking you won't like my baby?"

"It's possible."

I thought about it. "I think you'll like my baby," I said after a minute. "Nobody likes other people's babies. But I'm not other people."

"That's true," she said.

A guy wanted to know how much my bowling ball was. Meredith went into a spiel about how it had been owned by a South Texas bowling champ in the 1960s. He wound up paying about ten dollars too much. Meredith turned back to me and waved the money before she tucked it away.

"You have to like my baby," I said.

"I'll give it my best shot," she said. Then she took off her sunglasses and wiped the lenses on her shirt. "I'm just saying it doesn't look good."

Right around eleven-thirty, Dean woke up. He showed up on the porch, still in his clothes from the night before, which were wrinkled and emitting a thick odor of cigars. His boxers were edging up out of his waistband. He did not appear to have brushed his teeth. There he stood, hungover, unshaven, squinting. He was drinking a cup of coffee, undoubtedly from the pot I'd brewed for him at 5:00 A.M.—now a kind of burned black soup.

"Morning, ladies," he said with a hoarse voice that made Meredith turn her head away. "What can I do to help?"

soon as she glimpsed how unpleasant the rest of the day was going to be.

In the car on the way there, his unwanted recliner hanging out the back and secured with rope, I wondered if Dean was grumpy because there had been no takers for it. And, insult to injury, we were donating the thing to charity rather than just dragging it back inside. I wondered if his feelings might be hurt. Was it possible that he felt a special kinship with that stained velour found-by-the-road-on-trash-day chair?

I waited until after he'd dropped it off to find out. Pulling away from the Salvation Army, I asked, "What's going on with you?"

He was ready. He'd been waiting for me to ask. "I thought you were pretty rude this morning."

I was so dumbstruck, I almost ran a red light.

I screeched on the brakes and then had to back up a few feet. We sat, nose in the crosswalk, for a quiet minute while a pedestrian walked around the car. Dean had to be kidding. Finally, I said, "Are you staging a counterattack as a red herring?"

"I don't see what's so awful about me doing something fun once in a while."

"Okay," I said, hitting the accelerator perhaps a bit more violently than I should have. "Let's identify the asshole here. One person in this car promised to help another person with something that she was physically incapable"—here I patted my belly—"of doing. He then left her alone on a Friday night, went out, got drunk with a bunch of strangers, stumbled in at some insane hour, slept in his clothes, and, when morning came and his services were desperately needed, refused to even attempt to do the things he'd promised to do when the woman that he's supposed to love had no one else to turn to."

We flew over a set of train tracks. I didn't even brake.

Dean stayed quiet, in a locked-jaw "I'm not even going to dignify that with a response" way.

I eased us up onto the freeway. It felt better to go fast.

"Hello?" I said. "Do you have any kind of response?"

"I guess I'm just wondering if everything always has to be about you."

"Well," I said, "that's a hell of an accusation."

"I just don't think it would kill you to let me go out with the guys once in a while without acting like I'm violating your God-given right to access me at all times."

"Dean!" I shouted. "You let me down!"

"You let me down, too."

"How?" I demanded. "Exactly, how?"

"I don't think it's my job to spell it out for you."

I begged, then challenged, then dared him to spell it out for me. And then, somewhere around the I-10 interchange, after several miles of Dean staring out the window, I gave up. We drove a long way in silence. Until he said, "Just because you wanted to have a garage sale doesn't mean that I did."

At home, I took a long bath, with Dr. Blandon watching me from a perch on the toilet seat. Then he watched me towel off and put on a pair of chenille maternity sweats. He joined me on the bed, and we both curled up for a long, numbing nap.

When I woke up, Dean was out but had left a note that said BACK SOON. DEAN. It occurred to me to fixate on the note's lack of the word *love,* but I decided to pick up some Indian food for supper instead.

It certainly took more energy to fight than to make up, and I was low on energy these days. The more I thought about it, the more it seemed like he was picking a fight with me. Dean had a list of shortcomings as long as Meredith's arm, but things like being blatantly neglectful and being petulantly confrontational were not on it. Something was definitely going on with him, but frankly, a part of me didn't want to go looking for what it was. I decided that maybe if I ignored it, it would go away. I resolved to be sweet with him when I got home, and then to ply him with spicy food in the hope that we could recover enough to make our final childbirth class bearable. He had, after all, bowed out of a gig tonight so he could be there. That was something.

When I walked in, Dean was on the couch messing with his guitar. He looked up, then back down.

"Hey," he said.

"Hey," I said. "I got dinner." I held up the bag from the New Delhi Café.

"You know what? I just got a burger like an hour ago."

"Oh," I said, and watched him a minute. "Want to come and sit with me anyway?"

"I would like to," he said. "But I'm trying to get this chord progression down."

"Oh," I said, feeling kind of limp.

And then he continued, "For our gig tonight."

Tonight. "Hey, um," I said. I really was so tired of fighting. I was hoping that maybe he'd just forgotten. "Tonight's childbirth class. Did you forget?"

"Well," he said, "Sam called and the guy who was going to fill in can't make it, so I kind of have to be there."

"You also kind of have to be at childbirth class," I said, starting to gear up.

Dean closed his eyes, as if to block me out.

And then, deus ex machina, the bag of Indian food slipped out of my hand and hit the floor at just the right angle to pop open one side and splatter *saag paneer* and mango *lassi* all over the rug, the wall, my shoe, and my leg.

I had no choice but to cry. I bent down to start cleaning up, but I just sort of crumpled there on the rug instead. After a few minutes, I could feel Dean kneeling down beside me and purposefully scooping up spinach, moving containers, making trips to the kitchen for paper towels and water. He took care of it, even wiping my leg for me. And then his hands were on my shoulders, helping me up and over to the couch. And then his arms were around me, and his hair brushed my cheek as he gave me little kisses.

"I'm sorry," he whispered.

But what did that mean? It's easy to feel sorry when you've made someone cry.

"I've just had a hard week," he said. "I'm just tired."

I sat there on the sofa and let him kiss me and stroke my hair. It felt so good I could have stayed all night in that very spot. I was hungry, but also starving for affection. If I were Dr. Blandon, I would have been purring. But after a little while, he said, "We're going to have to get you fed if we're going to make it to childbirth class on time."

My eyes were puffy, and my lips, too. I said, "Both of us? To class?"

"Of course," he said. "Of course. Both of us."

"Thank you," I said.

Months later, it would occur to me to wonder if a person should thank another person for something she'd had to beg for. Wasn't the begging itself thanks enough?

But there he was, the old Dean. I was just grateful to have him back. In the kitchen, I ate the parts of the *saag* and *baingan bharta* that had survived the fall while he made me a cup of hot tea. On the drive to childbirth class, he told me about a song he was writing.

"It's kind of about lost love," he said.

"Oh," I said. Usually, his songs were about things that were specifically not love. Cigarettes. Cheeseburgers. Reality TV.

"You know, how people come into your life, and then they're gone."

"Sure," I said, committed to keeping everything pleasant and very glad that he was talking to me again. "That happens all the time."

"It's the human condition," he said.

"Uh-huh."

"That's the name of the song. 'Human Condition.' "

"That's a great title," I said. Lying, but what can you do?

By the time we got there, he was humming the tune to me. And in the parking lot, he paused to give me a little taste of the guitar solo, holding an imaginary guitar and strumming some imaginary strings.

Our time in the parking lot made us a few minutes late to class, but we did walk in holding hands.

The woman who ran our childbirth class was named Betty, and she moved like a hummingbird. She was so perky I worried she might explode. She looked about thirty (Dean had once made the unfortunate mistake of describing her as "hot"), but she had two grown kids. She was blond, and tan, and amazingly fit. And despite her Midwestern accent and blow-dryer hair, she was the most radical person I had ever met. Taking her class was an indoctrination. Breast-feeding was good, bottle-feeding was evil. Home births were good, hospitals were evil. Midwives were good, doctors were evil. Nipples were good, pacifiers were evil. Pain was good, epidurals were evil.

She'd given us article after article on all these topics, and others. She'd shown us videos of women giving birth in their own beds, giving birth underwater, giving birth on soft moss in a forest. She'd filled our heads with trivia. Women who had epidurals were more likely to have episiotomies. Babies whose mothers took pain medication during delivery were more likely to become drug addicts in later life. Formula-fed babies were more prone to allergies.

I was a good student. I took notes in outline form. I sat at rapt attention through the entire class, which was supposed to be two hours long, but was always at least three. I believed that there was a right way to give birth and a wrong way. And I was hell-bent on doing it the right way. Looking back, it's funny to think how easy it is to be sure of yourself when you have no idea what you're doing. It's funny to think that I was at my most confident about parenting when I had never even changed a diaper.

Dean was more relaxed. So relaxed, in fact, that he routinely fell asleep during our end-of-session meditations. I found myself, time after time, elbowing him in the ribs. I did not want Betty to think we were slackers. I wanted to be her star childbirthing pupil. I was looking for any signs that I'd be a good mother, and it couldn't hurt for her to like me.

Of the six dads, only one had made it to every session. A good half of the fathers regularly stumbled into class late and got the hairy eyeball from Betty. One of them was always taking cell-phone calls and disappearing out into the parking lot. Others asked her questions like "Are Big Macs okay for pregnant women?" the answer to which, if they'd read her handouts, they would have known: Fast food is never okay for anyone, least of all pregnant women.

I loved Betty. She was tall and strong, and she had great shawls. She wore them in class because she didn't know how to manage the air-conditioning in this borrowed office, and it wasn't something she was interested in learning. She brought a collection of lamps with her every week to warm up the lighting, and if someone accidentally flipped on a fluorescent light, she shrieked as if in pain. She believed in tending to all parts of the soul, even the ones we'd learned to ignore. She was a gentle animal with mothers, but absolutely fierce with anyone else.

Dean did not want to see pictures of botched C-sections or discuss the inner workings of the vagina. He did not want to question the way that Western women gave birth, or try to come up with a new paradigm by studying ancient cultures. If it were up to him, I would just show up at the hospital, get my epidural, and pop the baby out while drinking a beer and shouting out answers to *Jeopardy!* He thought Betty was making mountains out of molehills. When she talked about how the rate of C-sections had tripled in recent years, her voice rising in despair, I decided to write an editorial about it for the local paper. Dean, in contrast, glanced at his watch.

All of it was so much worse for him, knowing that at the very moments that he was trying to breathe deeply and imagine the birth canal in that dimly lit office building, his band was carrying on without him, grooving at a bar mitzvah or practicing for that elusive next

CD. If class had taken even a half an hour's less time, he might have been able to meet up with them after. But class never took less time. In fact, each week, it took more. Even to me, a total groupie, it was hard to make it to the end without stifling an onslaught of yawns.

Tonight was the last one. Our eighth and final. Betty had planned a "graduation" party, and she'd made us all promise to be there.

"I'll never make you take another birthing class with me again," I said to Dean as we pulled into the parking lot. "For the rest of our kids, I'll just take a refresher course."

"The rest of our kids?" Dean said.

"Yeah," I said. "You know, at least one or two more."

"Three seems like too many," he said.

"But two seems like too few."

"Two point five, then," he said, and I laughed, just to remind us both that we were not fighting anymore.

We had never spoken to anyone in our birthing class. There was never time. We didn't know their names, so we had nicknames for them. There was the Giraffe—very tall—and her husband, Abe Lincoln, who liked to say, "Now, wait a second here!" There were the Oompa Loompas: short and round. The Mute and the Talker were a well-matched couple. Julia Child spoke in a strange falsetto, and her husband, the Pirate, kept one eye closed whenever he heard his wife's voice. The Lizard licked his lips a lot and had beady eyes (Dean also claimed that he changed color depending on the color chair he'd picked for the night, but that point was up for debate), but his wife, Nipples, who should've brought a sweater to class, didn't seem to mind. And then there was me and Dean.

"What should our nicknames be?" I asked one night in bed.

"Beauty and the Beast," Dean said.

"Are you the Beauty?" I asked.

"No," he said, touching my hair. "You are the Beauty. You are the Beauty."

7

The baby did not come on its due date, which was March 11. The day came and went like any other. I felt as normal as any person in my condition could feel. I kept hoping for a cramp or a glimmer or a twinge. Something that said it was time. But there was nothing.

Betty had warned us that the hospital scene everybody sees in the movies was not the way it happened in real life. We would not have the drama of my water breaking, say, in the grocery checkout line, and then the frantic race, in traffic, to the hospital while I screamed in agony and shouted, "You got me into this!" at Dean. Birth would arrive in its own way in its own time, and we could expect many different signs to let us know it was here.

She was right, of course. Dean and I did not have the standard Hollywood birth drama. We had a very different one.

Many women, toward the end of pregnancy, can't wait to get the baby out. They are staggering under the weight of their bellies. Things that were once easy, such as putting on underpants, become riddled with complications. At birthing class, I once heard the Giraffe say to Julia Child, "It's time to get this thing out!" as if it were some frozen ham that'd been stuffed down her shirt. I was not one of those women. I was happy being pregnant, and I was in no rush for it to be over.

And I found that, as a very round pregnant woman, I was at ease in my body in a way I hadn't been before. Even though my breasts were bursting out of my old bras, I had taken on the characteristic pregnancy waddle, and my belly projected so far beyond the normal edges of my body that I routinely hit it while closing the car door.

Pregnant women aren't subject to the same rules as regular women. Pregnant women are allowed to gain weight and be round and move slowly. Oddly, in the most visibly sexual state I'd ever be in (you don't get knocked up like this by reading a book at the library), I felt totally shielded from roving eyes. I didn't have to look sexy. I could waddle all over the grocery store, or the mall, or the jogging track at the park. I was doing something more important than looking good.

For most of the pregnancy, Dean had been as randy as ever. That said, since that night he told me about the plane crash a month before, he'd been low on attention. I'd been trying not to talk about it, strategically staying outside the Cave, but after a while I couldn't stand it. Then, at last, my nervous-girlfriend questions came tumbling out: *How ya doin'? How's it goin'? What's up? What's shakin'? Are you okay? Are you feeling all right? Is something wrong? Is something not right? What's up? What's wrong? Just tired? Okay?*

"Is it me?" I tried again, two nights after my due date, out on the porch swing. There was a speckled moth orbiting our porch light with such energy I kept thinking it would exhaust itself and fall to the floor.

"Is what you?" he asked.

"Whatever's bothering you," I said.

"Nothing's bothering me," he said.

"Oh," I said. "You seem weird lately."

"Well," he said. "I'm not."

I was hesitant to launch these conversations because they only seemed to piss him off. He had already told me nothing was wrong so many times that he couldn't have anything new to say.

But something clearly was wrong. I wanted to talk about it.

Because it wasn't working for me. I was overdue. I wanted someone to rub my feet and tease me about my belly. I wanted a friend, a distraction from the interminable waiting, anything to give me some assurance about something.

"It's all because of his mother," my mother declared.

"Thanks, Freud," I said.

"She's the worst mother in the world."

"I think she has a little trophy for it, actually."

My mother and Dean's mother had met once, when Dean's parents visited from New York, right after we told them about the baby. It was the only time they ever visited Dean in Texas. They stayed at the Four Seasons, and his father remained in the hotel every day of their four-day jaunt, having declared he'd seen too many Westerns to want to see Texas for real. Instead, he played some racquetball, dined in the hotel restaurant, read faxes from work, and ordered French fries from room service.

Dean's mother was more adventurous. She even came out one evening to see our house, which I had been cleaning for a week in anticipation of her arrival. As we drove her from the hotel back toward our neighborhood, I found myself wishing I'd washed the car again after the rainstorm earlier that week. I also found myself trying, at the last minute, to figure out the most scenic route home.

Alas, there was no scenic route. Houston is a sprawling city, the ugly and the lovely all mixed up together. She didn't take it well. At each washateria, strip mall, or titty-bar billboard, she winced, gasped, or cried out. The occasional grassy parkway or gentrified historic avenue provided relief for all of us in the car, and though I hoped to hear happy noises to counter her moans of despair, in the scenic spots she was just quiet. I was glad to pull, at last, into our driveway.

But I had no sooner yanked up the parking brake than she took a gander at my beloved cottage and said, "My God! It's smaller than our apartment!"

And that's how our evening went. As we headed up our walkway, Dean's mother pointed out a drooping black-eyed Susan that needed watering, a bush that needed pruning, and, right in the middle of the porch steps like a welcome mat, a pile of dog poop. Dean and I exchanged looks. Him: *Why didn't you clean that up before we left?* Me: *It wasn't there before we left.*

Inside, she didn't want to sit down. Maybe she had done enough lounging at the Four Seasons and was ready to be on her feet, but I couldn't shake the feeling that she didn't want to touch my upholstery. As we waited for my mother, who was meeting us before we all headed out to dinner, she began to move around the house, narrating her own tour: "Paint needs a touch-up. Table leg's broken. Might want to dust that."

Dean never admitted he didn't like his mother. That said, he rarely called her, or talked to her, or told her anything. She was disappointed in his perverse guitar-playing behavior. And she was a fierce alcoholic, although Dean would never say so.

"She's nasty when she drinks," he once confessed.

"She's nasty all the time," I countered.

"That's really not true," he said. "You have to get to know her."

"I have to?"

She had once told him he had ruined her life, but tripped and smashed their glass coffee table before she got to telling him why.

"She didn't mean it," Dean said, backtracking after he let that story slip.

And there she was, in my house. Focusing not on its charm—its yellow stucco exterior and white window boxes with butterfly flowers in them, its working fireplace with dentiled molding, its built-in china cabinet with beveled-glass panes—but on its creaky floorboards and cracked ceiling. She made me defensive. This house had been a find! It had been a total fixer-upper that had not been altered in any way since it was built. It had its original kitchen, original hexagonal tiles on the bathroom floor, and original claw-foot tub. It had wavy panes of glass in the windows and transoms above the doors.

I'd bought it for a steal, making the down payment with money I'd saved from every job since high school. Then I added central air-conditioning, a disposal, and a dishwasher, refinished the floors and painted the walls, replaced the toilet and sink, and scrubbed every remaining surface until it gleamed. Buying and fixing up this house had wiped out my entire savings account. Everything about this house was me. Standing inside it was like standing inside my body. And Dean's mother clearly wished she were standing somewhere else.

"It's just so cluttered," she said, by way of explaining the look on her face. "I don't know how you stand it."

"It *is* kind of messy," Dean said.

"The clutter may be mine," I said, looking right at Dean so he'd know what I thought of him, "but the mess is Dean's."

I looked around the living room, trying to see it with her eyes. It was full of things: a wooden dartboard, a kidney-bean coffee table, an angular 1950s sofa, pillows with birds of paradise on them, curtains I'd made from flour sacks, old quilts, wooden chairs painted dark red and pale green, a lamp with a Dalmatian-statue base, a painting I'd once done of an old shoe.

My mother, who had slipped in behind us with her own key, defended me. "Jenny has such a funky sensibility. She's by far the most artistic person I know."

"Did you say artistic or autistic?" Dean's mother said, coughing out a laugh. Then she walked over to my mother, holding out her arms for their first meeting ever. "Hello, Phoebe," she said, clasping her hands and kissing her on the cheek. "You have such a wonderful Texas accent."

She was quite a thing to see. Her words were mean, but her body language was warm and open, as if she were about to start up a conversation with an old friend. But before my mother could even speak, Dean's mother had turned and walked off to inspect the kitchen.

I looked to Dean for explanation. "Did your mother just call me autistic?"

"No!" he said, knowing how lame he sounded. "She didn't understand your mother's accent."

"I think she just called me autistic," I said to my mother, who was watching the kitchen doorway.

"There's some kind of a dead bug on the floor in here," Dean's mother shouted from the kitchen, "but, Jenny, I do love these curtains."

Dean headed in to get the bug. "It was the accent," he insisted again before he opened the door.

It took me weeks to recover from her visit. The day she left, I couldn't even drag myself off the sofa to eat. Dean had to bring me soup and prop me up.

"Your mother!" I kept saying.

"She's not so bad," Dean replied every time.

"Keep telling yourself that, buddy," I said.

"She grows on you after a while," he said. And after watching my face for a minute, he added, "Like a fungus."

I tried not to smile, but I did, just a bit. "How did you turn out not to be a serial killer?" I asked.

"She has a loving side," he said.

"I hope I never see it," I said.

And I didn't. The best thing about her, as far as I could see, was that she sent Dean money every month. Or maybe the family secretary did. But I was grateful for the checks.

8

By the time I was a week past my due date, I was obsessed with Dean's distant behavior in a way that felt pathetic even to me. I was dreaming about it and talking about it nonstop. I was worried enough that I even decided to go watch his band play. I called Meredith on my cell phone on the drive over but didn't tell her what I was up to.

"You're making it worse," she said. "But I'm not allowed to say anything bad about Dean, so I really can't elaborate."

"Just talk!" I said.

"Talk freely?"

"Yes!"

So she did. She performed a concise and, even I had to admit, totally accurate analysis of my relationship with Dean. And "that mother" was her explanation for almost every struggle in Dean's life. For when he quit his job at the guitar store to take an office job he hated. For when he couldn't quit smoking. For when he talked about feeling trapped in our relationship and toyed with the idea of leaving me. And now that he'd gone into his Cave, apparently never to reemerge, Meredith blamed his mother.

"Okay," I said. "But that doesn't really help me."

Meredith was on the phone in the bathtub, and now she made me wait a minute while she toweled off.

"What am I supposed to do, send him to therapy?" I said.

There was a pause, and then we both decided it was a pretty good idea.

"Yes," she said.

It was totally preposterous. Therapy was something Dean would never do. In fact, he would resent the hell out of the suggestion. But after Meredith's analysis, it started to seem like the only possible answer.

"Where are you, anyway?" Meredith asked.

"Um . . ." I said.

"On your way to see the band," she guessed.

"Sort of," I said.

Meredith made a barfing noise.

"Cut it out!" I said.

"You said I could speak freely," she said.

The club was in sight. I did not want to go in alone.

"Come with me," I said. "I'll buy you a Tom Collins."

"I have a date," she said.

"Who with?"

"Dr. Blandon," she said in a "who else?" voice.

"He'll never measure up to the cat," I said.

"That may be true," she said, "but I'm going to let him try."

"I thought that first date was a disaster," I said.

"There can be a bright side to disaster," she said. Then she had to go. "Go tell Dean to change his life," she said as we hung up.

And that's how I came to shout the word "therapy" at Dean during a set break at a club called the Keg.

This place was the worst of the worst, in my opinion, though Dean did not agree. It was dead last on the list of places I was willing to go. It was small, suffocatingly hot, and absolutely filthy, even for a club. It had pool tables, beer, a dance floor, and a deck out back where people went to make out. The bartender wore his hair in a gray rattail braid, the women's bathroom had no toilet seat, and the college kids who piled in every weekend were so drunk that it was not possible to make it through the night without watching someone vomit into an empty beer pitcher. Still, to Dean, it was just fine. People danced. Some even tried to sing along. If you squinted, you could almost pretend it was a decent place.

I hid near the back—ankles as puffy as leg warmers, protecting my belly with my hands, toying with the idea of breathing through my shirt fabric to screen out the smoke.

There was the band, up onstage. And Dean, it appeared, was singing the lyrics of the ZZ Top song "Legs" to a very drunk coed in a halter top. She couldn't have been more than nineteen, and she had that kind of lean wild-animal body girls that age sometimes have. Later, she was grooving to the band's rendition of "Kiss" when she blew Dean a kiss of her own. I saw it happen. And then, as crazy as it sounds, I saw him wink at her. Maybe he just got caught up in his band persona. In any scenario other than this one, she was way out of his dating league. But whatever the circumstances, the vibe he was giving off on that stage was not one of an almost-married father-to-be, but of a horny, single band guy, working it with the ladies.

I could not have been more out of place in a bar like that, which was all about being young and drunk and skinny and wild. My mind, my whole life, could not have been more tame. I was up past my bedtime. I was wearing panties that came up to my rib cage. I had just taken up knitting. By the time I located Dean on the back deck, I was in fine form.

He was standing by himself, a beer in one hand, dragging on a cigarette so hard it seemed to burn all the way down in one deep, slow breath.

I showed up next to him. "I can't believe I'm here," I said.

"Hey," he said, glancing around. "I can't believe you're here, either."

"I saw you wink at that girl." I glared at him.

He took a deep sigh and closed his eyes. When he opened them again, I was still there, waiting.

"That," he said, shaking his head. "That's just part of the whole thing."

"Just part of the whole life-in-a-band thing?" I said. "Just one of those concessions you have to make for your cover-band art? Life on the road? Life as a rock star? What can you do if pussy just throws itself at you? You can't say no! You can't deny your sexy self to your cover band–loving, bar mitzvah–going fans!"

He was starting to look pissed. How was it that he got to look pissed?

"You need to calm down," he said.

"And you," I said. "You need to get into therapy."

"What?"

And that's when I shouted loud enough for half the people out on the porch to glance over at me. "Therapy!"

Dean started to walk away, but I grabbed his arm.

"Something is wrong. Something is really wrong. It's been this way for a month. I can't have a baby like this. Where are you? Meredith thinks you need to talk to somebody professional, and I think she's right."

All Dean could say was "You're telling me Meredith wants me to go to therapy?"

"Dean." My hand was still on his arm. "I'm begging you." Then I leaned in. "Dean," I said again. "We're getting married. You need to pull yourself together."

He put his head down then. He rubbed his eyes for a minute, and then he looked back up at me.

"Okay," he said. "Something is wrong."

There it was. I was right. But how good is it to be right about something being wrong?

"Okay," I said, bracing myself. Dean's kiss-blowing girlfriend was across the porch now, laughing too loudly as a boy in a backward baseball cap pretended to spank her.

"I guess we need to talk," Dean said. "But not here." The band was starting up again now. A cover of "California Girls." He glanced back toward the stage. "We've only got one more set. I'll finish up here, and then meet you at home. Take a good long bath, and I'll be there before you're even out."

I thought about staying to keep an eye on him. But I let him lean over my belly and kiss me on the forehead and then send me toward the parking lot with a very gentle push. Partly, I was tired. Partly, I did not want to stay there. Partly, a bath sounded like a great thing. But mostly, I think, it was the tenderness in his voice. I hadn't heard that in a long time. I drove home feeling oddly relieved. I drove home with this funny sense that everything was going to be okay.

He did come home and meet me. And I had taken a bath. I wore a maternity sleep shirt my mother had brought me that said JAMAICA ME CRAZY and was balancing a book called *Raising Your Kids to Be Smarter than You* on my belly. When he walked into the room, he headed straight for the bed and started kissing me. I couldn't imagine what had sparked such passion in him. It had been over a month since he'd shown any interest in anything. Our midwife had actually said that sex could help bring on labor—something to do with the chemicals—and tonight, for the first time since I'd gotten pregnant, I wanted to get that frozen ham of a baby out. I wanted to be my old self again.

He kissed me all over my neck, and I closed my eyes and tried to pretend that these were old times. His hands were on me, pulling me to him, and I let him slide my sleep shirt up over my head. His eyes were closed intently, and I unbuttoned and unbuckled him. In minutes, we were both naked on the bed, as we had been hundreds of times before. It should have been easy, but I couldn't keep my concentration. Dr. Blandon had hopped up on the bed and was watching us and purring. I wondered if I should move him, if he understood what we were up to, if Dean was distracted by the purring, too. Also, was I too big for Dean now? Was it scary for him to see this giant belly? Why on earth were we doing this, anyway, at this moment?

It became clear pretty soon that I was not going to get there, sexually speaking. He seemed to be stalling, too. We were losing momentum. I was just about to suggest taking another tack when he said, "This isn't going to happen. I'm sorry. I need to stop."

And then he turned away and sat up. I pulled our comforter over me, feeling suddenly bashful, like I didn't want him to see me naked. He moved to the edge of the bed and put his fingers on his eyes like he had at the club.

"Something is wrong," he said.

"I know that," I said. "I've been saying that."

He stood up, and Dr. Blandon and I watched him while he put his boxers back on, then his jeans. I thought he might stop there and sit on the bed to talk to me, but he went on to find his shirt and turn it back right-side-out and put it on. Then he sat on the edge of the bed and started on his shoes. Dr. Blandon tried to rub up against him, but he pushed him off the bed.

"What are you doing?" I said.

"I'm out of cigarettes," he said.

"So?" I said.

"I really need a cigarette if we're going to have this conversation."

"Can't smoke in the house," I said.

"We'll talk on the porch."

"I'll be on the porch. You'll have to stand out in the yard."

He stood up, shoes on. He grabbed his wallet and keys. "I'll be right back," he said. "Do you need anything?"

"I need you to hurry up and talk to me," I said.

He nodded and headed for the door. "I just have to clear my head."

"You're torturing me right now, you know that?" I said.

He turned and looked straight at me with his hand on the doorknob. "I'm sorry."

Then he was gone. I heard his car start up, and I put my nightshirt back on, plus a sweatshirt, with a strange feeling like I was suiting up for battle. Too bad my armor was cotton velour from Target. Then I peed, brushed my teeth, and tried to glam up a little for his return—a touch of mascara, some lip gloss—in case looking good would gain me any advantage. And then I sat back down on the bed with my book and waited.

But here's the unbelievable truth: Dean did not come right back. He did not come back before I finished my chapter. He did not come back before I tried his cell phone nine times and never got an answer. He did not come back before I gave myself a pep talk about giving him the space he needed. He did not come back before I accidentally fell asleep waiting for him on our bed. And he did not come back before I woke the next morning to find my full-term-and-one-week pregnant self completely alone.

9

~

At first, I stumbled from room to room, thinking I might find Dean sleeping in some crazy place. The sofa, maybe, or the guest bed. Maybe he'd forgotten his key and was out on the porch. Maybe he'd passed out drunk in the kitchen. I waddled laps around the house, my belly leading the way—checking rooms, trying to wake up fully and think straight. Maybe a car accident. I'd have to call all the hospitals. Or maybe—would he do that?—the halter-top girl. No. He wouldn't do the halter-top girl. It had to be an accident. He was in the ER. He was calling out for me. I had to find him. I headed for the phone book.

Then I saw the letter on the coffee table, and I stopped dead still. No ER. No accident. No one to find. Instead, a Crane's envelope in ecru. On my kidney-bean table. I picked it up and looked at my name on the front in his handwriting: the big sloppy *J*, the dumb little spiral at the bottom of the *y*. This is where we'd been heading for weeks. I knew what it said already. What else could it possibly say? I didn't even have to read it.

But it was impossible. I sat down carefully on the sofa and balanced the letter on my belly. I wanted to tear it open and devour every word. And, just as badly, I wanted to slip it into the kitchen garbage, and then maybe dump some old coffee grounds on top of it, and let it go out with the Monday trash. It was a pretty thin envelope. He'd never been much of a writer. I stuck my finger under the lip and, as slowly as I could, ripped one side to the other.

The letter was written on my stationery, which meant he must have tiptoed into our bedroom to get it while I slept. Had I been drooling? I hated the idea that he'd been able to stand in our room without my knowing it. That he might have watched me twitching through an REM cycle with a critical eye. That the events of my life had been unfolding without my participation.

The handwriting started out big and got smaller as the letter wore on, as if he'd realized how much he had to say only after he started writing. There were a number of scratch-outs, which would hold my attention weeks later as I tried to make out the words underneath them.

Most of the letter I can paraphrase. Standard stuff, really. Stuff I'd heard before, if not seen written down, in other breakups. And that's what this letter was: our official breakup. A document I had neither consented to nor participated in. But there it was. I had been served papers on my own stationery. A double-sided sheet, drenched in Dean's musings on the character of our relationship, with JENNIFER INGRID HARRIS embossed across the top, as if I'd sanctioned the whole thing. As if it had come from me, and Dean was just my penmanship-challenged assistant.

Dean had talked about leaving so many times before that I had built up a tolerance to the idea. Each time he brought it up, I felt less like he'd actually do it. Still, to be perfectly honest, I had never been a hundred percent certain that we would make it to the altar. Only, say, ninety. But that had seemed like enough.

So, he was leaving me. He was unhappy, this wasn't working for him, he felt trapped, et cetera, et cetera, et cetera. On and on about his malaise and his discontent. I wasn't the girl for him, and he'd known it for a while, but he'd been trying to stick it out for the baby, whose college tuition he still planned to pay (or, in truth, let his parents pay). He was sure I would be a great mom and he would try to help in any way he could. Blah, blah, blah. The words kept coming, the handwriting got smaller, and I felt completely numb.

Why on earth, if all these things were true, had he proposed? Why was it that this time last year he'd been so sure about me that he'd proposed all on his own—with no prompting or encouragement from me? I hadn't even suspected he was thinking about getting married. I wanted to, but I never even mentioned that fact to him, and I certainly never issued the dreaded "shit or get off the pot" ultimatum. I was just doing my thing. Working at the shop. Hitting the estate sales with Meredith on the weekends. Taking Spanish for fun. Teaching myself Italian cooking. Trying to take a good long walk at least once a day.

We were living together, and though I might have been a tiny bit of a control freak about home decor and which items he was allowed to bring into the house (i.e., none), he didn't seem to mind. He was slogging away at his awful financial job, trundling off in his suit every morning. But he came home to cannelloni and fresh pesto in the evenings, and on the weekends, we played Frisbee in the park.

And then, one day he took me out to dinner, to the seafood restaurant with the crab on top that we loved so much. He had a ring he'd picked out himself, and he couldn't wait until dessert, as he'd planned, to show it to me. That was it: He offered, I accepted, and then we drove down to Galveston, to the beach, and walked along the shore in the blue night, our shoes hanging from our fingers. It was easy.

So this was my question: How did we get from that night to this morning? And *why*. Why wasn't I the girl for him? Why wasn't it working? Why did he feel trapped? Why on earth did he think I would be a good mother, especially since he had never even seen me hold a baby?

And there, sandwiched between the awful, insulting "Dear Jane" text of this letter and his crazy, illegible signature, was a paragraph written in microscopic words that held a kind of an answer:

> *I didn't have an affair. That's the truth. But maybe I was in love. With the girl from the plane. She was going to see the band. I'd burned her a CD. I didn't sleep with her. Just gave her a ride home from work a few times. She never invited me in. But there was something there. And now she's gone, and I don't feel the same about you anymore. It's not my fault.*

And then, his conclusion: "I'm going to do some traveling. I'll be in touch. I'm sorry, I'm sorry. I'm so sorry. Dean."

And poof. I was alone.

So I called my mother. She thought I'd gone into labor, based on the tone of my voice when I said, "I have to see you right now." Fifteen minutes later, she showed up at the door with a baseball cap and a sport water bottle, ready for action. But I didn't even say anything to her at the door. I just pulled her in by the hand, led her over to the sofa, and handed her Dean's letter.

The rest of the day went by fast. The sobbing, the telephone calls to friends, the sobbing.

My mother tried to create an aura of calm acceptance. She stayed the whole day, fetching me Kleenex with lotion and going to pick up Cuban sandwiches for lunch. While I was on the phone, she did my dishes and swept the kitchen floor. She folded a giant pile of laundry that had been mounting on the guest bed. She even folded Dean's boxers.

"Just throw them away," I said when I found her holding the pair with mermaids on them.

"He'll be back," she said. "I'm putting them in the dresser."

During quiet moments, she sat by me and we processed it all

again, examining every angle up and down, trying to get a handle on things. She was very patient. She must have said "It's better to know now" a hundred times. She accentuated the positive.

But all I could say was "This can't be fucking happening."

My mother's favorite movie was *The Sound of Music.* At some point during the day, she began quoting from it. " 'Where the Lord closes a door,' " she said, " 'somewhere He opens a window.' "

"Thank you, Fräulein Maria," I said. And then I thought about it. "What if I don't believe in God? Do I still get a window?"

"Of course you do, darlin'. Everybody gets a window."

"Maybe like a drive-thru window for me, though. Not a nice wooden one with window treatments and tie-backs."

"Sugar," she said, her voice as soft as cotton, "if there's one thing I can guarantee you in this life, it's window treatments."

We paused in conversation long enough for me to go back to my lamenting. "This can't be happening," I said again.

My mother looked at me. "You really don't believe in God?"

I said, "I don't believe in anything today."

Meredith was at an antiques auction in Bellville that day and didn't get my messages until she started the drive home. She took the highway going ninety, made it back in a record fifty-three minutes, and then let herself in the back door, shouting, "I can't fucking believe it!" She paced the floor trying to figure out where he might have gone. As if we were going to hunt him down. As if knowing his location would change anything. "Look at you!" she kept saying, throwing her arm in the direction of my belly. "Look at you!" She had a lot of energy for ranting, and I was glad to let her take over for a while.

Meredith's approach was different from my mother's. Meredith wanted to pile his boxers, and indeed each and every one of his belongings, out in the street and light them on fire. She wanted to call up all his friends and tell them that he'd left me by the side of the road on the way to the hospital with the baby halfway out. She wanted me to get so angry, and stay so angry, that there would never be room for feelings of sorrow, or loneliness, or loss.

But after a while, even Meredith got tired. By ten o'clock, the three of us were collapsed in the living room, eating take-out Mexican food and listing all the things we hated about Dean in hoarse voices. Turns out, nobody had liked the styles of facial hair he'd sported over the years: a goatee, some mutton chops, a Fu Manchu. But both of their lists were far longer than I'd suspected.

"That ankle tattoo," my mother said.

"The little snort when he laughed," Meredith said.

"The pouting," I said.

Our list went on: his UP YOURS T-shirt, his smoking (and his insistence that he wasn't addicted), the way he shushed everybody when a song he liked came on, his collection of Matchbox cars, his affection for ZZ Top, his unwillingness to see any movie he deemed "too girly," his love of Budweiser, his crooked bottom tooth, his use of the word *dude* ("Who says that?" Meredith kept saying. "Who talks like that?"), his pretentious handwriting, his love of the Three Stooges, his refusal to eat any vegetables besides ketchup, his inability to appreciate Japanese woodblock prints, his dislike of cats, his occasional tendency to forget to flush, and, of course, unanimously, his penchant for air guitar.

And so we passed the time. Meredith didn't go home until one in the morning. My mother tried to leave then, too, but I begged her to stay. She had her purse on her shoulder and her hand on the knob when I started to cry. Without a word, she set down her things. We started to make up the sofa bed, and that's when Dr. Blandon, for the first time all day, decided to make an appearance.

He walked right into the living room, his belly almost dragging on the floor.

"What the hell is that?" my mother said, holding herself completely still.

"That's a cat," I said.

"What happened to its eye?"

"Hit by a car."

"What's it doing in your house?" my mother said, taking a step backward.

"He's staying with me for a while."

My mother took another step back, and Dr. Blandon took that as his cue to walk over to her, though she was tearing up just looking at him, and start doing figure eights around her ankles.

"Well, I can't stay here," my mother said. "I've been sitting in this house thinking I was coming down with a cold."

As soon as she said that, I started to cry again, and finally, bless her heart, she agreed again to stay the night. As long as the good doctor was locked up in my room. "I refuse to wake up and find that thing sleeping on my face," she said.

"He'll be on mine," I promised.

And then my dear mother made me a glass of milk, "to soothe your nerves," and she tucked me into bed. She sat beside me and smoothed my hair.

"Don't tell Dad yet that the wedding is off," I said.

"Dean may come back, honey," she said.

"Even still," I said. "The wedding is off."

My mother nodded, and then she kissed me on the forehead, and at that moment I wished like anything that I were still her little girl.

As she went out, Dr. Blandon tried to follow, but my petite mother gave him such a hard shove with her foot that he went scrambling off under the bed, his paws hydroplaning on the bare floor.

When I said the end began with a plane crash, this is the end I meant. The end of my engagement. The end of the Dean I thought I was going to marry. The end of the life I thought I was going to have. I wasn't sure if Dean would be back in the morning, out of gas and unshaven, or if I'd never see him again. And if he did show up, I wasn't sure if I'd shoo him off the porch and shut the door or let him squeeze his way in. But I was sure that something in me was a little bit broken, and that it was going to take me a good long while to figure out how to fix it.

I lay in bed for a long time after that, wondering what it felt like to go into shock, and then I fell asleep with the light on. As it turns out, I didn't go into shock. But I did go into labor.

10

About an hour after we went to bed, I found myself awake with stomach cramps. At first I thought maybe I'd just eaten too much. I was relieved when the feeling passed. Then it came and went again. It's amazing that after all those months of preparing for and reading about this moment it took me as long as it did to figure it out. But I was absolutely obtuse, sitting on the toilet at three in the morning. Until it hit me: It wasn't beans. It was labor.

Betty had told us how to handle it. We weren't supposed to rush to the hospital. In fact, we were supposed to wait as long as possible to go. Once we were there, she explained, we were in their hands. Once we were there, they were in charge. As long as we stayed home, we could still eat, if we liked, or take a bath, or curl up in our beds. Once we were there, we'd most likely be in a little gown that didn't close up the back in a strange, sterile room, a fetal monitor around our bellies and IVs in our arms. Home had certainly sounded more appealing at the time, but as I tried to wait, I found myself wishing I were in the hands of trained professionals. I suddenly didn't feel prepared.

Betty wanted us to enter labor calmly, as if from a tranquil sea. She wanted us drinking tea—preferably herbal, and mixed specifically for mothers-to-be. She wanted calming music, foot rubs, good conversation, hair stroking, back massages, swaying back and forth. Her whole approach was to avoid tension. Tension came from fear. It made labor slower, harder, and more painful.

Of course, I was already worked up that night. But as the cramps came, Dean's leaving started to seem like it might lose top billing. I woke my mother up and gave her the news. I went to put the kettle on while she pawed through my hospital bag and found my folder from Betty's class. She found a list of suggestions for dealing with the situation. She offered me a foot rub. She spoke in a soothing voice. She found me some very soft socks—of Dean's, actually, but I put them on anyway.

"I'm not supposed to do this alone," I said.

"You won't be alone," she said. "I'll be there with you."

"That's not what I mean," I said.

"I know," she said.

She brought me some tea called Super Soother, but I didn't want to drink it. I couldn't even imagine being calm and tranquil. And the thought of Dean out on the interstate in his SUV, listening to Creedence Clearwater Revival, his arm out the window, the wind ruffling his hair, thinking he'd done the right thing, congratulating himself on finally making a move—the idea of him tooling along like a free man made me so angry I wanted to punch a hole in the wall.

"This sheet of paper says you should do everything you can to relax."

"I don't want to relax," I said. "I'm too mad to relax. Relaxing sucks."

And then, before my mother could try to talk some sense into me, a real contraction. Up until that point, we'd been in the minor leagues. I'd been thinking I could handle labor easily because I'd always had such knee-buckling cramps with my period. It had seemed to me, all those years, like my body must have been preparing me for something. That I was going to be kind of a natural at the whole "giving birth" thing. Especially with my hips, which our midwife, Nicole, had described admiringly many times as "wide." But when this contraction hit, it was so much fiercer than I'd even contemplated, I was a little stunned. I bent over on the couch.

"Holy hell," I said when it started to subside.

"I know you don't want to relax," my mother said. "But you might think about changing your mind."

"Okay," I said.

I wasn't going to need a hospital to make me feel afraid. The contractions were going to do the job plenty well on their own.

My mother and I did some breathing. She, the most Texan woman I can even imagine, she, who ate steak four times a week and who confused yoga with yogurt, was telling me things like "Find your center" and "Hold the pain in your hands like a moonbeam." She was reading off the sheet and trying to sound convincing. Instead, she just sounded like my mother, badly cast in a play about people who talked this way.

We decided she should draw me a bath. "That I can do," she said. "A bath I can do."

I got hit with another one while she was turning on the water. I grabbed hold of the bookshelf. I wasn't supposed to be scared. I was supposed to know that my body was built for doing just this exact thing. But I felt like a volcano getting ready to blow. "I think this is bad," I said to my mother when she found me with my face pressed up against a boxed set of Jane Austen novels. "This is not at all how I thought it would be."

Part of me had wanted Dean to see me in such agony. It might break his heart to see me suffer, especially in the effort of bringing our own child into the world, and he might love me even more as a result. And even though Meredith had told me that I was "so fucked-up" when I told her this, I had insisted that the pain of childbirth made women noble and wise. Now the pain was so much worse than I could have imagined, and Dean had no idea. And instead of loving me more at this moment, he most certainly loved me less.

It seemed impossible to me that Dean had really left. My mother's theory was that he was panicking about the baby and that he'd turn around when he'd traveled far enough to leave the pressure behind. "He'll get to the state line," she predicted, "and suddenly feel okay again. And then turn around and come back and fall at your feet." And for her, if he was back soon enough, his leaving didn't count. Anybody could have a moment of panic.

She was sure that's what it was. This was not the time for a man to leave his woman for real. There were too many questions unanswered for him: What would it be like to see his child? To hold it for the first time? What would the child look like? Would it be healthy? What would it be like to be a family? It was like leaving a movie right before the end. Didn't he want to see how it turned out?

"The newness has to wear off before they really leave you," she said with total certainty. She herself, of course, had been left in the traditional way—with a child in middle school and no job. "That's the way it always happens," she said. "After the thrill is gone."

I agreed with her. There was simply no way that Dean had really left me. Not in this way, at this moment.

"Maybe he had a breakdown of some kind," I said, thinking how odd it was to be rooting for a breakdown. But it was hard to imagine. Truthfully, the only thing I could imagine was his pushing his way through the front door, his face contorted with remorse and self-hatred, begging my forgiveness as he clung to me. And maybe then I'd have another contraction, so he'd feel even worse.

Betty's packet suggested I eat something, and so I had some shredded wheat. After all the Mexican food, it seemed prudent to lie low gastronomically for a while. My hospital bag had been by the door for weeks, and my mother headed out to put it in the car. And, as instructed, I called Nicole to let her know we were heading in.

"Nicole's had to leave town for a family emergency," the answering service operator told me. "We have a doctor filling in. He's part of the larger medical practice."

I didn't speak.

"Hello?" she said.

"She left town?" I said.

"It was a family emergency," she said again.

"Where did she go?"

"I'm really only authorized to say that it was a family emergency and that Dr. Fred Hale will be filling in."

"Dr. Fred Hale?"

"He's very good," she said. "He's the best."

"But I'm supposed to have Nicole," I said, my voice starting to rise. My mother poked her head back in to see what was keeping me.

"I know, and I'm sorry, but she's not available right now."

"This is a fucking nightmare," I said.

"Dr. Hale will meet you at the hospital," she said firmly. "I suggest you get going."

On the drive to the hospital, my mother got feisty. "We could sue that midwife," she said, speeding along the highway, changing in and out of lanes, even though there were no other cars to speak of. "She sold you a bill of goods."

"Use your blinker," I said. The whole situation was making me limp.

"Don't get defeated," she said. "We're going to get her back one way or another."

"I don't want to get her back," I said. "I just want her to come and deliver this baby!"

My mom sped past a pickup truck going forty with three guys in the back.

"Slow down, Mom. This is not a race."

She pressed on the brake. "Sorry," she said.

"You're supposed to be a calming presence."

She thought about that a minute. Then she said, "Maybe this Dr. Hale really is the best in the business. Maybe he's a great doctor. Maybe you'll wish you'd had him all along."

Her words lingered as we tooled along the empty highway, my mother changing lanes randomly, but careful to use the blinker. We didn't talk the rest of the drive. Dr. Hale might be a great doctor. It was at least possible.

11

~

But Dr. Fred Hale was no Nicole. We had not even made it to a room yet when he found us in the corridor and introduced himself. "I'm Dr. Fred," he said. He was tall and redheaded, with a pillow-shaped torso and toothpick legs. He was maybe fifty. He opened the door of room 903 for us, and I had not even walked through it when he said, "Where the heck is your husband?"

I couldn't think of a reply. There was nothing at all I wanted to share with Dr. Fred. But he was waiting for an answer. And just when I was thinking I had no option but to burst into tears, my mother, using every ounce of charm she possessed, slapped her delicate hand up on Dr. Fred's big shoulder and said, "He's on a business trip, Fred. Wouldn't you know it? On a business trip to Florida."

Fred looked at me, then back to my mother. "I prefer Dr. Fred," he said.

My mother squeezed his arm. "Dr. Fred it is," she said, and went to set down our bags.

Dr. Fred, who seemed a little flustered by the arm-squeeze, flipped through my chart. After a few minutes, he said, "I see you've written out a birth plan."

"Yes," I said.

"Go ahead and kiss it good-bye. Nobody takes those things seriously here. And, a word to the wise, the 'birth-plan people' are far more likely to be treated as whiners." He patted me on the back. "I wouldn't bring it up with the nurses."

I thought about the time I'd spent trying to craft just the right letter to communicate my preferences to the vast, anonymous hospital staff that would deliver my child. This had been months ago, and I wrote draft after draft, trying to strike the perfect tone of both friendly and serious, both accommodating and steadfast, both in awe of their medical expertise and firm in my own wishes.

I wanted no drugs of any kind, no whisking of the baby off to the nursery, no plastic warming box, no formula. I wanted to walk around while I labored, to sit on a birthing ball and moan, to use gravity to help pull the baby down and out. It was my plan to birth him and then warm him against my own skin while he nursed. I didn't want them to cut the cord right away, either. Betty had said it was better to wait until it had stopped pulsating—a few minutes at least—so it could continue supplying blood until the baby was comfortable breathing on his own. I just wanted to do things the way nature intended, as much as was possible inside this ten-story hospital.

"And I'm ordering you an epidural," Dr. Fred said, writing something on a chart.

"No," I said. "I don't want an epidural."

He stopped writing and stared at me. Either he hadn't read the birth plan or he was being a drama queen. "I don't think you understand," he said, "just how very badly this is going to hurt."

"No drugs," I said.

He looked at me a second longer, then slapped my chart closed and said, "Okeydokey," in a "you're a nut job" kind of way. And then he walked out of the room.

I looked at my mother. "Where's he going? Was he mad at me?"

"No, darlin'," she said. "I'm sure he's just busy."

"We weren't done!" I said. "Were we done?"

My mother walked to the door. "I'll go see if I can find him," she said, and popped out into the hallway.

While she was gone, I had another searing contraction. This one had me down on my hands and knees on the slick, cool floor. I tried to breathe and relax like Betty said, but it's hard enough to decide to relax when you're sitting in a chair pretending. Relaxing now, in the face of the real thing, seemed like a quaint and almost comical idea. I lowered my cheek down to the floor and rested it there. This wasn't quite how I'd pictured things.

As the contraction subsided, I decided I might just stay down there awhile. Then two white sneakers appeared just inches from my eyes, and a rich, buttery woman's voice said, "Let's get you hooked up."

"I'm good," I said, my squished lips rubbery. "I'll just hang out here."

And then two hands were under my arms, pulling me up. I was panting for breath.

"Looks like your water broke," the woman said as I made it to my feet. My sweatpants were soaked. The floor was wet, too. I hadn't even felt it.

She leaned me against the bed and started to bustle around the room. I liked the way she moved—so confident, like she'd done this a million times. She wiped up the floor and then brought a gown over to me.

"No, no," I said, a little woozy. "I want to labor in my own clothes. It's in my birth—" I stopped before I said "plan."

"These wet clothes?" she said, touching my sweatpants. She didn't seem like someone who would think I was a whiner.

I paused. "I guess not."

She helped me change into a gown and wiped me down with a nubby washrag that she'd soaked in steaming hot water. It was too hot, but it felt good.

"I want to be able to walk around," I said as we got me into the bed.

"Okay," she said, the way you might talk to a feral cat under your porch. "We're just going to check on your baby first."

The nurse's name was Marie and she told me she was from Aruba. She looked about twenty, but her voice sounded much older. I closed my eyes while she fiddled with the machine, and she talked on and on in a kind of lullaby: the rain outside, the pinging sound in her car's engine, her little boy on vacation back home with her parents. My mother came back in then, and introduced herself, and she and Marie complimented each other on their earrings—my mother's small gold hoops and Marie's multicolored wooden fish.

While they were chatting, I got another contraction. This one was so blindingly painful that I pushed myself out of bed and paced the floor like I was in an asylum. I let out a moan that I'm sure people heard all the way in the parking garage. This one lasted longer than the others had, and a splash of blood came with it. As it subsided, Marie got to wiping up the floor. All I could think to say was "Sorry about the mess."

When we finally got me hooked up to the monitor, it turned out I was having a thing called "decels."

"That sounds bad," I said.

She said it meant that the baby's heart rate was slowing down with contractions. "We're just going to keep an eye on it," Marie said, patting my hand.

The baby's heart rate did not indicate that it was in distress. But something was a little bit wrong. Not necessarily badly wrong, but the umbilical cord, for example, might have been wrapped around his neck or his arm.

"That's sounds very bad!" I said.

"Not necessarily," she said. "Babies can be born with a cord around their necks and be fine. But it's something to watch."

Several contractions later, Marie had also determined that the baby was still facing the wrong direction. "Usually they've turned by now," she said.

"That can't be good," I said.

"It's fine for the baby," she said. "But for you, it's very painful."

I was steadfast in my desire for no drugs, so my mother, her Chanel handbag in one of the side chairs, was holding and rocking and patting me as I thrashed my way through each contraction. I couldn't bear to have anything touching me during them—especially that hospital gown—so I was pacing the room stark naked, splashing buckets of blood on every surface and person in the room. In between contractions, I was freezing cold and required three blankets. My poor mother, in her DKNY exercise togs, tended to me: blankets on, blankets off, bucket of blood, blankets on . . . The contractions came faster and faster, and they continued to attach a fetal monitor to my belly every few minutes to check on the little one.

During one particularly agonizing contraction, the phone in the room rang. The sound of it absolutely made me panic. I pointed in the direction of the noise and shouted, "Make it stop!" My mother walked over, lifted the receiver, and dropped it right back down. Whoever it was did not try to call again, and it occurred to me only later that it might have been Dean.

I had been at this for what felt like hours when Marie came in to tell me her shift would be over at six. She had been in the room almost constantly, wiping up the floor, checking the monitor, helping to hold me during the worst moments. We had not seen Dr. Fred since we arrived, and I hoped not to see him again. Marie was the person I wanted to deliver my baby.

"No!" I said. "Don't leave me!"

And just as I said it, another contraction. I put my arms around Marie's neck and she held me, stark naked, until it passed.

"I need to talk to you about something before I go," she said, helping me to the chair. Then she told me that Dr. Fred, who had been checking the printouts from the monitor, did not like the increasing frequency of the decels. He'd told Marie that it was no longer safe to monitor the baby only periodically. He wanted me hooked up to the monitor at all times.

"But I have to be in bed to be hooked up," I protested.

"Yes," Marie said.

"But I can't make it through the contractions unless I can move around."

"He wants you to have an epidural," she said.

"No drugs!" I said.

She put her hand on my hand. "This is what you need to do now," she said quietly.

I had spent many months imagining the birth. In my mind, I was always tough and noble, saintlike in my ability to endure pain. I just marched into the hospital and birthed that baby, the way my own mother had, the way all mothers in the history of motherhood had—up until recently. But in my imagination, it had not hurt like this. And in my imagination, it had not taken this long.

"This is not the kind of birth I want," I said.

And Marie, who might have been an angel, said, "It may be time to start thinking about what kind of birth your baby would want."

And so I relented. Dr. Fred won. I requested the epidural and, two contractions later, a very tall Asian man came wordlessly into the room with a rolling tray of tools. When he finally spoke, he said this: "It will be very important that you do not move after we begin. Even if you have a contraction, you must not move. Do you understand me?"

I nodded. One of the many reasons I had not wanted an epidural was that I hated the idea of a needle going into my spine. "I won't move," I said. "I promise."

Sure enough, I had a contraction as he was inserting the needle. I squeezed my mother's hand so hard I left a bruise that stayed there for almost a week. I trembled, and I held my breath until I felt dizzy. And as the contraction subsided, he said, "All done."

He said it would take a while to kick in, but I didn't have any contractions after that. I kept waiting for another one, but none came. And then, just as I was starting to wonder if my labor had stopped altogether, our new nurse showed me the monitor and pointed out the contractions that had been happening all along. I'd had four since the epidural. My body had been doing the exact same thing that had sent me reeling across the room time and again for hours, but now I no longer felt it. It was kind of wonderful. And it was kind of awful, too.

I was relieved for the pain to be over. And so was my mother, who pulled a clean T-shirt out of her overnight bag and threw her old one into the medical-waste garbage. But suddenly it was like nothing was happening. I lay in bed, watching the monitor for the next contraction, and I felt so quiet and still it was almost boring. After a while, tears were dripping onto my pillow. My mother, who had started reading a trashy romance novel, looked up at me and said, "Are you hurting?"

"No," I said.

"What's wrong, sweetheart?"

Her tenderness made it worse. Finally, I said, "I read an article that said babies whose mothers have epidurals are more likely to become drug addicts."

My mother didn't know what to say to that. She just squeezed my hand and waited for me to go on.

"I've ruined him!" I said. "He's ruined because I couldn't hack it."

"Darlin'," she said kindly. "He's not ruined yet. You've got his whole childhood to ruin him."

But I couldn't even give her a smile. Everything was all wrong. No

Dean, no Nicole. The awful Dr. Fred. Marie gone home. The pain, the blood. The fetal monitor. Nothing at all was right.

"It's not how you wanted it, but it's how it is," she said in her tenderest voice. "In truth," she added, "much of mothering is that way."

I was supposed to rest, so I closed my eyes. But then I had something else to say.

"Mom?" I said.

She looked up.

"The invitations have already gone out."

She knew that, of course. She'd mailed them weeks ago. But my mother wasn't one to linger on such details, so she just crinkled up her nose. Then she squeezed my hand and told me to close my eyes. After a bit, she started dozing in the recliner chair, but I couldn't sleep. Every time the door opened, I thought it was Dean. I had to open my eyes and look. Finally I gave up on sleep and turned on the TV.

It felt so wrong to be watching *Love Boat* in the wee morning hours when I should have been laboring. It felt so strange to be so immobile and for the room to be so quiet. It was so awful to think of all those invitations lying on people's desks. People had marked their calendars. Out-of-towners were booking hotel rooms. My mother had a collection of early gifts on a table in her living room. It wasn't how it was supposed to be, but it was how it was.

12

At about eight in the morning, just as I was dozing off, Dr. Fred arrived.

"Well, you're going to need a Cesarean," he announced, as if we'd been in midconversation, and startled my mother out of a deep sleep. "We like to play it safe around here. If you start to push and the decels get worse, the fetus might get trapped in the birth canal."

"What do you do then?" I asked.

He looked at me. "Nothing," he said. "There's nothing to be done."

He handed us some forms to sign and some handouts. "I recommend the C-section," he said. "It's the no-risk way to go." He stood up to leave. "But it is harder on the mother." At the door, he turned around and told us he was getting some coffee and would be back in five.

My mother went to the windowless bathroom and splashed some water on her face.

"C-section!" I shouted from the bed. "Nobody's even mentioned that at all!"

"He doesn't have the best bedside manner," she said as she reappeared.

As she sat on the edge of the bed and started combing through the pamphlets, there was a knock at the door. The nurses never knocked, just moved silently in and out. A knock. It had to be Dean. Who else would it be at 8:00 A.M.? Dean. Just in the nick of time to become a daddy, one way or another.

The door opened, and in walked Nicole, carrying her scrubs over her arm.

"How could you leave me with Dr. Fred?" I said.

"I'm sorry," she said, taking my hand. She said that her father had had a heart attack.

I thought about saying "That's no excuse," but decided against it.

"How is he now?" my mother asked.

Nicole said, "Stable." She was flying back to Chicago the next day.

"Where's Dean?" Nicole said, looking around.

"He left me."

"He left you?"

I nodded. My mother nodded.

"When?"

"Yesterday."

Nicole looked back and forth between me and my mother, and then said, "Well, that's a heck of a way to get things started."

Nicole excused herself after a minute and changed into her scrubs in our bathroom. When she came out, she was ready to get down to business.

"Now," she said, taking a long accordion of printouts off the fetal monitor's table, "let's talk about you."

Nicole wasn't convinced that I needed a C-section. But Dr. Fred was a doctor, and Nicole was only a nurse, so she couldn't really overrule him. But she could bring in a consulting physician.

A half hour later, a very fit, wide-awake, curly-haired woman named Dr. McKay was saying, "I've got a good feeling about you! Let's try some pushing!"

I was too tired to push. "Some pushing?" I said, stalling.

"Let's push!" she said cheerfully. "This is going to go well. You've got great hips."

"That's what they tell me," I said.

Before I knew it, they had me in a pushing position, all curled up like a shrimp. My mother and a nurse held my shoulders, while Nicole and Dr. McKay manned the nether regions. Nicole watched the monitor so that I could time my pushing to the contractions. Kind of like having turbo on your sports car.

"Okay!" Nicole said, and I pushed.

As soon as I started pushing, Nicole and Dr. McKay and the nurse who was standing behind them started shouting words of encouragement, telling me they could see the head, that he was just right there, almost out, and to keep going. I wondered if they were just faking to help me keep my energy up or if they really saw something. Finally I decided it didn't matter. It did help me to hear all that encouragement. And so I chose to believe them and pushed my little heart out.

It worked. Three pushes later, he was out. I didn't even feel it, but he came out, and I got the big news of the day: He was, in fact, a she.

"I guess this rules out 'Dean junior,' " my mother said.

I hadn't even left room for the possibility that he might be a girl. I didn't even have a name for a girl. I had just known that he was a boy. But, as with other things in my life, I'd been mistaken.

They pulled her up to my chest, and she started to nurse. Things finally seemed real. Her eyes were wide open and milky black, and she was looking at me as if to say, *Okay, I'm here! What's next?* I couldn't believe the tiny mouth, the little fingernails, the fuzzy hair on top. Eyelashes! I'd made eyelashes inside my body! How the heck had I pulled that off?

I had not even let myself think about giving birth. It had seemed so impossible, it was like trying to visualize outer space—more of a brainteaser than anything real. And even after I had just done it, it still seemed impossible. Once the baby was out, it was as if she had always been right there, pink-faced and wet, on my chest.

But here we were. I knew it was huge moment, and yet, at the same time, I couldn't seem to take it in. I felt like I ought to be having big "I just created another human being" feelings—weeping with joy or trembling with excitement. But instead, I just felt something I could only describe as pleased. I was very, very pleased. This was exactly right. She was exactly the little creature I had been waiting for. I watched her nursing, now with her eyes closed, and I knew right then: She was better than I ever could have wished for.

I did not want to ruin the moment by thinking about Dean. But when I thought about how I shouldn't think about him, I paused for a moment to marvel at the fact that he'd chosen to miss this. What was wrong with him? Granted, I'd done all the work, but we had made this human being together, and here she was. And he was in some truck stop off the interstate, buying Ding Dongs and paying for gas.

And I resolved right then and there that I would not be one of those single mothers who holds out hope of her child's father coming to his senses and coming home. This little person would not grow up with a hole in her life where a father should be. Nobody in our house was going to miss Dean. From here on out, he'd be nothing but a sperm donor. This baby's childhood was going to be a veritable parade of people who loved her. She was going to have more admirers than she knew what to do with. True, she would have no father—a big exception any way you sliced it. But, dammit, I was going to be so good, she wouldn't even miss him.

13

Despite my protests, they whisked the baby off to the nursery. I was too tired to fight them. My mother went along with the baby to make sure she was okay, and the doctor and Nicole were gone soon after.

It seemed like they all left at once. And then I was alone. A nurse was supposed to be coming to the room to clean me up and help me move from the labor-and-delivery room to one on the infant hallway, but she must have been taking a smoke break. She was nowhere to be found.

I just lay there in the silence, disliking the quietness, the smears of blood on the floor, the fluorescent lights. The lights had been dimmed while I was laboring to make it feel homey, but once the pushing started, those fluorescents came on like at a football field on a Friday night. Now the place lacked atmosphere, and voices, and people, and distractions.

I was desperate to see the baby, and I might have wandered down the hall to look for her—but I couldn't walk. I wondered what they were doing to her in the nursery. I hoped they weren't giving her formula, as Betty had said they would try to do. My birth plan had expressly forbidden bottles of any kind, so as not to interfere with breast-feeding. Not that my wishes carried any weight.

So I was paralyzed, wide-awake, and flooded with hormones. I thought about Dean. As mad as I was, I also just wanted to talk to him. There was a phone near the birthing bed, and I grabbed it and dialed his cell number. No answer, of course. I'd been thinking he might not recognize the hospital's number and pick up. But my luck didn't run that way.

Dean was gone. I had no job. This meant I had no income at all. How was I going to pay the mortgage? The taxes? The electric bill? What was I going to live on? I had a small bundle of stocks that my grandfather had left me, but I was never, ever supposed to touch it. And even if I decided to use it to live on, it'd be gone within the year.

My mother would help me some, of course. But she didn't have the cash for an extra mortgage lying around. And I knew better than to even think about my father. He was an up-by-the-bootstraps guy. His own father used to drop him at the freeway exit near their house and let him hitch to school. To *elementary* school. If you asked my father about it, he'd tell you he looked a lot older than he was. He'd tell you he met a lot of interesting folks that way. He'd tell you it was good for him, in the end. He did not look kindly on people who didn't take care of themselves.

I guessed I'd have to sell my house and move in with my mother. She'd take me. She'd have to. I'd sell off most of my stuff (oh—it didn't bear thinking about: the dinette, the Victorian fainting couch, the inlaid Art Nouveau bookshelf) and move back into my childhood bedroom. The baby and I would share. I could cook for my mom to earn my keep, and when the baby was old enough for day care (when was that, exactly?), I'd find a cheap apartment somewhere. It could work. I could make it work.

Or maybe I could rent out the house to cover my expenses and move back there years down the road. I actually couldn't stand the idea of losing the house. It was almost as bad as losing Dean. Maybe I could rent out the house, stay with my mother, and figure out a get-rich-quick scheme in the meantime.

Then my cell phone rang, and it was Meredith.

"You thought I was Dean, didn't you?" she said right off the bat, and I confessed I had. Then she said, "How are you doing?"

"Well," I said. "I'm less pregnant than I used to be."

"You had the baby?"

"I had the baby," I said. "She's a girl."

"I knew it was a girl," Meredith said. "What's her name?"

"I'm working on that," I said.

I gave Meredith the whole birth story, leaving out no detail, and then she did the *Reader's Digest* version of her third date with Dr. Blandon. He held the car door for her. He had a dimple she'd never noticed. He took her to a Moroccan place for dinner but accidentally drove right past the restaurant.

"Do you think that means he was nervous?" she asked.

"It sounds like a good bet," I said.

They were supposed to go to a jazz concert, but they talked so long at the restaurant that they went for ice cream instead. They sat on the hood of his car and licked their cones while he asked her all about herself. "I'm telling you," Meredith said, "he was Barbara Walters."

"Was that good or was that bad?"

"Everything about him," Meredith said, "is good."

I was about to ask if he'd kissed her good night when a skeletally thin nurse came in and made a distinct "hang up the phone" motion with her hands. So I did.

"Time to get you cleaned up," she said, and started pulling my sheets down.

She removed my catheter as she gave me her opinions on everything from raising children to air pollution.

"I've seen hundreds of births," she said. "Women come, birth the babies, and then we wheel 'em out of here with the goofiest looks on their faces. You've got one. All the moms do. It's got to be the hormones, because I don't see how those wrinkled little baked potatoes could make anybody that happy."

I was quiet. She was not a person I wanted to share with. I just watched her swish around the room, getting the place squared away with remarkable speed.

When we were ready, she and an orderly moved me to a new bed and tucked me in with some pillows and blankets. Just before she wheeled me off to my new room, she suggested I might want to put on some makeup.

"You look a little droopy," she said.

We went past the nursery on the way. I could see my mother and the baby in there. My mom was wearing a hospital coat and gloves. "That's her! That's her!" I said, pointing at the window, begging to stop for a minute so I could see better.

But the skinny nurse just kept on walking as if I hadn't said anything at all. She parked me in my room, hit the brake, and I was alone again.

I waited a good half hour after that. Finally, my mother arrived, and behind her, a nurse with the baby wrapped up like a papoose in a plastic box on wheels.

"Is she sick?" I said, instantly terrified.

"No, no!" my mom said. "She's just in the warmer."

The nurse left strict instructions not to take the baby out of her box, and though I'd had my own instructions not to put her in one in the first place, I was afraid to take her out. What if I took her out and something terrible happened? She could get hypothermia. She could start screaming and just refuse to stop. A whole team of medical professionals could rush in and yell at me to put her back.

I watched her while my mom told me about what they'd been up to: a bath, some shots, some glop for the baby's eyes.

"The glop is in case you have venereal disease," my mother explained. "So the baby doesn't go blind."

"I don't have venereal disease!" I said.

My mother shrugged. "It's the law."

I could not imagine what kind of shots a one-hour-old baby could possibly need. This place was so weird. They just popped 'em on a conveyor belt and sent them through a Rube Goldberg machine.

My mother pointed through the box at the baby's forehead. "And she has a little birthmark above her nose," she said.

I could barely make it out.

"It's called a stork bite," she said. "It should be gone by kindergarten."

I looked up to see if she was kidding.

"But mostly gone in a year," she added.

We studied the mark.

"I think it's cute," my mother said.

"I'm taking her out," I said to my mother, who glanced furtively at the door as she helped me get the box open, working quickly so we wouldn't get caught.

And out she came! I felt desperately relieved. I'd known this baby less than two hours, and already my arms felt empty without her. I held her snugly and touched her forehead with my nose. I couldn't believe how tiny she was. She was fast asleep in her swaddling blanket, and her eyes were closed in a little crescent of lashes. She was easy to hold in this little wrapped-up bundle, and I made a note to learn how to swaddle before I left the hospital.

It was almost noon. I should have slept, but before I could settle, the visitors started to arrive. They kept up a steady parade, one after another throughout the day, and with them came the question

"Where's Dean?" My mother, who stayed for most of the day, did her best to distract them.

My cousin Sarah, who burst into tears when she saw the baby, burst into tears a second time when I told her Dean had left me.

After that, I lied to my aunt Lindy, who brought a yellow blanket she'd crocheted and who wanted to see Dean. I didn't have the heart to tell her. I said he'd gone down to the cafeteria to get me a snack. "He's going to be such a great father," she told me.

I also lied to both of my ex-stepmothers, two perfectly nice women who had, like my mother, failed to make it work with my dad—and both of whom came with cookie bouquets and missed each other by minutes.

My cousin Peter and his wife, Anna, traded off shifts watching their kids in the hallway. They didn't want to bring in any germs. I told them Dean was out buying a car seat, and they went on and on about how we should have thought about that sooner, about how having kids is all about thinking ahead.

Meredith had been the first person to arrive, peeking in on her way to work. She showed up with a bottle of champagne and a stack of Dixie cups and insisted I take a sip. After our toast, she peeked over my lap to get a good look at the baby.

"Do you want to hold her?" I asked.

"No," she said.

I must have looked disappointed, because she went on.

"You know, she's asleep. I don't need to mess with her. And what if I dropped her? You guys are all settled there. I'm not great with babies. Plus"—she held up her Dixie cup—"I'm drunk."

I nodded. There was a short silence, and then she held up the tweed jacket that was over her arm.

I gave her the curious look she wanted, and she said, "It's Dr. Blandon's. He's going to stop by work and pick it up. Thought you'd like to see."

She had me. "How did he happen to leave it with you?"

"He came in for some ice cream."

"After you got back from the ice cream shop?"

"Well," she said, twinkling, "we had some more."

Turns out, he got a crazy back spasm not too long after they walked in, and they spent a couple of hours with him flat on his back on her new rug from Ikea.

"He has a bad back?" I said.

"No," she said. "He had to carry a Great Dane up a flight of stairs that morning."

I looked at her.

"This dog weighed a hundred and sixty pounds."

She gave Dr. Blandon chocolate-chip mint and they talked about his life as a vet. Then they rolled him over and she gave him a massage.

"So," she said. "No first kiss. But a first massage."

"Meredith," I said, "you look smitten. You look smitten in a way that you never, ever do."

"It's just the champagne," she said, waving her Dixie cup again.

My father, in contrast to Meredith, was the last visitor of the day, hitting the hospital right at my late-afternoon sinking spell. He'd had a cold, so I made him wear a mask and sit in the armchair across the room. My mother "went for coffee" when he arrived. He asked where Dean was right away. What he actually said was, "Where's the genius who got you in this trouble?"

"He's catching up on some sleep," I said, which could have been true. Dean's leaving seemed so much worse now that I was holding a baby in my arms. And my father, a rifle owner, might actually have tried to hunt Dean down. It occurred to me it might be best not to tell him at all and spend the rest of my life pretending Dean was in the bathroom or working late.

After the basics of asking about me and the baby, my dad took off the mask to go, but then lingered. He paced around the room, reading the cards and examining the flowers. I watched him for a while, then I said, "What's going on with you?"

He sat down on the edge of the armchair and said, "I've got a question for you."

"Let's hear it," I said. My epidural was really wearing off.

He leaned forward, elbows on knees, and said, "Do you think your mother would go out with me?"

I looked at him. "I don't understand the question."

He nodded and looked around the room like he might find some kind of guidance among my leftover hospital-issued Jell-O bowls and plastic cups.

Then I said, "She just invented an excuse to leave the room, if that gives you any sense of her feelings."

He nodded again.

I continued. "Isn't there anyone else in the entire city you could date?"

"The thing is," my dad said, "I may be in love with her."

"Again?" I asked.

"Again," he said.

A number of responses ran through my head, but I went with "You might want to rethink that."

"I can't help it," he said. He put his head down and squeezed a fistful of his hair. "It just hit me."

Then a nurse came in.

"Hi," she said to me, glancing over at my dad. "We're going to need to get you in the shower." My dad looked up then, and she recognized him.

"Doc Harris!" she said, moving quickly to shake his hand. He stood and put on a smile, flirted a little, and then got himself out of there pretty fast. When he was gone, she said, "That's your dad? He's so dreamy! Every nurse I know has a crush on him."

"He's quite a guy," I said.

My mother returned midshower, just as the baby was waking up and starting to fuss. She picked her up out of the bassinet and did her best to quiet her.

"How's your daddy?" she asked.

"He's okay," I said. Then I added, "Nurse Martha says all the nurses around here have a crush on him."

My mother just snorted a laugh and paced the baby around the room.

Later, after my mother went home to get some rest, Meredith showed up with a requested spread of sushi takeout for dinner. I gobbled down California rolls while she watched with distaste, reminding me each time I held out a piece to her that she didn't "do seafood."

"Hey," she said when I was about halfway done, "can lactating women even eat sushi?" I was not the first friend Meredith had watched walk down the baby path.

"Opinions vary," I said. "But I'm going with 'Yes.' "

She was holding the baby while I ate. The baby was so asleep, she might as well have been a throw pillow.

"She's not so bad, huh?" I asked, gesturing at the baby with my chopsticks.

"No," Meredith said, thinking about it. "They're not too bad when they're sleeping."

Meredith handed her back as soon as I was done, reminding me that I needed to get some sleep. She gave me a little kiss on the forehead as she headed out. Then, at the door, she stopped and said, "I have a present for you, by the way."

I said, "You got me a baby present?"

"It's not for the baby," she said. "It's for you."

"Well, hand it over," I said.

"Soon," she said. "It's not quite ready."

She blew me a kiss, and then she left, and it was quiet for the first time all day. But just as I was settling my head back, and just as I started to feel the aftershock of exhaustion start to hit me, the baby woke up. Really woke up. I guess she'd had enough sleep. And, I learned that night, whenever she was awake, she was crying. Meredith was probably already in the parking lot when it started, but the fussing was so loud, she may have even heard her.

The crying made me nervous. I'd nurse her and she'd get quiet for a while, and then she'd doze off, but she'd wake up and cry again a short while later. I was all alone, and I started to worry that something was wrong with her.

I pressed the NURSE button on my bed.

Nurse Martha showed up, and I said, "Why is she crying so much?"

Nurse Martha looked like she felt very sorry for the baby. "She's just hungry," she said.

"But she's been nursing all day!"

"But you don't have your milk yet," she explained. "So there's not much for her to eat."

I knew about this. Before the milk, there was a thing called colostrum, which Betty had said was very nutritious, but was only doled out in drops.

"Why don't you let me take her for a while so you can get some sleep?" she offered.

"No!" I almost shouted, as if she'd suggested selling the baby on eBay. "We'll be fine. Thank you."

That had been in my unread birth plan, too: "rooming in." The baby was to sleep in my room, and in my bed, with me—not with all those sleeping babies (who, looking back, also had sleeping mothers) in the nursery. Hell, no. We were better than that.

And so the night began. I knew that having a baby involved sleep deprivation, and a friend with kids had even described it as "brutal," but I wasn't at all prepared. We were up every few hours, all night. She'd wake, and cry, and then nurse back to sleep.

During one of her wake-ups, she didn't fall back to sleep easily. I panicked—until it occurred to me to sing her a lullaby. That's what lullabies had been invented for, after all. But at that moment, with the pressure on, I couldn't think of any. A million lullabies in the world, and I could not come up with one. The only song, in fact, that came to my mind was "I Will Survive." So I ran with it. In a hoarse whisper, I started to sing.

That seemed to get the baby's attention, so I kept going. I stroked her head and sang the words as softly as a person praying. It occurred to me that this song should be my anthem. Gloria Gaynor had been dumped—but look at her now! She was kicking ass! But even though that song was all about triumph when it came from Gloria's mouth, with my broken little middle-of-the-night voice, it just sounded kind of hopeless. By the time I was singing the lines "Did you think I'd crumble? Did you think I'd lay down and die?" my voice was faltering so much I had to stop for a sip of water.

I spent that whole night with the baby in the bed with me, my arm asleep, my whole body hurting. I was afraid to take pain medication in case it might get into my not-yet-arrived breast milk and hurt her, so I left the pill they'd assured me was safe on the nightstand.

My stubbornness was, perhaps, some kind of half-dead-with-exhaustion, hormone-induced attempt at self-esteem renewal through mothering. I was going to be the best, most perfect goddamned mother in the history of the human race. I was not going to do one thing that would harm my baby, even if doctors said it wouldn't harm her anyway, like take pain medicine. I wanted to do everything better than right.

Around three in the morning, I gave up and took the pain medicine. The whole space between my belly button and the tops of my thighs hurt so badly it felt like I was being crushed in a vise, and, needless to say, I couldn't get comfortable. In the bed, I moved and twisted and rearranged constantly, repositioning the baby each time, terrified she'd wake up.

I was going to need a name for this girl. She wasn't going to be Dean Murphy, Jr., anymore. I'd have to come up with something beautiful and feminine yet strong and fierce. Something appropriate for a tiny person of seven pounds, eight ounces, but also right for an adult woman out showing the world how things are done. Something distinctive to her (I spent my childhood as "Jenny Harris"—pronounced like it was all one word—or "Jenny H."). Distinctive, but not trendy. Although, of course, lately, according to the baby-name books I'd read, being distinctive was trendy. I didn't want to call her Catelyn or Ruby or Olivia, only to have those names fall out of fashion before she hit kindergarten.

Dean Harris Murphy. It had been an easy name, a perfect name. We were going to call him either Dean or Harris, depending on his personality. Boys were easy to name. Girls were harder. It seemed to me that I ought to do something to honor my mother, who had put up with so many of my crises. My mother's middle name was Maxine, and that seemed like a good middle name for this little one. And the first name should be something sensible, intelligent, classic. As the painkiller kicked in, I ran through names in my head, and as I finally started to drift off, I settled on one: Elizabeth. And no nicknames, either. She would be Elizabeth Maxine Harris. And she'd go by her full name, Elizabeth.

"You may call her Elizabeth," said Meredith, who brought me breakfast the next morning. "But everybody else is going to call her Maxie."

"They'll call her whatever I tell them her name is," I said.

"No," Meredith said. "They'll take one look at her and call her Maxie."

And so, over breakfast, she became Maxie. In the light of Meredith's absolute certainty, it was easy to give in. And people loved it. "Her name is Elizabeth Maxine," I'd tell them. "But we're calling her Maxie."

Talking about her name was a great distraction for the visitors who came on Day Two asking about Dean. By the end of the day, I was liking the name so much, when people saw her and said, "And what is your name?" I just tilted her toward them, like a ventriloquist, and said: "Maxie."

14

The next day, a nurse wheeled Maxie and me to the curb. We waited with my mother for the hospital valet to bring my car around. I had installed the car seat at around Month Six and had been driving around with it, empty and waiting, ever since. I'd researched all the brands thoroughly and then bought the one that matched the interior of my car. As my mother and Maxie and I stood on the sidewalk in the mild sunlight, I felt confident that I was prepared for the ride home at least.

But after we'd tipped the valet and my mother had put my bag in the back, I realized I had no idea how to get the baby into the car seat. Here's where I panicked: Should I leave the basket in the car and slip the baby into it? Or should I take the basket out, snap the baby in, and then pop the whole thing back inside? The choice was paralyzing. She was so tiny, and her head seemed like it was attached to her body on a macaroni noodle. I had no idea how to get her in.

"Don't ask me," my mother said. "We didn't even use car seats when you were a baby."

Finally, I popped the basket out and put it on the sidewalk. Then I arranged Maxie in the seat, clipped all the clips, lifted it by the handle, and used every bit of strength I had in me to stretch across the backseat and snap the basket into the base. Days later, when I was no longer taking pain medicine, I would discover that doing this actually hurt quite a bit.

By the time I got her in, she was all slumped over—almost folded in half—and I didn't know how to reposition her without starting all over, so my mother drove and I sat in the backseat holding Maxie's head up and hoping for the best.

Every bump on the drive home gave me a jolt of adrenaline. Maxie seemed far too small and far too precious to be out in the world, zooming along at thirty-five miles an hour like this. How could I protect her from anything out here? We were sitting ducks! I was also terrified that she was going to start to cry, and I'd be helpless to soothe her until we made it home. The sound of her crying made me absolutely frantic to stop it. It was like I had an emergency siren going off in my head, with a blinking sign that said HELP THE BABY! When she cried, I could think about nothing else.

But Maxie fell asleep and stayed that way for the drive.

My mother pulled into the driveway a bit too quickly for me, but then we stopped moving, and Maxie was still out. I'd half expected to see Dean's Explorer parked out front, in part because I was just used to seeing it there, and in part because I could not believe he was missing all this. But there was no Explorer. No sign of him at all.

My mother started to open the door, but I stopped her.

"Wait," I said.

She knew what I meant. There was no rush. Soon enough, we'd

be inside the house and catapulted into a whole new life. Maxie had given us a few minutes to take a deep breath, and it seemed crazy not to take it. I was in the backseat, and I watched my mother lean her head back against the headrest.

"Are you going to stay with me?" I whispered. And then, before she could answer: "I don't want to be alone."

"You won't be alone. You'll have the baby."

"Okay, that's worse than being alone."

I had never changed a diaper before. I had never babysat or been around children. Any confidence that some simian knowledge of what to do would just rise up in me when I needed it had blown out the window on the drive home.

"I will stay with you," my mother said. "Until my allergies get too bad."

"What is the definition of 'too bad'?" I said. This was not a time to let some sniffles get in the way of doing the right thing. This was a real emergency. This was life or death.

"Well, I've got a whole package of Benadryl in my purse, so I'm planning to stay at least a week."

A week. That was something.

"Thanks, Mom," I whispered, just as a car with racing stripes and no muffler came tearing down the street. The vibration was so loud, I could actually feel it pulsing against my skin, and though it didn't wake Maxie, it startled us enough to decide to go inside.

Getting out of the car was painful in a way that I hadn't noticed on the way in. I hadn't had an episiotomy, but I had ripped, as Nicole put it, "from stem to stern." She had sewed me back up while I cuddled the baby, and I was now under strict orders to take at least two warm baths a day to help myself heal. I took things slowly, and I let my mother pop the infant carrier out for me and head up the walk with Maxie.

The house was my house, and everything about it was the same. I was different, though, and so it felt like a whole new place. It was like someone had tinted everything a slightly different color. Not a bad color—just not the one I'd been used to before.

Dr. Blandon greeted us at the door by rubbing all over my mother's pant legs. She set sleeping Maxie on the floor in the living room and headed to the bedroom with my suitcase.

"You're just going to leave her there?" I whispered.

"She'll be fine," she said. "Keep an eye on the cat."

It was true. Maxie was at cat level. And spider level and lizard level and cockroach level. I lifted the basket up and set it on the dining table, coming eye to eye with the warning notice, standard on all baby equipment, that detailed in yellow and black the many ways in which that car seat could maim, mutilate, torture, or kill my baby. DO NOT LEAVE CHILD UNATTENDED IN SEAT! it read like the voice of God. DO NOT PLACE SEAT ON ANY SURFACE HIGHER THAN FLOOR. INFANTS CAN BE KILLED IF SEAT FALLS TO GROUND.

I moved her back to the floor. I had to pee, but I was afraid to leave her there alone. How on earth could that seat fall off the table? The cat could knock it off, I decided. The table leg could dislodge. A great gust of wind could come along. An earthquake. None of these things was likely, but all were at least possible. And I was not taking any chances, so I finally took the baby into the bathroom with me, peed, and didn't flush.

When the phone rang, I was afraid Maxie's eyes would pop open and I'd soon hear the cry that sent me scrambling to appease her. When she didn't stir, I had another jolt: It was Dean. I could feel it. I couldn't wait to forgive him and tell him the great news that we had a girl, of all things, and tell him we'd named her Maxie.

I was close, but it wasn't Dean. It was his mother.

"We heard the awful news about what our son did to you," she said, without saying hello or identifying herself. "Dean's father and I want you to know that sometimes that boy is a stupid idiot, and after you have the baby—"

"Mrs. Murphy," I interrupted, "I had the baby two days ago."

There was a silence. Then she said, "Is it healthy?"

"It is!" I could feel myself starting to gush. "She is! It's a girl! She's a girl! And she's perfect and absolutely gorgeous!"

The next words from her mouth sounded almost dreamy. "A girl," she said.

"Seven pounds, eight ounces!" I announced.

"That sounds fat to me," she said. "Is she fat?"

"She's not fat! The doctor says she's perfect." Dean and I had agreed months ago not to tell her about the midwife.

"And what are you calling her?"

"Maxie," I said.

"That's an awful name," she said. "The kids at school are going to call her Maxi Pad."

I didn't know what to say.

"Well," Mrs. Murphy said, seeming eager now to end the digression about the baby, "I was calling to let you know that Dean's father and I would like to help you and our grandchild out financially. Since our son has left you in the lurch, we'd like to send a little something every month to cover your expenses. We know you had hoped to stay home with the baby, and we hope this gesture will enable you to do that."

A thousand responses ran through my head, including "Hell, no"; "Are you fucking crazy?"; and "I can always eat my fat baby if I run out of food"; but the words that came out of my mouth, despite any other instinct I might have had, were "Thank you."

"You're so welcome," she said, sounding oddly affectionate. And just as I thought she was hanging up, she said, "About the last name. Is it Murphy?"

"It's Harris," I said. "Elizabeth Maxine Harris."

"Of course," she said, and the line clicked dead.

15

My mother had started boiling water for pasta, a food she insisted on calling "noodles." She poked her head out from the kitchen.

"Who was that?" she said.

"You're never going to believe it," I said.

But then Maxie woke up, and I couldn't concentrate on any conversation until I had nursed, changed, nursed, rocked, nursed, held, nursed, and sung to her, then nursed her back to sleep.

By then I was tired, too, and I figured I'd nap when she did. I closed my eyes. Seventeen minutes later, she was up again.

"It seems like she should be sleeping longer," my mother said, pulling her out of her bassinet.

"The nurse says she's hungry," I said.

"Well, where is your milk?" she asked.

"It's coming!" I said. "It takes two to four days."

"So any minute now," she said.

"It'll probably be in by tonight," I told her. "That's what the books say."

But the milk didn't come that night, or the next night. Maxie was frantic, and she couldn't sleep. And neither could I. She nursed like a piranha, and my nipples became so sore I couldn't wear a shirt or even pull up the flaps on my nursing bra. My gentle nipples, for whom I'd always had such affection, were so raw they looked like they'd been in bad contact with a cheese grater. Every time Maxie latched on, her wet, toothless mouth felt like it was made of razors. I had to squeeze my eyes closed, make a fist, and count to twenty before it subsided. And she wanted to latch on constantly. Because she was hungry. My newborn was hungry, and I had no milk.

We called a lactation consultant named Rhonda, who on Day Three of the Milk Watch suggested a phone consultation. She was, it turned out, all booked up for the week. She could squeeze us in after supper that night, but only for thirty minutes.

My mother took dictation while I prepared a list of questions to use our minutes effectively. Topping the list was "Why do my nipples have scabs on them?" and just underneath it, competing for top billing, was "Where the hell is my milk?"

The phone call was quite hurried. Regarding the mauled nipples, she suggested many tips for a better baby "latch-on." Regarding the milk itself, she stressed it was important "to get the milk flowing." I resisted the urge to tell her that there was not one single person in my vicinity who did not understand that simple fact. Instead, I wrote down her list of instructions for making it happen: First, and most important, we had to rent a medical-grade breast pump from a breast-feeding specialty store. We had to pump at least five times a day. She warned us that it was the frequency of the pumping that brought the milk. I couldn't just hook myself up, watch *Oprah* for an hour, and be done with it. She told me to pump during every spare minute.

"I don't have any spare minutes," I said to her.

"If you want to breast-feed, you'll have to find some."

I did want to breast-feed. I loved the idea of the closeness, the skin-to-skin contact, the cradling. I loved the novelty of being a source of food for someone. And, of course, I had read all of Betty's handouts about the differences between breast milk and formula. Breast milk seemed to be a kind of miracle juice. It was free and always available. It required no washing or sterilizing. It changed its taste depending on what I had eaten, so Maxie was less likely to turn out to be a picky eater. If she got sick, my breasts would know it and produce extra antibodies for her to help fight the infection. And, mainly, it was just part of my plan. Looking back, it was crazy to think that. Spewing milk out of your nipples has little to do with how much you love, nurture, cuddle, or treasure your baby. But at that moment, the idea that I would not be able to breast-feed was enough to bring tears to my bloodshot eyes.

And so I decided to pump. My mother drove across town and returned with a carload of equipment: sterilized bags, tubes, bottles, nipples, instruction books, and a compact, square suitcase that was, she informed me, the pump. She had to take the baby out on the porch while I read through the pamphlets and tried to figure out which tube connected to what, because I could not concentrate on anything with the baby near me. Only when I was alone could I clear my fuzzy brain enough to do tricky things like read.

I got it all set up and then I spent some time trying to decide which breast was less likely to actually bleed. It was a toss-up. They both looked ghoulish. I picked one and pressed it delicately into a clear plastic funnel that was hooked to a tube connected to the machine. I hesitated before flipping the switch, and then I closed my eyes and pushed it with my toe. The *swoosh!* noise that it made popped my eyes back open just in time to see my sweet, innocent nipple being sucked down into the funnel, elongated in a way I had never imagined possible, and then released to pop back into place. I had not recovered from the sight when it did it again. *Swoosh,* and there it went, the delicate bud that had over the years given me so much pleasure. It was not painful as much as it was humiliating—I could not for the life of me imagine why the inventors of this contraption decided to make the nipple-funnels see-through. No one could possibly want to see her tenderest parts treated in this way.

Nothing came out, by the way. I sat and watched for a good twenty minutes, mesmerized like a rubbernecker at a pileup. But no milk ever came.

Then there was a perfunctory knock at the door.

"Sweetie," my mother said. "Can I bring in a visitor?"

There I was on the sofa, my raw breasts hanging out of my unfastened nursing-bra flaps, as they had been day in and day out since the baby was born. My unwashed hair was flat and stringy. My face was speckled with postpregnancy acne. I was wearing the clothes I'd worn the day before. I had a foot-long, full Maxi Pad in my underwear that I'd not found the time to change. I wasn't sure if I'd brushed my teeth that morning, or the morning before. And my eyes were so puffy you'd think I'd had them collagen-injected.

"Hell, no!" I shouted, dropping the pump and grabbing for something to cover my boobs with as I watched the door opening wider. All I found was a cloth diaper with pink ducks on it.

My mother poked her head in. "Not receiving visitors?"

"Didn't I just say, 'Hell, no'?"

She looked at me, and her face confirmed that I looked as bad as I thought I did. She said, "Well, sweetheart, yes, you did." She disappeared and shut the door behind her.

Rhonda had also told me to start eating almonds by the truckload, drink as much water as I could force down into my belly, get plenty of rest, and imbibe a licorice-smelling tea from the health food store called Lactation Delight.

The water and almonds were pretty easy, and the tea I could get down about twice a day with a great exertion of will, but the resting was simply not possible. Even the idea of rest was like a mirage. The baby just cried all the time. Whenever she was awake, she was crying. And every time I heard her cry, I was jolted out of whatever I'd been doing—eating, going to the bathroom, trying to sleep—and raced to her side as if possessed by a mothering demon.

I was not eating anything I could not swallow by handfuls while holding her. Dry cereal, grapes, raisins, and, lately, almonds were it for me. Utensils, plates, condiments—all were things of the past. As well as sitting down. I had not sat down to a meal since before Maxie arrived. My mother was helping me as much as she could, but I was triaging my time. What was essential? Sleeping always ranked first. Tending to my stitches was up there at the top of the list, as well as brushing my teeth, showering, and changing into clean clothes. Food was way down.

But I could pump, and I did. We figured out a way to prop the baby up on one boob and the funnel on the other, and I pumped like heck. On the morning of Day Five, when there was still no milk in sight, when the baby was unable to sleep longer than twenty minutes before waking to suck at my empty breasts, when I had developed a mysterious, all-over body rash that had me scratching uncontrollably and later turned out to be an almond allergy, I lost my composure.

The specifics of what I said to Rhonda on the phone are a blur to me now. I remember her answering the phone and me shouting her name in the way a drowning person might shout up to a passing ocean liner. I remember tears coming out of my eyes and a Woody Woodpecker–ish laugh coming out of my mouth. I remember saying something along the lines of "I have not been hauling these breasts around my whole life for nothing." And I remember the tone in her voice after I finally fell silent, when she said, "You know what? I'll be right over."

I was shirtless and sobbing when Rhonda arrived. Rhonda, who was about sixty and had the leathery skin of a tennis player, took one look at me and said, "Ouch." She did not hesitate to sit herself down next to me and take a good gander at my breasts. "Well," she said definitively, "this is just bad latch-on." But I'd read all the books and followed her suggestions. I couldn't fathom that I could be trying so hard and failing so miserably. "It's fixable," she said, and set about giving me a hands-on demonstration of proper technique. "Doesn't that feel better?" she said, after we got Maxie hooked up.

"Actually, it hurts like hell."

"Just be sure her mouth is open like a baby bird before you stuff your nipple in. You want her to get a big mouthful of breast every time she eats."

" 'A big mouthful of breast,' " I said. "It sounds like a pop-up book."

About the latch-on, she was confident. I could fix it. I just had to pay attention.

The milk, or lack of milk, was a little trickier. "It should be here by now," she said. "This baby is hungry. You're going to have to supplement with formula."

Betty had warned us about the evils of supplementing. It's the sucking that tells your body to make the milk, so if your baby is sucking on something other than you, like a bottle, it becomes a vicious cycle. The more formula you use, the less milk you make. A troubling rule of thumb for me, since I wasn't making any milk at all.

"Supplementing is bad!" I said.

"There's really no choice here," she said. "Her health can go downhill after this long."

They had given me formula at the hospital, "just in case," and I'd lectured my mother about the evils of psyching women out so that they were set up to fail at breast-feeding. And here I was, failing at it.

"You're not failing," Rhonda said. "Your body's just taking its time. Let's help out your baby in the meanwhile."

My mother found a bottle of formula in my bag of hospital freebies. She shook it up and screwed a nipple onto the top. Then, as

Rhonda looked on, I let Maxie drink. Her eyes closed after swallowing two and a half ounces, and she fell deeply, limply asleep.

Rhonda looked at me. "What's the longest stretch of sleep you've had since the baby was born?"

"An hour and a half?"

"Go get in bed," she said. "You need to do many things to get your milk going, but sleep is the biggest one."

"I can't sleep," I said, looking at Maxie. "She'll be up in twenty minutes and want to nurse again."

"I'm betting she'll be out for hours," she said. "Milk is like a sleeping potion."

"It's not milk. It's formula."

"Close enough," she said.

I did what I was told. I rolled into bed and slept for five glorious hours before I woke, as I always did now, to the sound of crying Maxie.

I scrambled out of bed and was standing in the living room, shirtless and still rubbing my eyes, before I realized that while I had slept my breasts had filled up with marbles. My mother was holding Maxie, but was not able to comfort her. "I think she's hungry," she said.

"I think my milk came in," I said.

My mother stared at me. "It's either that or you've sprouted some pretty aggressive tumors."

I couldn't take my hands off my breasts. "Toss me that baby," I said. I latched Maxie on as best I could and then watched as she drank furiously. When she was done, the marbles in my breast were gone. I switched her over and she began doing the same thing on the other side.

And so we were breast-feeding! It was amazing. I'd had these breasts for years, and they'd never been able to do anything like this. I was mesmerized by Maxie, and the little swallowing sounds she made. This was a whole different thing from the raspy, dry nursing we'd been doing before. Before the boob was drained, Maxie fell asleep again in my arms, her mouth still attached.

"She just finished sleeping!" I said, looking up.

My mother was blowing her nose with a tissue. "That's what they do in the beginning. Eat, sleep, poop. You just had a rocky start." She looked up then, and I saw that her eyes were bright red and puffy. Her whole face looked pink, actually.

My mother saw me noticing and said, "I think I'm hitting my allergy threshold."

"Did this just start?" I was shocked.

"No, sugar, it's been like this for days."

And that was it. She was leaving. She had put Dr. Blandon out on the back steps (where he'd been sitting at attention for days, waiting to get back in), but even the residual fur and dander was enough to take my mother down. She'd been taking the Benadryl at night, but in the day it made her too sleepy. So she was just struggling through. Apparently, during my breast-feeding crisis, she'd discreetly gone through three boxes of Puffs without telling me.

"Headaches, too?" I asked.

She nodded.

I couldn't make her stay. The rational, adult part of me knew it was time to send her home with a grateful hug. The rest of me was catatonic with fear at the prospect of facing all of this by myself. And facing my life, my new real life, without Dean. My house, without my mother or a good postpartum drama to distract me, was going to feel pretty empty. Even with one and a half people living here, the fact remained that there was no longer a couple.

"I'll keep my cell phone on at all times," she said, "and I'll come by morning and evening to check on you." She was already setting her red rolling suitcase by the front door. She headed into the bathroom to get her toiletries.

"You're leaving now? Right now?"

"I'll be back in the morning."

"I don't want you to leave," I said.

"Honey," she said. "Look at me. Look at my face."

Her things gathered, she stood by the door with her purse over her shoulder. I was paralyzed on the sofa, afraid to move and wake Maxie. I couldn't give a grateful hug. Not even a wave. All I could do was let her go. I met her gaze. "Thank you," I said.

And then my mother was gone. I was alone in the house. Alone with my sleeping daughter, who had still not let go of my nipple. This was what I had hoped to avoid. My whole life, I had nurtured friendships, carefully maintained relationships, and called my mother once a day, hoping, in the end, to avoid just exactly this kind of being alone. And here I was in the middle of it. Pinned to the sofa by a sleeping baby, unable even to lift my arm to grab the cordless phone.

I watched Maxie for a bit, and then I put my head back, too, and, for a little while, we dozed.

16

People told me before I had Maxie that I would not be able to manage a shower once I had a newborn. At the time, I did not believe that could really be true. I figured, in my cocky, childless way, that if I really, really wanted a shower, I'd be able to find a way to get one.

The truth is, after my mother left, I did not take a shower for five full days.

I'd take Maxie into the bathroom and put her in the bouncy chair, get her all strapped in and hit the vibrating button, cover her with toys, and before I could even get my clothes off she'd be wailing with such desperate abandon that I'd abort the mission and take her back out.

The first time my mother came to visit, I went to my room to nap, but only after reminding her to wake me if Maxie started to cry, to take a blanket if they left the house, to use the brakes on the stroller, and to look both ways before crossing the street.

She took the baby, pushed me toward the bedroom, and said, "It is a wonder you survived your own childhood."

"It's a different world these days, Mom," I said.

"It's exactly the same world," she said. "You're just the mother now."

And so went Life with Baby. Betty had warned us in class that motherhood was a process of "immersion and reemergence." But I wasn't so much immersed as obliterated. I ate, drank, and slept motherhood. That was the thing about it. It was so unbelievably hard, and the learning curve was so steep that there was no way to do anything but figure out how to do it.

I thought about explaining all this to my father when he came for a visit about three weeks after the baby was born.

"How are your nipples?" he asked as I opened the door.

A question, needless to say, I'd not been expecting.

I stared at him, Maxie's sleeping head on my shoulder, trying to figure how not to give an answer.

He shrugged and said, "Your mother told me about it."

"You and mom are talking about my nipples?"

"Among other things," he said.

"What other things?" I said, gesturing him in.

"Um," he said, crossing the threshold, "how much she hates me, how much I still owe her for my remainder of the wedding that's not happening."

"Not my fault," I said.

The wedding had been planned for this weekend. I hadn't even noticed. I remember my mother dealing with it some during the breast-feeding crisis. She'd argued with Rosita Rosenstein over her invoice. She'd released the sculpture garden to the O'Gorman wedding, which had been wait-listed. She'd organized a telephone tree to let people know not to come, specifying that folks use the word *post-*

poned instead of *canceled*. I remember trying to apologize, and my mother was appalled at my attempt. I was not, she said again and again, the person who should be apologizing.

Much of what my parents had spent was just plain lost. At this late date, there was nothing to be done. The down payments on almost everything: vanished. I think my mother donated the flowers to a retirement home. The cake and the food were also done deals, and they went to a homeless shelter. No one ever picked up my gown. As far as I knew, it was still hanging in a closet at the dressmaker's. Perhaps she had a special closet for these types of dresses, the ones that were forgotten.

My mother didn't give me too many of the details. With her usual poise, she just handled it. My parents were out many thousands of dollars, a vast quantity that had seemed outrageous even when it was paying for my safe passage into the future. And now, with not even a wedding to show for it, the money had disappeared, as if it had been dropped into the ocean and scattered among the fish.

The life I'd had with Dean seemed like it had belonged to somebody else. What I was doing every day was so radically different from the activities that had filled my time even a month before, I didn't even feel like the same person. That girl, that still-pregnant, still-optimistic, so-much-younger me, had had an embarrassment of luxuries: time, freedom, rosy young nipples, salads for dinner, glasses of San Pellegrino, telephone conversations, lunches out with friends, a man beside her she believed in, a future to look forward to.

Now I was just making it through each day, one sore nipple at a time.

"I guess Mom told you Dean left," I said.

"The florist did, actually," he said.

I nodded.

"I never liked him," my father said.

"Dean, or the florist?"

He wrinkled his nose at me. "Either," he said.

"Did you ask Mom out yet?" I asked.

"I'm waiting for my moment," he said.

"But you guys are talking on the phone?"

"A little. It seems to take her about a week to call me back."

"She may not be too eager to talk to you," I said.

He nodded. "But I'm going to change that."

I just looked at him.

"There's something there," he said. "I can feel it."

"I think it's bitterness. Or anger. Or possibly thoughts of violence."

He thought about that a little.

"This place is a mess," he said, looking around. "Don't turn into me."

"That's a good tip," I said.

He had a present for me in his hand, but he seemed to have forgotten about it. He moved around the room as if he were in an art museum, contemplating each view as if he'd paid admission. It struck me how little we know about our parents. I knew he was a surgeon, that he was dedicated to his work in a way that eclipsed all else, that he had a wall full of awards and fellowships. I knew his father had never gone to see a single one of his football games, even after he got a full scholarship to the University of Texas. I knew something was missing from his life that he kept searching for. But a daughter's perspective is limited.

"I'll help you, if I can," I said. "With Mom."

"Just put in a good word for me now and again," he said.

I offered him juice, crackers, and a place on the sofa, all of which he declined.

We stood in the living room, me swaying back and forth to keep the baby asleep. He looked far too tall for my house, and his shoulders seemed to slump down to compensate. So different from when he was doing his TV spots, or strutting around the hospital, or even in sneakers for his 7:00 A.M. squash game. He was larger than life, and somehow that made him too big for my house. Even though he'd been here many times before. It was always this way.

"Want to see the baby?" I said.

"Yes!" he said, as if he'd forgotten why he came.

I turned my shoulder so her little sleeping face was near him.

"Isn't she something!" I heard him say to himself.

When I turned back around, he remembered his present. "Here," he said, putting a shopping bag that said ST. JOSEPH'S in my hand. "It's for the baby." And then, "It's from the gift shop."

"Nice wrapping job," I said.

I pulled out a little onesie with the hospital logo on it.

My dad shrugged. "Impulse buy."

And then he was moving toward the door, thanking me for letting him stop by, kissing his fingers and pressing them to my head. "Good luck, kiddo," he said. "This is the hardest thing in the world." He clicked the door closed behind him and I was left wondering why he'd even come by at all.

"Little babies make your father nervous," my mother explained when she stopped by that evening. "As do older children and adults."

"He seems introspective lately," I said to her. "I think he's growing."

My mother pulled down her glasses and shot me a "give me a break" look.

My father had left my mother in the typical way. New wife waiting in the wings. Younger, blonder, bustier. She wanted kids of her own, of course, and so within a year of my parents' divorce, I had a baby half brother. Eighteen months later, another. I didn't see them much. Any of them. In the standard way, my father fell out of touch after he'd moved on to his new family. I was thirteen when he left.

When he married Melinda, they bought a big house in a brand-new suburb. They lived there until he left her for his next wife, whose name, unfortunately, was also Melinda. We called them the Mellies, or, if we needed to differentiate, Part One and Part Two. Two more sons from that marriage. Then another divorce. And now he was single again, and dating from a wide pool of nurses at the hospital.

Standard stuff, really, for men of his generation. But the thing is, my mother never saw it coming. She never, ever imagined that he would leave her. When she married him, she married him forever.

So he broke her heart when he left. And, worse than that, he took away the future she thought they'd been building. Once she got him out of her system, which took a few years, she never looked back.

The part of me that was like my mother disliked my father for leaving her. But my dad was also one of my favorite people. Lots of nights, he'd call at dinnertime and say, "They're grilling up some great catfish over at the Cajun Cage." Twenty minutes later, we were there, him in his scrubs after a long day, his eyes bloodshot from his contacts, each of us holding a catfish po'boy the size of a sneaker. He'd rest his elbows on the table and lick ketchup off his fingers. He always wore his black leather wristwatch, the one my mother gave him on their first anniversary. Even when he'd been married to other women, he wore it. He had a way of hanging on to things.

Despite all the money my father made now, and the shiny car he drove, catfish was still his favorite food. And those picnic tables by the highway were still his favorite place to eat. Meeting him there, the sun setting on the parking lot, the wind blowing my hair, the slight stickiness of the painted picnic-table boards—something about it felt like the best parts of my childhood. He had a kind of intuition for offering you just exactly the thing you were longing for most.

In the weeks after I had Maxie, he called me often. I'd swing on the porch with the cordless and strategize with him about ways to woo my mother. I maintained that it was hopeless, but I also found myself rooting for him. And one thing I was sure of: If anybody in this world possessed enough charm to pull it off, it was my dad.

17

By the fifth week of motherhood, I had a sense of the terrain. There was no predictability or rhythm to the day, but I had at least become familiar with the mechanics of mothering. The diaper system was in place. The onesies were all in a certain drawer. I had learned how to stick Maxie in the kangaroo-pouch carrier, even though she never looked comfortable.

Part of the sheer terror of those days was figuring out how to comfort her. When she cried, I ran through a checklist of things she might want: Hungry? Dirty diaper? Too cold? Too hot? Sleepy? A hair wrapped around a finger or toe? (This last one never actually happened, but I'd read about it in a book and I checked for it every single time she cried.) My mother always thought she was crying because her diaper was poopy, but I swear she could have sat in a poopy diaper for days. She didn't notice or care.

Mostly what soothed her was being walked. I walked her around the house, making laps from the kitchen to the front door. I'd leave the TV on and catch pieces of whatever was on. My stitches were still hurting then—I'd be cauterized at my six-week checkup because "this should have healed ages ago"—and my muscles were still sore. Nothing about me felt right at all.

I'd hoped that after the birth, my old self would just pop back into place, but there was no pop. I still looked and felt pregnant for weeks after the delivery, except that now, instead of a taut, round belly, I had a droopy one. Everything else was the same: the stretch marks, the loose ligaments, the swollen ankles. Then add sore stitches, headaches, and a couple of unexplained bouts of explosive diarrhea, and I was actually worse off than I had been before. But still, I walked. It was what she wanted, and I was in no position to deny her anything. No matter how much spit-up was caking my T-shirt, or how long it had been since I'd showered, I paced the block with her in the carrier or in my arms for what seemed like hours.

It was lucky for me that Maxie also liked the porch swing. When I just couldn't walk anymore, or when it was too late or too early to be out and about in the neighborhood, we did the swing. And Maxie turned out to be an early riser, so, many mornings at five, after I'd paced the living room until I thought I'd lose my mind, we wound up on the swing. It was there, in the early mornings, that we discovered that my garage-sale neighbor was a predawn jogger.

The first time I saw him, he was running down the block, his dog, Herman, trailing leashless behind him. The second time I saw him was the first time he saw us. He stopped short when he noticed us on the swing, even though he'd just started running, and walked up the front walk.

"Morning!" he said.

The sun had not even started to rise. "I'm not convinced that it is morning," I said.

"This must be your baby."

I held her up and said, "Maxie."

He smoothed his big palm over her head.

"She's a morning person," I said.

"And so are you," he said.

"I am now."

Herman the dog was lingering near my bushes, eager to get going on the jog.

As always, I was starving for someone to talk to. Even at this early hour.

My neighbor started to move back toward the road. Then he turned back and said, "Where's your husband? I haven't seen his SUV."

"Oh," I said. "He wasn't my husband."

"Oh," he said.

"He was scheduled to be," I offered. "But the plan got—" I paused. How could I talk about this without seeming like a wounded animal?

"Revised?" he suggested.

"Yep," I said. "That's pretty much it."

He got it. In twenty-five words or less, he knew my whole, sad, clichéd story. And knowing the story seemed to make him angry. Most people seemed angry when they found out. But there was something extra nice about his response. A touch of big-brother protectiveness. I breathed it in like a good aroma. Cookies baking, say. Or onions sautéing in butter.

"He left you after you had a baby," he said incredulously.

"Day before," I corrected him in a voice that was both perky and bitter. "He left, and then I went into labor. My midwife said it was all the—" I stopped myself for a second. He was all ears, waiting. Fuck it. "All the sobbing."

"His baby," he said. It was a question, but it was also a declaration, because he already knew the answer.

When I nodded, he looked away in something like disgust.

I got lots of disgust from the women I told, but the men just usually seemed uncomfortable. In this story, men were the enemy. I was the Good Woman, an archetype for all the Good Women out there who were done wrong by their men. Men heard this story and averted their eyes. They may not have been bad men, but they were certainly no match for a Good Woman. They felt guilty by association. But this man looked right at me. It didn't even seem to occur to him to feel guilty. And at this moment I suddenly knew that he was decent and kind and—

Herman the dog took off trotting down the street. Tired of waiting, he was starting without my neighbor. My neighbor moved to follow him. Time to get going.

"You must be exhausted," he said, walking backward. "My older sister has two kids fifteen months apart."

"So you know all about it," I said.

"Brutal," he said.

"Yeah, that word comes up a lot." I was stroking Maxie's soft, bare legs. "But parts of it," I said then, "are better than the best thing in the world." I waved Maxie's little hand at him.

He started off after his dog, and then he turned to call out, "If you ever need anything, let me know."

"You bet," I said, with no intention of ever doing it.

It had been nice to have some conversation, and I stayed out on the porch for a good long while, hoping we might catch him on his way back in. But he must have been quite a runner, because an hour later, there was still no sign of him.

It was worth waiting, though, because I was lonesome. Getting out was far more difficult than I had ever imagined, especially because I felt shy about nursing in public. So we mostly stayed home and hoped for visitors. Of course, my mother did come by twice a day, though she often stayed out on the porch with Maxie to avoid dander. And other folks made an effort to check in. And I talked on the phone some. Occasionally, I'd see Meredith, but she had fallen in love with the real Dr. Blandon, and that was keeping her pretty busy. They spent every free minute together and called each other six times a day. When I did see her, she smiled a lot and said things like "He really does have a washboard stomach. I've never seen one of those in real life."

I wasn't the greatest company, either. I was totally preoccupied with tending to the baby. And since I had little interest in Dr. Blandon, and Meredith had little interest in Maxie, we were kind of at an impasse. I missed her, though.

That day, Maxie and I walked up and down the street a lot, sat on the porch swing, napped, chatted on the phone with a friend living in Paris, and ate an entire bag of shelled pecans. It was a pretty typical day.

When night came, Maxie went down easily. She nursed to sleep in five minutes flat, I rolled her into the bassinet by my bed, and we were done.

She wasn't turning out to be the greatest sleeper, though, and most nights we were up three or four times, nursing and walking and singing. I had two or three hours, roughly, between wake-ups. That night, I chose not to do the dishes, even though I'd suffer for it the next day. I chose not to take a shower, even though I had not managed to change my underwear yet. I just crawled into my unmade bed and pulled out a couple of home-decorating magazines.

I piled pillows up all around me and savored the anticipation of two whole hours stretched out ahead and no one to worry about but myself. It was eight-thirty. She'd be up by ten-thirty, ready to nurse again. The pleasure of flipping pages gave way to the pleasure of anticipating sleep, and I dropped *Country Home* on the floor after about fifteen minutes and closed my eyes.

And then the phone rang. I sat up and grabbed it on the first ring, terrified that the noise was going to wake Maxie.

"Hello!" I said in a hoarse whisper, trying to make clear that the caller had really caused a problem for me by calling after bedtime. Then I looked at the clock. It was two-thirty in the morning. Maxie had slept straight through. What a brilliant, fabulous, beautiful child.

"Jenny?"

I held my breath.

"Jenny?"

It was, unbelievably, of all people, after all this time, Dean.

"Is this who I think it is?" I whispered.

"Jenny, are you okay?"

"Do you know what fucking time it is?" I was still whispering.

I could hear him suck on his cigarette—could actually hear it crackle—before he said, "It's late."

"It is two-fucking-thirty in the morning."

And then that was it. Maxie had heard the phone. And me talking. She started to cry.

"The baby's up now," I said, attempting to convey in that one sentence that the only chance I'd had of getting even a bad imitation of a normal night's sleep was now gone. And that I was fucking exhausted. And that everything, absolutely everything, was his fault. And that even still, as pathetic as it was and as much as I didn't want to, I missed him. Stupid me. "I've got to go, Dean," I said in a normal voice. "She's crying."

"Wait!" he said.

I paused.

Then he said, "It's a girl?"

"You don't know one fucking thing," I said, and hung up. That was all I had time for. I could have asked him a thousand questions at that moment. But Maxie was crying, and that was that.

And then I was reaching for her, swooping her up, and settling the two of us in my rocker. She stopped crying the minute I touched her, and as I gathered her in my arms I felt her ribs under her baby fat, all tucked inside the soft casing of her cotton pajamas. The feeling of her little self was like a tonic, and I felt so grateful to her that she'd let me sleep so long. It was as if she'd given me a gift. She was wide-awake as we settled into the chair, and looking at me with those big eyes that always looked so black at nighttime. I closed my eyes, hoping she would, too, and we nursed there. I was holding her, but she was holding me, too.

And so, the big question: Why was he calling? Was he just drunk and overly emotional, perhaps boasting to some bartender that he had a wife and baby at home? Or was it better than that? Was he thinking about coming back? Was he calling to test the waters? If so, my multiple uses of the word "fucking" had, perhaps, not conveyed any encouragement. But why would I even want to encourage him? Maybe he'd call back tonight to finish the conversation. Or in the morning, to apologize for waking me. Maybe this was it. Or maybe not.

How was it possible that he did not know about Maxie? His parents knew all about her. I'd even sent them some pictures of her in the pink onesie with the tulip on it they'd mailed. I figured at least he'd be getting reports on us from them. Even if shame, or confusion, or a narcissistic focus on his own life to the exclusion of all else had kept him from calling me, I figured he must at least have been talking to his folks, hearing about us, safe in the knowledge that we were okay.

Apparently not. Apparently, he was truly carousing around the country. Maybe dreadlocking his hair and smoking dope. Or maybe he'd joined another bad band in a new city, repeating his old mistakes in new surroundings. Maybe he had a new girlfriend, one who thought he was brilliant and talented. Dean was in my thoughts every day, as sad as that was. If he had been thinking about me even a tenth as much as that, he'd have found a way to check up on how Maxie and I were doing.

But he hadn't. That was the amazing thing. He was gone, and we were forgotten. Out of sight, out of mind.

So that was it. The call I'd been waiting for, even though I never would have admitted it out loud, and now it was over. The truth was, even though I fully recognized that he was a bastard for the way he'd left me, letting him go was not as easy as it should have been. I wanted to believe that I was the type of woman who never looked back at any man who did not meet her high standards, but that wasn't exactly the case.

With Meredith and my mother, I put my hands on my hips and said, "Good riddance." But in some crooked little place in my heart, I waited for him to come back. My plan, if he ever called, had been to (a) describe my pain to him in such a vivid way that he would feel the pain, too, and then (b) move on to other topics and be so witty and fabulous that he found himself desperate to be near me, then (c) tell him about Maxie in such glowing terms, perhaps sugarcoating the experience a bit, that he'd ache to come home and be a proper father. It was a three-pronged plan many late-night nursings in the making, and I hadn't even gotten to prong one. No caller ID. No way to find him or call him back. But what was I going to do, leave Maxie screaming while I tried to lure her unwilling father back home against my own better judgment? It couldn't have gone differently. Unless Dean had thought to call at a normal, decent, human hour.

18

Dean did not call back that night, though I slept with my hand on the phone just in case. He did not call the next morning, either. Though it had been my plan to act like the call had meant no more to me than any chat with an old acquaintance, I called his cell phone three times the next day. No answer, any time.

Maxie and I walked up and down the block for most of the morning, then took a nap together on my bed, then scrounged around for some lunch for me. I was still doing the handfuls-only diet—only eating things I could grab with one hand while I held her.

I could not put her down. She was not fooled by the vibrating bouncy seat, or the swing, or the Mama Motion bassinet. All activities for me now were one-handed. My favorite meal of late was a handful of sunflower seeds, a piece of toast, a piece of string cheese, several strawberries or grapes, and any chocolate I could find. Though, to be fair, chocolate was not restricted to meals—if anything eaten standing at the kitchen counter could be called a "meal."

Since Maxie, my relationship with chocolate had intensified into something of an addiction. Now I needed it, wanted it, had to have it. If I ran out, I returned obsessively to the cabinets, Maxie over my shoulder, using one hand to look for old Halloween candy or stray packets of hot cocoa. This was how Dean must have felt that night I happened upon him fishing a mostly smoked Marlboro out of the kitchen trash.

I read in a women's magazine that chocolate had mild antidepressant qualities. But if I was depressed, I couldn't feel it. I felt other things. An overwhelming, heartbreaking, euphoric love for Maxie. Gratitude toward my mother every time she let me have a shower. Numbness about Dean. And, every minute of every day, hollowed-to-the-bone exhaustion.

Which is why, when the Giraffe from childbirth class called to invite me over, I almost said no.

"We thought we'd all get together next week with our new babies," she said.

"Kind of a show-and-tell," I said.

"Exactly!" she said. "How did your birth go, by the way?"

"Torture. How was yours?"

"Wonderful. It was more spiritual and moving than I could have hoped for."

I paused.

"You think you can make it?" she finally said. "We're ordering a pizza."

She sounded so perky. She did not sound at all like a capsized person in a stormy sea of sleep deprivation and lactation hormones. I wasn't sure I could stand to be in a whole roomful of women whose lives were going just exactly as they had planned. But I had nothing else to do, and wasn't in a position to be picky about company. At least it would kill an afternoon.

When the day finally came, I had nothing to wear. Every single thing I owned made me look frumpy. As I tried on my fourth T-shirt, I gave up and decided with an internal wince that the trouble probably wasn't the clothes.

It was supposed to be our entire childbirth class—all the moms, anyway. But the Talker had already gone back to work and the Oompa Loompas lived so far out in the country that the drive was too much.

"Lee Ann really wanted to be here," the Giraffe said as each of us walked in, "but little Kevin refuses to be in the car for more than ten minutes."

Sure, sure. We all understood that. Our new lives were circumscribed from every angle by things our babies would not tolerate. Everyone compared notes and I learned that Nipples's son loved the car and rode most places without a fuss. The Giraffe's daughter screamed her head off from ignition to parking brake. And Julia Child's son, who had been born two weeks premature, only slept when he was in the car, so she and her husband, the Pirate, were taking turns sleeping in the driveway.

The group of us arrived at the Giraffe's house with enough gear for a camping expedition. Diaper bags, strollers, baby slings, car-seat baskets, changing pads, and nursing pillows littered the living room. We were all nursing, so each of us found a place on the oversize twin sofas or matching chairs, plugged babies up to boobs, and got to chatting. At this point, it was what most of us did most of the day, anyway: nursed and nursed and nursed.

The Giraffe was really the leader of the group. Not only had she taken the initiative to organize this get-together, but she seemed to know everybody's name, the name of each respective spouse, and the name of each baby. And she made sure folks felt included by bringing them into the conversation. I learned later that she'd been a corporate seminar facilitator before she went to law school and started raking in the big bucks. But at the time, when she looked at me during a pause and said, "So, Jenny, how does Dean like being a daddy?" I admit I hadn't expected to be brought into the conversation so directly.

I could have lied. I could have made up an idyllic life for the listening pleasure of the other mommies, complete with a very helpful fictional mate who changed the diaper pail and brought me hot tea while I was nursing. It didn't seem likely that I'd see these women again. The idea of telling the truth was not appealing. I hated the idea that, months from now, if Dean returned to me and Maxie, and if we pieced back together a life that looked pretty good, and if I was trying to forget that this awful time had ever happened, these women would know the truth and remember. I'd run into Nipples, say, in the grocery store, and try to convince her that everything was all put back together now. But she'd have the goods on me.

I'm not sure what compelled me to be honest. It may just have been that it made for a good story. But I answered the Giraffe as plainly as I could: "He left me the day before I went into labor, and I haven't seen him since."

Suffice it to say, there was outrage all around. You haven't seen outrage until you've seen a pack of breast-feeding women hear about one of their own getting abandoned.

"I don't understand," Julia Child said.

"He left me," I said.

"You're all alone?" Nipples asked.

"I am all alone," I answered. "Except for Maxie and my obese cat."

The Giraffe had gone to the kitchen to get me a chocolate-chip cookie immediately upon hearing the news. "How on earth are you surviving?" she asked, thrusting it so close to my mouth it grazed my lips.

With most people, I tried to accentuate the positive. I'd point out that my mother was helping and that I'd been getting pretty good at things. But suddenly something about these women made me want to be accurate. Maybe it was the fact that we were strangers sitting in a room with our boobs hanging out. Maybe it was the fact that not one of us was getting more than four consecutive hours of sleep. Maybe it was all the hormones in the air. But it was a relief to just look around the room, nod, and then say, "It really sucks."

I learned a lot of things that day. Their real names, for one. But everybody had her share of heartbreak. Nipples, whose real name was April, had had four miscarriages before a pregnancy finally stuck. Julia Child, whose name was Paige, had moved to Texas from Maine in her seventh month, had no family anywhere, and her husband worked fifteen-hour days and Saturdays. And the Giraffe, whose name was Claudia, turned out to be a single mother like me. Though not exactly like me, because she had a full-time nanny and a three-day-a-week housekeeper. Her husband, Abe Lincoln, had not, in fact, been her husband. He was her brother, who had only reluctantly agreed to be her partner, and he had almost missed five out of six classes.

"You're not married?" I asked dumbly.

"No," she said. "I'm thirty-eight. I haven't found the right guy. I have plenty of money, and I was ready."

"Did you go to a sperm bank?" Paige asked.

"Actually, I was going to. But I wound up doing it with a guy from my office at the company picnic—"

"At the picnic?" April asked.

"It was actually a square dance. They were giving everybody lessons. We were do-si-do-ing and swinging around and out of breath. Who knew that square dancing could be so erotically charged?" We all nodded at her. Who knew, indeed? Claudia continued. "Before I knew it, I was out in an alleyway with this guy who'd always been kind of flirty with me, next to a dumpster that smelled like rotten bananas."

"That sounds like bad sex," somebody said.

"We wound up on top of his jacket on the pavement," Claudia said.

"Better than up against the dumpster," someone else added.

"You'd been drinking?" I asked, and she nodded.

"I had been planning to do the whole thing so carefully—find a donor, check his medical history, where he went to college, make sure he was height-weight proportionate."

We all watched her for a minute.

"When I told this guy I was pregnant, he said, 'You can't have this baby. You will ruin my life.' He started ignoring me at the office, and a few weeks later, he transferred to Cleveland." She looked around at us.

"So he doesn't know about the baby?" April asked.

"I think he chose to believe that I did what he wanted and had an abortion," Claudia said.

We all chewed our cookies for a little bit.

"So anyway," Claudia said. "I'm single. If you know anybody looking for a girlfriend with a baby."

For a moment, I felt so sorry for her. I thought, *How's she ever going to meet someone now? Her body's all messed up. She's lactating like crazy and riddled with stretch marks. Her old underwear doesn't fit. She's exhausted. She'll have to get a sitter if she wants to go out. And men barely even like their own kids.* I'd gotten just about that far before I realized that she was me.

"You'll find somebody," I said.

"I knew for sure I wanted a baby," she said, and we all nodded.

Conversations sprang up and fell back, crisscrossed and converged. We talked on and on.

There on the sofa, as I nursed Maxie and her eyes slid closed, I said to the girls, "I think nursing is where kisses come from." I had been thinking about it. Nursing had to be the place where nurturing and sweet milk and soft skin and mouths and warmth all came together and started to mean something about love.

I had always assumed kissing was a learned thing, like waving bye-bye or speaking a language. But since Maxie, I'd decided that it was innate, the adult version of something we know to do from the moment we're born. All of it tied together in the cycle of life.

The other moms liked this idea. They said I should write a book about it.

We'd arrived for lunch at eleven o'clock. At five-twenty-five, we were still there. Somebody noticed the time, and then everybody jumped up, snapping up nursing bras and buckling the babies into their carriers. I, myself, could have stayed the night. We had told our birth stories and had talked about sleeping, eating, nipples, pumping, spit-up, unexplained crying, and the varied meanings of poop. It was addictive to be around other people who were in the same time-warp baby world that I was. Their life circumstances may have been different, but we were all on baby time now, and I had to force myself out to the car when it was all over.

Driving home with Maxie wailing in the backseat, I found myself thinking about Meredith. I hadn't seen her in weeks. I'd left three messages on her cell that she had yet to return. These days, I was as lonely as I'd ever been, and she was MIA. Being in love was no excuse. I really needed her. Where was she? Where was this present she kept promising me? I was glad I'd found some new friends. Maybe now I wouldn't need her. If she was going to leave me, I would just leave her, too. I resolved to start a weekly get-together with the other mommies. Starting the next week. And, as soon as next week was, I wondered how I would ever wait that long.

19

That night, Maxie fell asleep late, and had her wake-up even later, and by the time I got myself into bed, it was almost midnight.

But I was feeling pretty good. Being around the other moms had given me a little perspective, and I was feeling like maybe I was getting a handle on this parenting thing. I thought to myself, *Maybe I can do this. Maybe I'm going to turn out to be good at this.*

And then the power went out.

It was pitch black. I heard the air-conditioning fan cut out. The hum of the dishwasher stopped. Even the quiet buzzing noises that the lightbulbs and ceiling fans made all fell silent.

I had a flashlight in the kitchen, so I felt my way in there, moving very slowly while my eyes adjusted, sliding my feet across the floor, feeling ahead of myself with my toes, praying I wouldn't kick Dr. Blandon or knock over a floor lamp and wake Maxie. At the junk drawer, I felt around for the flashlight, but it wasn't there. Would Dean have taken it? My eyes were adjusting and I looked out the window. All the houses on the street were dark. It was a strange feeling, as if they weren't alive anymore, somehow. Of course, there were people inside them, hunting for flashlights like I was, but it felt like I was all alone in the world.

Flashlight, flashlight. Who stops to take a flashlight when leaving his pregnant girlfriend? And then I remembered: I'd taken it into the bathroom a few weeks back to look in Maxie's ear to see if she had an infection. (She didn't, but here's a tip: You can't tell that by holding a flashlight to a baby's ear.) I shuffled my way back to the bathroom and kicked the little plastic tub that I'd forgotten to hang up after the bath. There was a loud honking noise as it moved, and then water splashed out onto the floor, onto my pajama legs. I held still, waiting for a cry from Maxie. Nothing. I probably stood there for ten minutes, afraid to move, before I finally reached over to the sink to get the flashlight. I flicked it on. Light! I aimed it toward the doorway and followed it out into the living room.

I needed to find the phone book and call the power company. I headed to the kitchen, but before I got there, the beam of light started to fade. "Fuck!" I said out loud, and then, almost that fast, the light was gone. Batteries.

I didn't have any spares, so I stood in the dark for a minute, watching the shadows. And then I remembered that Dean and I had received sterling-silver candelabras as wedding gifts from a patient of my dad's. My mother had brought over all the gifts that had come in before the wedding was "postponed," and told me that I'd have to return them and then write thank-you notes anyway. "That's just insult to injury," I'd said. I still hadn't written the notes, and I was toying with keeping the gifts as consolation prizes. Those candelabras were something to see.

I lit some emergency candles and set them in the candelabras on the dinette table. This could so easily have been me in a different life, a newlywed me, whimsically breaking in my wedding candelabras with a romantic dinner at the dinette table. I watched the candles drip wax in spots on the table. Now, in the light, I saw Dr. Blandon watching me from a perch on the kitchen counter. Crouched in that position, his belly fat completely enveloped his paws.

Then there was a knock at the door. All I could think was *Please don't wake the baby!* and I went running to answer it before it happened again. I kicked my toe on a chair leg on the way and muffled my yelp of pain with my hand over my mouth.

I tried to look through the peephole, but with no porch light, it wasn't much use. Against all single-woman-alone-in-a-house advice, I cracked the door open to peer out. It was my garage-sale neighbor. He was in his pajamas. Again.

"The baby's sleeping," I whispered, to underscore the point.

"Okay," he whispered back.

I gestured toward his pajamas. "You must wear those things a lot," I whispered.

"Mostly at night," he whispered back.

"Did you lose your power?"

"Yes."

"Why are you here?" I asked.

"I thought you might need some help."

I didn't need help, but I did want company. I had never paused to reflect on how comforting the auxiliary components of my life were until they were gone: no lights, no clocks, no phone, nothing. None of those lively electronic friends that populate the house. Just walls, furniture, a baby, and me.

Inside, he insisted we stop whispering. I led him back to the kitchen, and we sat at the dinette in the light of the candles. "That's one badass cat," he said, eyeing Dr. Blandon. Dr. Blandon started to purr.

We both looked around at my messy kitchen, and then, after a while, my neighbor said, "Nice candles."

"My flashlight died," I said.

Then he told me the whole neighborhood was out, and wait times just to report the outage were over thirty minutes. "So probably a big one," he said.

"Probably so," I said.

"I thought I might stay with you until the power came back on."

I thought about faking it and telling him I was fine. But then I said, "Okay."

I offered him a can of warm grapefruit juice from the pantry, and he whipped out a deck of cards.

"You think of everything," I said, and he started to shuffle.

"I'm good in emergencies," he said. Then he looked up at me and said, "I'm good in other situations, too."

"I don't doubt it," I said.

As he started to deal, I said, "The baby might wake up, and if she does, I'll have to go nurse her back to sleep, and that could take some time."

"And I'll still be here when you get back," he said. Then he glanced up. "If that's what you were asking."

I nodded.

And then we played gin rummy. I couldn't remember the last time I'd played cards. It reminded me of being a kid.

My neighbor lost every hand, but he talked trash the whole time and made me laugh. He was a funny kind of pseudo-competitive.

After a bit, we started building a house of cards. He told me that he renovated houses. He found bargains, fixed them up, and sold them at a profit. He did three houses a year. He lived in them while he worked, and then went up to stay with his parents in Dallas while the houses were on the market. He left his furniture, to make the houses feel homey, but nothing else—no stacks of junk mail, no tangle of computer cords, no dirty socks in the hamper.

"You sell them the house they wish they had!" I said.

"That's the idea," he said. "It's working pretty well."

I asked about his parents. "They don't mind you mooching off them?" I said.

"We don't call it mooching," he said. "We just call it visiting."

"How's this house going?" I asked.

"This one's got a ways to go," he said. His project for the week was to tear off a rotten screened-in back porch.

"You should save it," I said, and then I told him about the one my grandparents used to have when I was little. He really seemed to want to hear about it, so I went on and on: It was a big outdoor room, with a long table on one side and wicker sofas and chairs on the other. There were two ceiling fans, and my grandmother had a collection of potted plants in the corner that got all the sun. We ate almost every meal out there and played board games at the table after dark, the June bugs congregating by the light on the back steps.

We had built a seven-story apartment complex with the cards and were discussing adding a gym for the tenants when the lights came back on. First the lights, then the sounds. We knocked the cards down in a satisfying flutter, then leaned in at the same time to blow out the candles. I petted Dr. Blandon while my neighbor stuffed the cards back in the box. "Next time, I'll let you win," he said.

I walked him to the front door and thanked him. And then, as he was headed down the front walk, I said, "Hey—"

He turned.

"I'm embarrassed to say I forgot your name."

"It's John," he said. "But everybody calls me Gardner."

"Is that because you garden?" I said.

"No."

I looked at him, waiting to hear how he got "Gardner" as a nickname for "John." And he looked back, waiting for me to figure it out.

Finally, he walked back to me and leaned over to my ear. I could feel the tickle of his breath as he whispered, "It's my last name," and headed off again.

John Gardner. Good name.

And Maxie, bless her, waited until after I'd turned the dead bolt before she woke up and cried.

The next day, during my mother's morning visit, we chatted a minute before I went in to shower. She was sitting on the porch swing and holding Maxie.

"He brought a deck of cards?" she asked.

"Yep," I said.

"He's very cute," she said.

"He is," I said.

"Much cuter than Dean," she said.

"Much cuter."

"And taller."

"Yep," I said.

She arched her eyebrow in a triumphant way.

"Guess what?" I asked her, unwilling to concede. "I am too tired for love."

I had a hard time making myself get out of the shower that morning. I shampooed my hair twice and did some shaving. Then I just stood under the water for a while, telling myself firmly it was time to get out, but staying put all the same.

When I made it back out to the porch, my hair up in a Carmen Miranda towel-hat, my mother was antsy. She handed Maxie back and was putting her purse on her shoulder when I asked her if she'd seen Dad lately.

"Actually, yes," she said. "He showed up at my house a few nights ago."

"He showed up at your house?"

She frowned a little. "It must have been almost ten o'clock. Of course, he never had any sense of time."

"What did he say?"

"He had some leftover papers from your wedding he'd been meaning to return."

"That was it?"

She nodded.

"What happened?"

She couldn't imagine why I was asking. "I took them and went back inside."

Then I said, "Are you ever still attracted to Dad?"

She laughed out loud, startling Maxie, who I then had to shush and bobble a bit.

"Are you?" I asked again.

"Attracted to your father? Hell, no!"

"Why not?" I asked.

She thought about it. "Well, sweetheart, he just disappointed me too hard."

I followed her to the car, and she pulled out a cooler with vegetable-soup containers inside. She'd made them for me to freeze. I thanked her with a kiss, wondering how many months would go by before I'd be able to actually sit down with something like a hot bowl of soup and eat it.

20

By August, the armpit of Houston's long summer, Maxie was over four months old and still getting up at the crack of dawn. Sometimes five o'clock, sometimes four, sometimes even earlier. I'd go in to try to nurse her back to sleep, but if those eyes didn't close after about half an hour, I knew that was it. We were up.

And we'd wind up out on the porch. Many mornings, Gardner stopped by with Herman before their jog. A couple of times he even skipped the jog altogether because we talked for so long. Herman got used to the detour pretty quickly.

On one such morning, I found out why Gardner was not married—anymore. His wife, a former ballet dancer, had cheated on him with her dentist.

Apparently, she'd gone in to have a crown made, but the Dentist, a perfectionist, couldn't match the color of her other teeth exactly. She went back again and again and was sent home each time so he could try for a better match. On the day he finally got it right, she was the last appointment of the day. They walked out to the parking lot together, but her car didn't start, and he waited for AAA with her under an oak tree. Before they knew it, they were kissing, and he was making jokes about inspecting her new crown.

"She certainly gave you a lot of details," I said.

"I asked for them," Gardner said.

"Why on earth would you do that?" I asked.

"I thought I might learn something."

"And did you?"

He nodded. "I've learned a lot of things."

They'd been trying to get pregnant for two years by then. They'd had two miscarriages, and Karen, his wife, had become obsessed with her fertility cycle. Even she called herself a Sex Nazi.

"It did take some of the fun out of it," Gardner said.

He was working a lot then, and he was almost never home. Looking back, he said, he realized she must have been lonely. But he really hadn't been paying that much attention. Three months after that first kiss with the Dentist, Karen woke Gardner at two in the morning to say that she was leaving. She told him the whole story, and then she left in her pajamas.

It had been five years since then, and he hadn't dated anybody seriously. Lots of blind dates, but no keepers.

"She has two kids now," Gardner said. "With the Dentist."

"She was wrong to do that to you," I said.

"She was unhappy," he said.

"It doesn't matter," I said.

"I was a bad husband."

"That's not possible. I barely know you, but I know that's not possible."

"I was," he said. "I had a different job then, and I was always working."

"What was your job?"

"I was a pediatric nephrologist."

I nodded like I knew exactly what that was, which I didn't. Then I said, "Five years is a long time."

He agreed.

"You need to get back out there," I said. "It's a waste of a good man."

"When are you going to get back out there?" he asked.

"Never," I said. "But women like me are a dime a dozen."

It was good to have a new friend in Gardner. Meredith was still distracted by love, and my mother had been hired by the St. Regis hotel to redo their lobby. I was scrambling to find enough conversations to fill up the day. I called the mommies pretty frequently, and I had also made a real friendship with Claudia, who lived within walking distance. My mother couldn't remember Claudia's name and just called her my "other Meredith." It was true enough.

The other person I saw quite a bit was my dad, who had taken to stopping by a few nights a week on his way home from the hospital. Sometimes he brought takeout or we ordered Chinese. He thought Maxie was "cute enough for TV" and offered to take her on his show. Every time he saw her, he'd grab her by the cheeks and kiss her on the nose, prompting me to say, "Germs!" Mostly, he'd tell me stories from the hospital. But every few days he'd want to talk about my mother, and I continued to give tips and encouragement, despite my better judgment. I could imagine nothing worse for my mother than striking up a fresh liaison with my dad, and I wasn't so sure this minor obsession was great for him, either.

But he was so eager, and so sweet.

The night he'd gone by her house with the paperwork, he'd actually had flowers in the car, but at the last minute he'd chickened out about taking them to her. "Boy, was I glad, too," he said. "She didn't even invite me in. Just took the papers and closed the door."

"Isn't there anyone else in the city that you could date?" I asked again.

"There's no one else I *want* to date," he said.

"Every nurse in town has a crush on you," I said.

"It's not the same."

So we strategized, and psychoanalyzed, and I gave him the woman's view of things. I encouraged him to be up-front. To tell Mom that spending time with her in the past year had stirred up his feelings, and that he'd like to take her out sometime, that he feared leaving her might have been the biggest mistake of his life.

"You think that'll work?" he asked.

"I think she'll turn you down flat," I said.

He nodded and nodded.

My mother had not remarried in the fifteen years since they'd split up. After my dad left, she fell apart a little bit and forgot to pay bills and go to the grocery store. We had a swimming pool full of leaves, an unmowed lawn, and a cashier at Jack in the Box who knew our names. It was the only time I've ever seen my mother anything other than pressed and perfumed by 7:00 A.M. After she pulled herself together, she never looked back. She'd had a series of semiserious boyfriends. People to travel with, see movies with, and spend the night with. But not to marry. She was done with that.

It was hard to be as fond of my dad as I was and not feel a bit disloyal to my mother. For my mother, he was Dean. Worse than Dean. It made me wonder if Maxie would grow up to love Dean the way that I loved my dad—if Dean deserved a chance with her, even though he had blown it with me. He wasn't a monster, after all. Just a jerk. And a coward. And a disappointment.

But I loved Maxie enough not to want to deprive her of a daddy, if she wanted one. Which she would.

In a way, Dean's timing when he left me was pretty good. Because I was right on the verge of falling in love with someone new.

Granted, a newborn baby isn't going to rub your back before you fall asleep at night or take you out for an expensive dinner, but the love I felt for her filled up my entire body. Time and again, as soon as I got her down for a nap, no matter how much I thought I wanted to be alone, I'd go look at pictures of her. Just because I missed her little face.

Maxie had lost her newborn hair now, but only on the top, so she had a kind of Friar Tuck hairdo of fringe around the bottom. Her eyes, which had been a milky black, were settling into a deep blue just like my own. She had pink, pouty baby lips. Her legs were like little sausages, and she loved to kick them. Everybody said she looked just like me. "She does," I'd agree. "But she's cuter."

And the way I loved her was like nothing else. This, I decided, was the love all other loves were measured against. They say girls look to marry their fathers, but I decided after having Maxie that we all, every one of us, were looking to marry our mothers. Sitting on the sofa with her wrapped in a soft blanket in my arms, I'd think, *This baby has it so good.*

It just seemed that the love I'd been searching and hoping for all my life was what Maxie already had right now: two big arms and a lap, a warm blanket, the background music of a heartbeat and a pair of lungs, food at a moment's notice, sleep at every urge, and a person totally obsessed with her, whose every moment—waking or otherwise—was devoted to her comfort and care. Was that so much to ask for?

In comparison to this, the things I'd felt for Dean seemed kind of paltry. He hadn't called again since that one night, and I was finally starting to think that he might not be coming back.

I'd said it to my mother on the porch one morning.

"I think he's gone for good," I said.

"Oh, God," she said. "I hope so."

21

The weeks went by fast, but the days went by slowly. I changed four thousand diapers a day, replaced Maxie's outfits after every meal of applesauce (unless I was very tired), and nursed, rocked, and sang to her. We took endless walks around the neighborhood during the day and drives when she couldn't sleep at night. As much as I carried a kind of hollow spot, I also didn't have time to think about too much. When I wasn't busy with Maxie, I was fast asleep.

Sometimes, when I was rocking Maxie, I found myself thinking about running a trash-and-treasure shop out of our garage. Our house was on a corner, and the garage faced a pretty big street. I could hang a sign out and see who came by. Just in a casual way. Just maybe on the weekends. To have something to do and some reason to interact with people. I imagined making little price tags with 1950s illustrations on them and using an old cash register I'd seen at a junk store on Nineteenth Street. The garage would need a fresh coat of paint. And some better lighting. And some shelves. And maybe a clean floor for Maxie to crawl around on, when she learned how.

Usually, as I rocked Maxie and let my thoughts wander, I floated from topic to topic, but lately I was caught on the idea of this little shop. It would just be open when I was in the mood. And it would only have to make enough money to pay for itself—here in the beginning, at least, while Maxie was so small. We'd get established and, in a few years, turn it into a moneymaker. For now, though, if Maxie was napping, or I was, we'd just hang up a sign: TAKING A NAP! COME BACK LATER! I could scour garage sales on weekend mornings, fix up and price the treasures at night, and set them out in the shop when I was ready. I wouldn't buy anything that I couldn't carry with the one arm that wasn't holding Maxie. It could work.

"It'll never work," my mother said when I told her about the idea one morning. I'd caught her on her cell phone at a brunch with some of her decorator friends. "You're so tired, honey. You're falling asleep in your oatmeal."

"But I have to be awake anyway, so why not be at a shop?"

"I think you've got your hands full right now, don't you?"

"I do. I definitely do," I said. "But I can't quite get the idea out of my head."

"I just don't want to see you get excited if it's not going to work out."

I thought about that one for a minute. "But wouldn't it be nice," I said, "to see me excited about something? Anything? Even if it's not going to work out?"

She paused, and then she said, "Sweetheart, the shrimp cocktail is here."

"It could be this funky, great place," I continued.

My mother had to go. She said she'd call me later. But her parting words, with a mouth full of shrimp, were "Trust me on this. It'll be a disaster."

And that was it. It was decided. I was opening a shop.

Maxie and I had spent the morning lying on a blanket on the living room. At five months, she was great at rolling over, but sometimes she'd get stuck midway and grunt like a piglet until I picked her up. The whole time I'd been on the phone with my mother, she'd been complaining, and by the time I hung up, she was launching into a full-out cry.

"Come on, muffin," I said. "Let's prove your nana wrong."

I popped on the baby carrier and marched outside, barely remembering to take my keys with me. In minutes, I was standing on Gardner's front porch, rapping on the door. It wasn't until I'd already knocked that I paused to think that maybe I should have brushed my hair, or put on some lip gloss, or done any tiny thing to keep from looking like a pasty, dried-out, crazy neighbor. Too late. He was unlocking the dead bolt. I licked my lips and tucked some hair behind my ears. Maxie let out a big belch. We were ready for action.

But it wasn't him. The door pulled back and it was a woman. An attractive, clean, about-my-age, not-insane-seeming woman, who smiled and said, "Hi?"

"We are looking for Gardner!" I said, overly cheerful. My confidence started to fall away. I had just marched over, certain he'd want to see me and Maxie first thing on a Sunday morning. Me and Maxie and Maxie's possibly now-full diaper.

"He's in the shower," she said. God, she was so clean.

"Oh," I said. *A new girlfriend!*

"Would you like to come in?" she asked.

Hell, no! "We'll just swing by another time," I said, starting to back up.

She started to ask if she could get my name, but before the words were even out, I had accidentally stepped in Herman's water bowl, lost my balance, and pitched sideways. I suppose a person never wants to trip and fall. But a person with an infant in a carrier on her belly really, really never wants to trip and fall. Some kind of primal maternal protectiveness roared up in me at that moment and I twisted myself around in midair like a cat to make sure that whatever I hit the ground with, it wasn't Maxie.

I did hit the ground. On my left knee. So hard it felt like I'd crushed the kneecap. But Maxie, to my relief, escaped unscathed. That said, I did everything I could not to cry as I scrambled back up into a standing position. Maxie took another approach.

Her screams must have been pretty loud, because in seconds, Gardner appeared on the porch, dripping wet, fastening his towel around his waist. He had a little soap still on his neck. I was cringing a little, trying to comfort Maxie, but also not totally able to stand up, and before I knew it, Gardner's hands were unsnapping the baby carrier and then Maxie was in his arms. I was about to protest, thinking a baby could not possibly want to be with a total stranger more than her own mother at such a time, but he started doing a little dance with her and within seconds she was quiet with her head against his chest.

Herman came out to check out the commotion, and the clean woman led me to the porch swing to sit down.

I couldn't take my eyes off Gardner and Maxie. He was like an animal trainer hypnotizing a wild beast.

"Hey there," I said. "Whatcha doin' there?" He had started humming a little song, and was hopping from one foot to another.

"I kind of have a way with babies," he said.

Maxie was in a trance.

"That," I said, "is a hell of an understatement."

Maybe it was the fall that did it, or maybe Maxie's cries, but in any case, my shirt was spotted with milk. In any other context, I'd be nursing her. But this nonlactating neighbor, this man, had it under control. I crossed my arms over my chest.

"You've got a rare talent there," I said. "Usually only people with working nipples can have that effect on her."

"Yeah," he said. "I'm being studied by a team of scientists."

He went on with his humming a minute, and then his new girlfriend put her hand on my shoulder. "How are you?" she said.

"Oh." I waved my hand. "I'm fine." I wasn't sure I was fine, but it seemed like a good answer. And I wasn't bleeding, so there was no real evidence to the contrary. I looked her in the eye. "You're very kind," I said. And she probably was.

"I'm going to get you some ice," she said, and she went inside.

Maxie was starting to doze off now. It was the most amazing sight I had ever seen.

"You are a genius," I said to Gardner.

"I just have a rumbly voice," he said. "Babies like it."

"But you weren't talking when you first took her," I said, "and she just went limp."

He shrugged. "It's a gift."

I watched him with her for a few more minutes. To be honest, I so rarely got to hand her over to anyone that, even though my knee was throbbing, I was very happy to just sit on the swing.

"Did you need something?" Gardner then asked.

I didn't know what he meant.

"You knocked? At my door?"

"Oh!" I said. "Yes. I was coming to you with a proposition."

"Hit me," he said.

"Well, you're handy, right?"

"I am," he said. "I am handy."

"I was wondering if you might be willing to help me with my garage."

"Help you how?"

I said it quickly, to make the request sound smaller than it was: "A new coat of paint and some new light fixtures and maybe a few other things."

He just looked at me.

"I'd pay you, of course," I said.

And then the girlfriend appeared on the porch with a plastic bag full of ice. She pressed it up against my knee. These people were too perfect. Kind, nurturing, stable, not-sadistic people who would get married and raise cheerful, high-scoring, polite children who would grow up to have jobs as urban planners or famous chefs. They were going to live in the best-looking house on the block and have the best lives.

"She's out," Gardner said to me, of Maxie. "Why don't I walk you home and pop her in the crib?"

"Can you do that?" I asked, but I was just making conversation. After that performance on the porch, I was convinced he could do anything he wanted.

He waved to the girlfriend. She said, "Feel better," to me, and then we were off, me limping just a little, Gardner in his blue bath towel, Maxie like a kitten against his chest, and Herman following behind.

On the walk to my house, I couldn't think of anything to say. I led him inside and felt embarrassed by all the unfolded laundry and teething toys and half-eaten apples everywhere. He followed me to Maxie's room, rolled her off his shoulder and into the crib, and the two of us crept out. After I shut the door, I gave him a high five.

"Nice work!" I whispered.

"Just good luck."

Then I said, "What is a pediatric nephrologist, anyway?"

He tilted his head like he thought I should know that.

"Okay, *pediatric* is kids," I offered.

He nodded.

"And *nephrologist*?"

He frowned like he still really thought I ought to know.

I said, "You want me to come up with the Latin root *neph*?"

"Kidneys," he finally said. "Kidney problems."

"Oh," I said. "Of course."

He looked at me for a minute, then said, "I'll probably go back to it. Sometime."

He started back toward the front door and paused at the handle. It was a strange scene, for us to be standing so close, me in my milk-drenched pajamas, him in nothing but a towel. In another world this could have been our house, our baby, our blue towel around his waist. He was looking at me, and I knew I looked pale and bloodshot and tangled. I didn't like the picture of me I imagined he was getting. I wished again I had at least paused for some lip gloss. At that thought, I sucked on my bottom lip to wet it. He looked down at my mouth.

"I should take a look at your knee," he said, still staring at my mouth.

"Oh," I said, waving my hand. "It doesn't even hurt."

He didn't argue, though he could have.

"Go put some clothes on," I said, by way of a good-bye.

And he nodded, still staring at me, lingering there in a way that any girlfriend would not have liked. He had me under a spell, too, I think. Maybe it really was his rumbly voice. Maybe it was how calm he was. Maybe it was how good he was with Maxie. But I felt relaxed. I felt rocked in a gentle sea. I felt like we were friends. And then suddenly I heard myself saying, "So is that woman your new girlfriend?"

And as soon as I said it, I was out of the trance. My eyes must have popped wide open when I heard myself. *Don't ask him that! What kind of question is that? None of your business!*

Before he could answer, I was covering. "Because I thought you were single. And I have a friend who is also single I'd been thinking about setting you up with. But if you're seeing somebody, I won't. Set you up with my friend."

He paused. He was studying me like he was trying to read me in some other language. "That girl is not my girlfriend," he said. "She's my . . ." And he waited for me to guess.

"Sister?" I asked.

As he nodded, he touched a finger to his nose.

Of course, of course. They looked alike in a way, now that I thought about it.

"So, sure. You can give me your friend's number," he said.

And then, before we had finished talking about anything, he waved and headed off, back up the street in his blue sarong, looking every bit as good as he had in his pajamas.

22

So that woman was not Gardner's girlfriend. I had the information I wanted, but I'd had to pay big to get it. Now I had to come up with a "friend"—and her phone number. I considered just "forgetting" to give him the phone number, but then I thought better of it. He probably suspected I was covering, anyway. I had to go on the offensive and prove to him that I was earnest and trustworthy—even, apparently, if it meant catapulting him into a relationship with someone other than me. Given the situation, Claudia seemed like my only option.

The problem with setting up Gardner with Claudia was twofold. One, she would really like him. What was not to like? And, two, he might like her, too. Claudia was definitely better-looking than me. I had my good qualities, sure. Excellent, perfectly proportioned toes that, in my former life, used to have shiny red pedicured nails. A pretty good smattering of freckles. Perfectly straight teeth—perhaps even too perfect. Sometimes I thought about trying to create a gap between the two front ones just to give myself a bit more of an edge.

But Claudia bore some resemblance to a movie star. She had shoulder-length red hair that she sometimes wore up in a loose bun. She wore cutoffs and clogs and had a kind of tranquil, California-girl quality. She also had lost all of her baby weight long before I saw her again for our first mommy group. And—I could certainly vouch, after all those afternoons nursing with the ladies—she had great tits.

We had taken to meeting frequently. She was back at work on weekdays, but on weekends, we were both husbandless and looking for companionship. Almost every Saturday, and sometimes Sunday, too, we'd meet at the zoo to stroll around with the babies. We started with the zoo because it seemed kid-friendly. The babies, of course, could have just as easily been at the opera. As long as they could doze and nurse, they were good. But Claudia and I found that we liked the pace of strolling, and the mild distraction of seeing the animals. And with driving all the way down there, parking, getting in, walking around, and then doing it all in reverse to go home, it was a great way to kill an afternoon.

Both of us, I think, were waiting for our babies to get older. I for one had never expected that Maxie would be so noninteractive. When I thought about babies before she was born, I imagined the things on TV that crawl around and coo and smile at you. But those babies are much older than the cantaloupes that had come out of our bodies. When they first arrived, they were red and cranky and toothless. Sometimes they'd stare pleasantly into space while we held them, and then we could marvel at the little people that we'd made with our very own bodies. But mostly, it was a hustle to keep them happy.

Claudia had admitted to feeling a little off-center about this stage, too. Though we loved our infants, we couldn't wait to see our two-year-olds and then our six-year-olds. And then, as much as we wanted to see what would come next, when our toddlers came, we'd be sad to see our infants go. I read that somewhere about motherhood: that it's bittersweet, because each new stage means letting go of the one before it.

Claudia and I got along very well. She had lots of opinions, and it was lucky for me that I agreed with them. I decided early on that if I ever stumbled upon a subject we disagreed on, I'd keep my mouth shut. Claudia was not a person I wanted to cross. Even still, I liked her more and more. She was someone I would have been friends with even before Maxie. She was no Meredith, but she was someone I would have gone to coffee with a couple of times a month. Instead, now, as single moms, we talked on the phone every day.

"I have something to tell you," I said to her the next time we saw each other.

We were in the monkey jungle. "Let's hear it," she said. She was pushing an empty stroller for little Nikki, who, like Maxie, had refused to ride in it and was now nestled, fast asleep, in Claudia's sling. Claudia had mastered the sling.

"I accidentally set you up on a date with my neighbor."

"Okay," she said. "Is he a person I'd want to date?"

"I don't know," I said, treading carefully. "I don't really know your taste in men."

"Well." She looked up, as if reading off a mental list. "Not insane. Not a Republican. Not a lawyer. At least as tall as I am. And, preferred but not required: funny."

"Those are some tough restrictions," I said.

"You know," she said. "When I was in college, my list was like a mile long. I rejected perfectly decent boys for reasons like 'bad facial hair.' Now look at me. I'll take anybody."

I felt strange as we walked around, talking about Gardner. On the one hand, it made me happy to be able to offer my friend this decent, cute, handy guy. On the other, I couldn't believe I was doing it.

"Why'd you give him my number, anyway?"

"It just kind of happened," I said. Normally, I was pretty honest with Claudia. With most people. But I didn't know how to talk about Gardner. She'd insist that I liked him, I'd insist that I didn't. She'd refuse to go out with him on principle, and I'd feel guilty, months later, when some girl as sweet as his sister but not, obviously, his actual sister, came along and nabbed him. Then neither of us would have him, and that seemed just plain wrong.

"You take him," I said aloud.

"What?"

"He's there for the taking," I said.

I hadn't, actually, given Gardner Claudia's number yet. Part of the reason I told her that day was that I feared I'd never do it unless I knew she was going to ask me about him. Driving home from the zoo, I resolved to take her number straight over to him at the next opportunity. After all, Claudia was a good woman. She deserved some happiness. And I wasn't even sure what I'd do with him if I had him. Who was I to put a good man on the shelf in case I wanted him later?

A few hours later, feeling like a good friend, I headed over to his house with Maxie on my belly. We'd eaten and then had a blowout-poopy diaper that got all over me, the sofa, Maxie, the changing table, and everything in between. It took about a box of baby wipes, but I managed to take care of it. I was getting better at multitasking. I could sing "Farmer in the Dell" to a screaming Maxie while wiping down every surface in arm's reach, stripping the changing-table cover, tossing poop-covered items in the laundry, and choosing a fresh outfit for my little one and then myself. All without getting flustered.

It was a quality that many mothers I knew had—the ability to seem calm when the shit was literally hitting the fan. I was getting the hang of it. And as crazy as it made me to hear Maxie cry, I'd learned to pause from my little song to give her life lessons: "Just a poopy diaper. Part of life!"

Gardner wasn't home. I left the number, written on stationery my mother had given me that said MAXIE'S MOM at the top, in his mailbox. We walked home. All cleaned up and no one to talk to.

And then, rounding the driveway, I saw Gardner come out of my garage. He waved.

"You want me to paint the whole thing?" he called out.

I suddenly felt embarrassed that I'd even asked him. He wasn't a handyman. He was a doctor! Or some kind of an ex-doctor. He had friends, a life, and a sister who visited him. He didn't want to paint my garage!

"You don't want to paint my garage," I said.

"I don't?"

"I'm sorry I even asked you. I was just excited about an idea."

"I do want to paint your garage," he said. "And I will let you pay me. In food."

"In food?"

"I thought of this plan," he said. "I'll come over on Sunday afternoons and paint—which I find relaxing—and you'll be inside cooking me a delicious meal to suck down when I'm done for the day."

"I like that plan," I said. "Except I don't cook anymore."

"You don't cook?"

I pointed down at Maxie, now holding a strand of my hair in her fist.

He nodded. "Okay. How about I finish up a little early on those Sundays and take this one for a walk so you can cook?"

"I think you're getting the short end of the stick, buddy."

"Can you cook?" he asked.

"I'm actually a very good cook."

"Then everybody wins," he said. "Because I can't cook. I subsist on canned beans and takeout. I'd give a lot for a home-cooked meal."

"Well, it looks like you're going to be giving up your Sundays," I said.

And so he talked me into it—or I talked him into it—and that next Sunday he was out in my garage in his overalls, painting and, I was charmed to hear, whistling as he worked.

I myself had gone to the market with Maxie that morning and had gotten the fixings for spinach risotto. I had not cooked one thing since Maxie had come along, and as I pawed through the basil bunches in the produce area, Maxie asleep against my chest, I felt an emotion that couldn't have been anything other than happiness.

That afternoon, after four solid hours of painting, Gardner went home, showered, and appeared back at my front door in under ten minutes. Maxie was wide-awake, cooing like she was onstage. And as we got the stroller ready, I suddenly felt nervous. "She doesn't always like the stroller, so you can put her in this carrier if she fusses. Or sometimes I just hold her and push the stroller with the other hand. I wouldn't go too far, if I were you, in case she really starts to cry and you need to get her back to me. Maybe just laps that stay close to the house. And she likes 'Old MacDonald,' if you need a song. Don't forget to look both ways before crossing the street. And, seriously, if she starts to cry, just bring her back. We can always order pizza."

Gardner watched me with a kind of awe. "Did you just tell me to look both ways before crossing the street?"

"I'm not sure," I said. "It's possible."

He popped Maxie in the stroller, quite expertly, I thought, and before I knew it they were off.

I paused for a moment to wonder if Gardner was actually a baby thief who would disappear with her as soon as they turned the corner and then sell her to the highest bidder. Although, of course, as he rounded the corner, it was too late. Unwilling to chase him down, I had to hope for the best.

Alone in the kitchen, I put on a CD and boogied around a little while I washed and chopped. Here I was! It was like being the old me. I was awake, and cooking, and listening to music. I was alone in the house for the first time in months, and the smell of melting butter and sautéing onions filled the kitchen and I found myself feeling homesick for my old life. And so when Gardner made it back, and I heard the key in the lock and then the door slam shut, I thought—for just a minute, before I remembered where I was in time—that he was Dean.

Dinner involved some baby juggling. Gardner claimed that Maxie had been perfect on the walk, but here at home she decided to fuss. I held her and bounced around while Gardner ate his meal, then he did the same for me. I was a little relieved to see that she fussed even with him. That day on the porch he had made it all look way too easy.

We didn't talk much, over Maxie. I'd imagined somehow, when he'd suggested dinner, that cooking dinner for him would feel almost like a date. But I'd forgotten about Maxie and her feelings about early evening. It was hard to keep her happy then, and I don't know where my head had been when I'd imagined her resting in the bouncy seat and letting me talk to anyone at all.

He left early, waving away a stream of thank-yous from me, and I found myself wondering, much later in the evening as I finished washing the dishes, if he was still thinking about me, too.

23

I waited to hear about Gardner and Claudia's date, but nobody told me anything. Four whole Saturdays at the zoo went by without a word from Claudia. I deliberately didn't ask her. Officially, it was the type of thing that could slip my mind. And the more time that went by without her saying anything to me, the more I worried that they had met for coffee or some other normal thing—since Claudia, with her nanny and housekeeper, could still do grown-up activities like that—and hit it off so amazingly well that neither of them even wanted to tell me. It was so good, they couldn't tell another living soul without creating horrible envy.

After a while I decided they'd gone not for coffee, but for a night out. Claudia had fastened on some earrings and left Nikki home with the nanny and a freezer full of breast milk. I imagined them at that corner Italian restaurant where amateur singers performed light opera on Saturdays. They drank wine and filled their bellies with warm pasta. It was a cool night with a blue sky. They started with current events, like the article about the bear attacks in Los Angeles, then moved on to something more personal, like his college major (botany) and how his father had tried to make him change it, and then wound up on something touching and meaningful, like her grandfather's funeral near Lake Placid in the snow.

I just knew that they were seeing each other. The more time that passed, the more certain I became. They were seeing each other and didn't want to tell me. Maybe they sensed that I would have mixed feelings. Maybe they thought it was fun to have a secret. I didn't know, and I damn sure wasn't going to ask.

And what if Claudia had finally found love? She'd been searching all these years. Was it fair of me to pout in the corner? I did not want to be that kind of friend. They were dating. They were happy. God bless.

Gardner still came over on Sundays to paint, and still took Maxie on walks afterward while I cooked for us. And we always still ate one at a time, taking turns holding Maxie. But I treated him now like he was somebody else's man.

After a while, I told myself that my choice to give him Claudia's number had probably been an act of self-protection. My unconscious mind, or my inner child, or something in there, had known I wasn't ready to start anything new. The thought was inconceivable. I was barely learning the ropes with Maxie, and I wasn't over the Dean debacle—that was for sure. I needed to be a good mom, and to learn how to get at least one shower a day, and heal my heartbreak, and become self-sufficient. I did not need to fling myself at the next available man I saw. Just because he pranced around the neighborhood in his pj's. Or even just because I was lonesome.

I'd known kids whose mothers had been left, and those mothers often became so desperate to find new mates that they forgot about their kids. The kids became a barrier to love. And then they'd find some irritable, balding accountant who had left his own first wife, and they'd date for a while, and then suddenly he'd show up at Christmas with some perfunctory and deeply unexciting gifts for the kids, and the next thing you knew they were engaged. But those weren't his kids. He didn't care about them. The mother would bend herself into a pretzel trying to pretend that they were a family, the kids would start hot-wiring cars in the neighborhood and parking them at different houses just to be a little naughty, and that marriage, too, would eventually fold under the strain.

I wasn't going to be one of those mothers.

I'd made my choice, and my choice was Maxie. I was not going to pine for Dean, and I wasn't going to put Maxie second to finding a new man, either. My die was cast. I was a mother now, and that was all I was going to be until Maxie was, at least, in college.

"That's too depressing," my mother said to me when she came to take Maxie. "Don't ever say that to me again."

"Well, that's the way it is," I said.

"A new man can be an asset to your little family if you find a good one," my mother said.

But even she wasn't convinced. There just weren't a lot of good ones out there. Everybody knew that.

It was liberating in a way. I could chat with Gardner in his paint-splattered overalls and notice his neck, and the way his Adam's apple bobbed when he talked, and not feel anxious. He was a steak sandwich, yes, but I was a vegetarian. I was eating off a whole different menu.

I was, in fact, feeling particularly tranquil and free of desire at the zoo one afternoon with Claudia when she said, "That friend of yours never called me."

"What friend?"

"Your neighbor. He was supposed to call me."

I was slow on the uptake. How could they be dating if he never called her? "He never called you?"

"You gave him my number, right?"

I nodded. "I put it in his mailbox."

"Maybe he never got it."

"Maybe it got lost in the junk mail."

"Or maybe he saw that picture of me on your fridge and got scared away."

"Trust me when I tell you: If he'd seen that photo, he'd have raced to your house and knocked down the door."

"You think too much of me."

"You think too little of you."

We were at an impasse.

"Maybe he found someone else," she tried again.

"Or maybe he saw that picture of you and got intimidated."

"Please."

"I'll have to ask him."

"No!" she said. "Don't ask him. Then I'll feel pathetic."

"I have to ask him," I said.

"If he doesn't want to call me, then I don't want him to call me," she said.

"But what if it was just a mistake? What if he never got the number?"

"Then it wasn't meant to be," she said.

"You don't really believe that. Nobody believes in fate that much."

"I sort of do," she said. "But I don't believe in much else. Just fate, a little. And horoscopes."

On the drive home, I couldn't locate my easy, detached, live-and-let-love self. My mind was racing instead. What was he thinking? Was he calling my bluff? Or did he snub my friend? Maybe he was feeling shy. Or had met someone else. The old me would have called him as soon as I got home to nose it all out of him. But in this life, I had a very tired and crabby little person in the car with me who had other ideas.

I raced her into the house as soon as we landed in the driveway.

We nursed for a while and that calmed her down, and then we went to change her diaper.

I was a close watcher of poops. It was one of Maxie's only forms of communication. Unable to just ask her how she was, I inspected her diapers like they were mood rings.

By the time she was changed, it was almost bath time. I held her in one arm and ate some spaghetti my mother had made and stored—sauce and all—in separate, meal-size Ziploc bags. It had seemed so over-the-top when she arrived with them. But now that I had only two left, I was wondering if she'd make me some more.

The next day was Sunday. Gardner had not let me in to see the garage while he'd been working—in the same way that he had never let me inside his house because it "wasn't finished yet"—and I hadn't wanted to go out there for fear that the fumes would harm Maxie's brain development. But today, he said he was ready to let us look. When Maxie and Gardner got back from their walk, the three of us headed to the garage.

I waited as he unlocked the dead bolt. The potted plants on my back steps were so dry and dead that they could have been wisps of paper. Oh, well. Priorities.

Gardner started to open the door and said, "So, this is it. I'm pretty much finished."

"You are?" I said. "That was fast."

"I have a special brush. You know, 'cause I do this type of thing a lot."

I was thinking I'd have to come up with something new for him to do.

"Don't you want to see it?"

I stepped in. I didn't know what to say. "Holy cow" was what I finally came up with.

He held Maxie while I looked around. I had expected him only to slap on a coat of paint and replace a few fixtures. And he had. The walls were the French Gray Linen I'd picked out. But he had also repainted the window frames, trim, and ceiling a clean white. He'd replaced the light fixture—a single bulb that had hung like an interrogation lamp—with a gorgeous Craftsman-style one that had four bulbs and shined a warm light into every corner. And in the center, up near the front door, was a display case, handmade, from the looks of it, with a glass front and top and a place for a register.

I didn't have the heart to tell him that I'd been wondering lately if my mother had been right and opening a shop might be a mistake.

I walked over to the display case. "Did you make this?"

"No," he said, waving his hand. "I found it in a junk shop." There was a pause. "But I did refinish it."

"This is too much," I said. "How did you get all this done?"

He came over to me and started playing with Maxie's feet. "You know." He shrugged. "I'm handy."

"I don't know what to say," I said.

"Say 'Dinner's ready,' " he said.

And so I did.

24

We were barely inside when the doorbell rang. I hadn't heard the sound of the doorbell since I'd put up the sign that said SLEEPING BABY! KNOCK! DON'T RING!

I opened the door to see my father standing there. Before I even said hello, I checked the bell to see if that sign had fallen off. It hadn't.

"Hiya, Jen-Jen," my dad said. He was still in his scrubs.

"I have a note here on this bell that says not to ring it."

My father was waving his pointer finger at Maxie.

I continued. "You have to move this note to get to the bell."

"Nah," my father said. "You can just press the note itself."

"The baby could have been sleeping," I said.

"But she wasn't."

"But she could have been. And you would have woken her."

"But she wasn't."

"You're missing the point."

"And you're fixating on it."

We stared at each other.

Then he said, "Smells good. What's for supper?" and let himself inside.

Gardner had been standing back, watching—not intruding, but keeping an eye on the situation. My father marched right up to him and said, "You the new boyfriend?"

"He's just a neighbor, Dad," I said, and felt instantly like I'd said the wrong thing. I glanced over at Gardner, who looked away as soon as I did.

"Good," my father said, making his way back to the kitchen. "No more boyfriends for you. Even if I have to sit on the front porch with a shotgun."

"No shotgun necessary," Gardner said.

I'd made a Cajun shrimp étouffée, a dish of my mother's.

My dad spied it in the pot and said, "Now, that's just torture."

We were ready to eat, but my dad had an announcement. "I did it," he said as I was ladling bowls. I set my ladle back in the pot. Gardner, who was holding Maxie, waited to see what, exactly, my dad had done.

"When?" I asked.

"Just now. On the way over."

"On the cell phone?" I asked, wrinkling my nose.

"You're supposed to ask me how it went," my dad said.

"How did it go?"

And then my dad just smiled.

I couldn't believe it. She'd said yes.

"You're a miracle worker," I said. "Is there ever anything you want that you don't get?"

My dad got serious. "Yes," he said.

"But not today!" I said, and we slapped high fives.

Gardner was still trying to figure it out. My dad looked over and said, "I'm trying to get Jenny's mother to fall back in love with me."

"After leaving her high and dry on her birthday many years ago," I added.

My father nodded, his face tight with guilt. It was true.

"I did leave a present for her on the hall table that day," he offered.

"I don't think she ever opened it," I said. "I think she gave it to Goodwill still in the wrapping paper."

My father had not heard this before. "There was a gold bracelet in there!"

"I'm sure it went to a grateful recipient."

We all thought about it. Then Gardner said, "Trying to get her back, huh?"

My father, still thinking, nodded.

"How's that going?" Gardner asked.

"Well, son," my father said, straightening his shoulders a bit. "Today, it's going pretty well."

Gardner and my dad ate étouffée while I held Maxie and asked every question I could think of. He had followed my advice and confessed all his feelings, most likely while driving fifty in a thirty and shaking his fist at drivers who got in his way. She had listened to him without saying anything and then, when he finally got to the big question, she paused for what he insisted was a full three minutes and then said, "Okay."

So they were going out for Brazilian food at this new place that had a "real rain forest" in the middle. "It's nicer than it sounds," my dad insisted. "And the steaks are so good they bring tears to your eyes."

"She can't resist a good steak," I said.

He wanted suggestions about what to wear, how to act, which topics of conversation to introduce. And he'd need all the help he could get. So I gave him some tips. I told him no cigars, no French food or wine, no knock-knock jokes. I told him to be early for everything. She did not tolerate waiting for people. I told him to compliment something she was wearing every time he saw her, to put his hand on the small of her back when walking through a restaurant, and to watch her eyes and her mouth when she answered a question. I told him not to check his watch at dinner, not to run yellow lights, and not, under any circumstances, to even glance at another woman in my mother's presence. Even if that other woman was the waitress and speaking directly to him. "Avert your eyes," I said, "order your food, and get it over with."

My father raised his eyebrows at Gardner. "Are you getting this all down?"

Gardner tapped his finger against his head. "It's right in here."

They finished their bowls, then Gardner held Maxie while I had some myself, and then they both started on seconds. Maxie was getting restless, so I took her out in the backyard and paced around, catching snippets of the conversation whenever I was near the door.

My father asked Gardner all about himself, and I noticed that Gardner never mentioned that he, too, like my dad, was a doctor. My dad made Gardner laugh several times. He had a way with people. It's why he was such a beloved doctor. We used to get fan mail at the house when I was a kid. One guy even sent us a Thanksgiving turkey that he'd raised on his own farm.

"I've told every one of my kids that they're my favorite, but Jenny really is," I heard my dad say.

As happy as I was for my dad, I couldn't help thinking that if he weren't there, I'd be alone with Gardner. I wanted to be gushing to him about how great the garage looked, thanking him over and over, and praising his painting, light-installing, and furniture-refinishing skills. I stepped back into the kitchen to see if I could subtly encourage my dad to be on his way. Instead, I listened to him talk about fly-fishing. Gardner seemed interested. Was he faking? Who could be interested in fly-fishing?

"Now, Jenny," my Dad said, pointing at me, "there's a fisherman."

"You fish, Jenny?" Gardner said.

"No," I said. I looked at my dad. "You must be mixing me up with one of your other children."

"You don't remember that time we all went down to Galveston Bay?"

"No," I said.

"You must have been about seven," he said. "And me and you and your mother, we drove down in the station wagon with a whole coolerful of chicken necks. And we stopped at the bay and your mother set up a picnic while the two of us tied our chicken necks to strings and headed out into the water with our sneakers on."

"You went fishing with chicken necks?" Gardner said.

"Crabbing," my father said. "The crabs go after the necks, and you scoop them up with a net. It's easy!"

"That's not really fishing, though, is it?" I said.

"It's all the same," my father said, intent on telling his story. "And your mom and I caught a few of them, here and there. But you! You caught a bucketful. One right after the other! Like you were calling them to you!" My father had stopped looking at Gardner and me, and now was gazing into space as if he were watching an old home movie. "I couldn't believe it!" he went on. "Your mother went to read a magazine after a while, but you and I stayed out there until the horizon turned bright pink. Crab after crab. We had sandwiches on the beach that night, but the next night, at home, I boiled those crabs and we licked every one of them clean."

"I have no memory of this," I said.

"There's a picture of us on that shore. I have it somewhere. I'm going to find it to show you."

"Okay," I said as Maxie started to fuss.

And then dinner was over. My last dinner with Gardner, and I wasn't able to thank him properly. My father left almost as soon as his second bowl was empty and Gardner left a few minutes later, and just as I was thinking I might stand at the counter and eat some seconds out of the pot, Maxie started to melt down for real and it was time to get bedtime going.

For some reason, it took me almost an hour and a half to get Maxie down that night. I just kept rocking and rocking and rocking, and humming. I hummed every song I could think of, and made my way from "You Are My Sunshine" to "Just a Gigolo" before starting over. When she was finally in her crib, I cleaned the kitchen quietly and slowly, thinking about my father. He did seem to get everything he wanted. I wondered if he would get my mother. And I wondered if he would still want her when he had her.

Dishes done, I pulled some double-A batteries out of the junk drawer and put them in the baby monitor. Then I took it and the cordless phone out the back door with me. I had never left Maxie alone in the house before, and if I were to, say, have a heart attack while I was out there, I wanted to at least call my mother in my last seconds of consciousness so that she could be there at the midnight wake-up with a bottle of frozen breast milk.

I walked barefoot through the grass in the backyard. Then I unlocked the side door and stepped into the garage. Even at night, it felt clean and bright. I decided to call Gardner. I had to call 4-1-1 for his number. I was so nervous that I almost forgot the number before I could dial it.

"How can I thank you for this?" I said when he answered.

"Come out to the movies with me," he said.

I paused. "I don't go to the movies anymore."

"Oh," Gardner said.

"I don't do fun things anymore," I explained.

"I bet your mother would babysit," he said.

"Not as long as there's a cat in my house," I said.

"So put him in the garage," he said.

He had me there, but I still hesitated.

"Just friends," he said.

I didn't say anything.

"Why don't you just say yes now," Gardner suggested, "and then change your mind later?"

"That sounds good," I said.

"So that's a yes?"

"Yes."

25

I did change my mind later. Mostly because I could not shake the feeling that Maxie would not be able to sleep if I left the house, even though my mother had put her down for naps before. Nighttime was a different thing. And she still woke up so frequently. Babies are supposed to get "organized" not too long after they're born and figure out that they, like the rest of us, sleep at night and run around during the day. But I still feared that Maxie hadn't figured it out yet, and that without my elaborate bedtime rituals and cajoling, she might just stay up all night every night.

Plus I hated the idea of leaving her. How could she feel safe and secure if I was out at the movies? Every hormone in my body made me feel like I had to be within ten feet of her at all times. And so I was.

But another part of me just ached to go out and do grown-up things. Every taste I got of my old self made me hungry for more. So then I changed my mind back.

I laid it all out for Claudia at an emergency weekday meeting at the zoo, and instead of focusing on my dilemma, she said, "So he never called me because he really liked you."

"It's possible," I said.

"And you like him, too?"

"I'm not sure. Maybe. I'm too tired to have any feelings."

"Why on earth did you give him my number?"

"It was kind of a desperate situation. Let's just say I panicked."

"What would you have done, though, if we'd started seeing each other?"

"Started therapy to learn to support your happiness."

"Really, I was kind of a pawn," she said.

I put my hand over my face and peeked through my fingers. "Kind of."

"Why didn't you just talk to me about the whole thing?"

I shrugged. "I wasn't sure what to say." I reached over and touched her sleeve—just a little tug. "Are you mad?"

"The thing is, I haven't had a date since before I got pregnant."

I nodded.

She continued. "So I was pretty excited."

"And now you're let down."

"Yes," she said. "By you. The person who now has my date."

"But I guess he was sort of my date all along."

"But you didn't tell me that!" She really did seem irritated.

"I wish I could take it back, Claudia," I said.

She accepted my apology. But she stayed irritated for the rest of the day.

"Where is *my* dream neighbor?" she asked later. "The only single man on my block is eighty-five and drives a Plymouth." And, as we passed the lions, the unfairness of it all seized her again. "Who do I have to fuck to get a boyfriend?" she shouted.

She was gracious enough, though, most of the time, to let me continue to process about Gardner.

"I really thought I had given him away and made myself miserable," I explained to her in the bat cave.

"Do you do that to yourself a lot?"

"Do what?"

"Make yourself miserable with men?"

"Oh, God," I said. "All the time."

"Well, then, he broke a pattern for you."

"He did?"

"Instead of liking me and allowing you to be miserable, he's liking you and forcing you to be happy."

"I don't want to be happy," I said.

"Yes you do."

"I'm not even going to go out with him this weekend. I'm going to fake an illness."

"Oh no you're not."

I tried to get her to support me and give me permission to chicken out. "I'm on shaky ground here," I said. "I don't know what to do with a nice man. Nobody's this nice. I keep thinking he's a serial killer." I told her that the heartaches Dean gave me were at least familiar. We'd been at it so long I was used to them. I probably could have categorized them by type and made a chart. I wasn't ready for new heartaches, I said.

"But there'll be new pleasures, too," she said.

"Just more things to miss after he leaves me."

"You're such an optimist," she said, putting her arm around me as we walked on to the porcupines. "How do you stay so sunny?"

On the porch the next morning, my mother was much less gentle. "There is no dilemma. You're going. If I have to tie you to the bed of his truck."

"You know what?" I said. "I'm heartbroken. I'm weak. I may not be ready."

"Everybody is heartbroken," she said. "It doesn't matter. That's life. Get out there and shake a tail feather."

"Well," I said, "I hear you're going to be doing some feather-shaking yourself."

She knew what I meant. She took a deep breath. "He caught me off guard with the tears."

"The tears?!"

She nodded. "Just as I was thinking about hanging up on him, he started to sob."

"That's what made you say yes?"

She shrugged. "Yes."

"Does he have any kind of a chance?"

"Well," she said, "I once loved him so much that I climbed out my bedroom window to neck with him behind the gazebo in Granny and Grandpa's yard. So he has that going for him."

She was lost in thought for a minute, remembering. And, I thought, even the sassiest of us couldn't resist getting a little bit hopeful about love.

26

On the Wednesday before we were supposed to go out, Gardner called to reconfirm.

"We're still on?" he asked.

"Still on!" I said.

"This is your first night out since Maxie was born?"

"It is."

"You should wear something festive, then," he said. "We'll celebrate adulthood."

"Okay," I said.

"And," he added, just before we hung up, "I've thought of something better than the movies."

When Friday finally came, I was anxious about leaving Maxie. I dreaded it from the moment she woke me up that morning.

But I began our bedtime rituals that night as usual. My heart felt anxious, and I wondered if she could sense it. All during bath time, I tried to seem like it was just any other night. But of course, it wasn't. Because tonight, after I tiptoed out of her room, I was going to leave her alone in the house with my mother. Who was a very capable person, and who, I'm sure, could get her out if the place started to burn down, but who was not, in fact, me.

I tried not to think about the unlikely but distinctly possible scenario that Maxie would wake up and cry out for me, but get my mother instead. I tried not to imagine Maxie jumping to the conclusion that I'd left the country and her forever, that no breast milk would ever come to her again, that she was not loved or cared for. When I thought like this, my eyes filled with tears and I had to blink them back and remind myself to seem cheerful and normal.

It seems odd, looking back, that I had such a hard time leaving the baby. All I can say is that when a tiny, fragile creature depends on you all day every day for every sense of safety and comfort she has, you start to feel that every moment is vital, and that you better not screw up. Abandonment was clearly a loaded issue for me as well.

My mother had no patience for me. She'd arrived and left her things hooked over my bedroom door, hoping to safeguard them from cat fur. Now she was standing in the bathroom doorway, watching me dab my eyes.

"You are acting like a crazy person," she said. "She's going to be fine."

"You don't know that," I said. "You don't know for sure."

"If she wakes up, I'll rock her."

"But you aren't me."

"I'm pretty damn close."

I reminded my mother to wash her hands every ten or fifteen minutes. "You don't want to get cat dander on them," I said. "And don't touch your face or your eyes." I'd kept Dr. Blandon locked up in my room for a week in hopes that my mother could make it through a few hours in my house. Now he was out in the garage, and I hoped he was far enough away.

"I'll be fine," my mother said, holding up a baggie full of allergy remedies. "Just go."

It was time to do it. I pulled Maxie out of the tub and toweled her off. We had this routine down by now. A touch of diaper cream, a diaper, left foot in the pj's, then right, *snap, snap, snap,* and she was all suited up for bed. Then off we went into her darkened bedroom and settled into the fancy rocker I'd splurged on—or, to be more accurate, Dean's mother had splurged on. I pulled out my boob and she was like a tiny hungry bird waiting for it. In it went, and she nursed and nursed. I hummed and hummed. Her eyes were closed.

It's a rule that if you let yourself think about anything fun that you're looking forward to after you've nursed your baby to sleep, it will take twice as long to get there. I tried to keep my mind completely blank, but I also worried a little that I might fall asleep, too. It was 7:14. I was due at Gardner's at 7:30, and I wasn't dressed. I'd just have to call him as soon as I got out. I hoped he hadn't made reservations. I felt reasonably sure that Maxie would be asleep pretty soon. She'd been rubbing her eyes since five o'clock.

But when I went to put her in her crib, she woke up and cried.

I picked her back up and went back to the rocker. She nursed some more. It was 7:32. Did Gardner think I was standing him up? Surely he knew how crazy things were with a baby. He wasn't going to give up on me that fast. I wondered where we were going. The idea of being outside after sundown was almost intoxicating. Maxie was asleep again, her mouth slack, her eyes peaceful and closed. I gave her five more minutes to get settled, then I tried again.

It was 7:40. I eased myself up out of the chair and crept across the floor, carefully avoiding the spot with the creaky floorboard. She was completely limp. I made it to the crib. I leaned over and set her in, rocking her gently to pull my hands out from under her body. She was out. I was done. It occurred to me that I didn't even have Gardner's phone number. I thought about sending my mother over there while I dressed.

I pulled up the railing and turned to leave, and, *schuuuumpffff*—the railing fell from position. It hadn't latched! Maxie's eyes popped open. When she saw me, she started to cry. I had no choice. I lifted her up, walked us back over to the rocker, and settled back down. I'd already tucked my boob back into my bra, so I had to wrestle with the snap and get my shirt up. She took the nipple impatiently and began the process of putting herself back to sleep. 7:47.

I finally made it out at 8:02. I raced to find my mother. I was pulling off my shirt as I swept into the living room when I saw Gardner sitting on the couch.

"Hey there," he said.

I pressed my shirt tightly to my chest and said, "Hello. Gardner, I see you've met my mother."

"Again," he said.

"Sweetheart," my mother said. "Why don't you go put some clothes on?"

"I'm sorry I'm late," I said to Gardner. "The baby didn't want to go down."

Gardner was waving me away. "It's all okay. Go get dressed. There's no rush."

I backed out of the room. What was my mother telling him? I hoped she wasn't acting like we were going on a date. She was a matchmaker, my mother. But I'd explained that it wasn't a date. Just one friend taking another friend out of the house. Friends did that kind of thing all the time.

Something festive. I had a red skirt that was silk and kind of swirly. Red skirt and black shirt. And under the shirt, a plain-old regular nonlactating bra. Was that the kind of outfit that friends wore out on the town with other friends? Fuck it. Who cared? I took a few minutes to wash my sticky face, brush my teeth (had I even remembered to do that yet today?), put on some deodorant and perfume, and shake my hair to fluff it. I threw on the clothes and some black high-heeled sandals. Then red lipstick to go with the skirt and a little mascara.

Just then, my engagement ring caught my eye, and I pulled it off in one decisive yank, tossed it in my jewelry box, and slammed down the lid. Truly, I'd forgotten I even had the thing on. How long had it been since I'd even noticed it on my hand? But that ring had no right to be there, and it certainly wasn't coming with me on a nondate with Gardner. I took a deep breath, turned off the light, and left the room.

Gardner stood when I showed up. He was all decked out in flat-front khakis and a button-down shirt. "You look fancy," I said.

My mother nudged Gardner and he started escorting me by the elbow out the door.

"Wait!" I said. "I've got a list of instructions to go over, and I haven't shown you—"

My mother said, "I've got the list. I'll be fine. You survived with me taking care of you, and I'm sure this little one will, too." She gave me a push toward the door. "Go, Cinderella. Your clock is ticking."

And then I was out on the porch. Alone. With Gardner. He took my hand and started pulling me down the sidewalk. "Let's go," he said. "You need a beer."

"I can't have a beer," I said, pointing at my boobs.

He looked at them and said, "Maybe it's me who needs the beer."

We walked up the gentle slope toward his house. It was warm and a bit humid out, which was kind of a shame for October, but it was breezy, too—and that made it seem like the ocean was somewhere nearby. The dark sky was a pale autumn color, and something about the way the night air was touching my arms made me pay close attention to everything around me. My heels knocked along the sidewalk. The palm tree across the street rustled.

"It feels oddly thrilling," I said, "to be out of the house after dark."

His pickup truck was very clean and had leather seats. He had a well-used notepad attached to the dashboard. I relaxed into the seat as he drove. He was a good driver—measured, considerate of the passenger. Not once did I feel nauseated or anxious. He used his turn signals and deferred politely to other drivers.

"So. Where are we going?" I finally asked.

"Angelica's Cantina."

"That's better than a movie?"

He nodded. "It's better than many things."

Angelica's was probably bigger than it seemed, because it was packed. The ceiling was low and decorated with multicolored doilies. There was a bar near the front and some tables near the back, but mostly the place was just for dancing. On Fridays, it appeared, Angelica went all-out and hired a live band with more musicians than the stage could really hold.

At the table, I rested my chin in my hands. I was tired. I had not eaten dinner, although I'd told Gardner I would eat before we left, so I was hungry. A movie had sounded good to me. I hadn't seen a movie since before Maxie. I wasn't sure I had the energy for a cantina.

When the waiter came, I ordered a virgin margarita, babbling and, yes, gesturing for illustration about how I was breast-feeding and couldn't have any alcohol. He nodded and brought me the most relaxing virgin margarita I'd ever had. "I think this virgin margarita is spiked," I said halfway through.

"I'm not sure the waiter was totally with you on the no-alcohol concept," Gardner said.

But by then I was too relaxed to care. Something that under different circumstances would have me poring through my parenting books, scanning the index for "alcohol, accidental ingestion of," felt like not such a big deal in the warm noise of the cantina.

The music was so loud it reverberated in my chest, and I could feel it massaging out all the mother-worry that I carried around every minute. The baby seemed like part of a distant world, and I found myself thinking, *She'll be fine*. I had brought my cell phone to call and check on her, but soon, with all the noise and the cigarette smoke and the warm bodies making waves of motion in the room, I forgot all about it.

Gardner leaned in close and yelled into my ear, "Do you know how to dance to this?"

"No!" I shouted. "Do you?"

"Yes."

"You know how to salsa dance?" I gave him a look.

He said, "What?"

"It's just a little—" I was going to say "cheesy," but it seemed too mean.

"Cheesy?" he offered.

I nodded.

"I took lessons in college to impress girls."

"And are girls impressed?"

He set down his beer. "It really depends on the girl."

He leaned in closer. "I studied with the master: Ferdinand Cervantes." When he said "Ferdinand Cervantes," he made his voice very deep and spoke in a Spanish accent. He was drinking a Tecate. He was cuter than I remembered.

My margarita was almost gone. I'd sucked it down like it was an Icee. Gardner took a big swig of his beer and pulled me up. "Let's do it," he said.

I thought he was going to take me toward the dance floor, but instead he took me to a back patio that was pretty quiet. We could still hear the music, but we could also hear ourselves.

"So this is the basic step," he said, putting me in position. "Start with your feet together. Like this."

I was feeling goofy from the drink. "I'm a great dancer," I said.

"I don't doubt it," he said, staring at my feet. "Put your hands here."

We danced for a bit, him watching my feet and me watching his. Then he said, "Now look up."

"Oh, no," I said. "I have to look down."

"No, you don't," he said, putting his arm around my waist. He pulled me to him, and we were pressed together.

"Hey!" I said. "My feet!"

"Just imagine them," he said.

And so I closed my eyes and imagined my feet in their festive black sandals. And he moved me around the patio, the muted music in the background. I had never done that kind of couple dancing before. The feeling was like nothing else. A strong arm holding you, guiding you to the next move, the sense that everything was taken care of, the pleasure of two separate people moving at the same time to the same music. It was, in fact—as he had promised—better than going to the movies.

He showed me a few more steps and then pulled me toward the door. "Okay," he said. "You're ready for the big time."

"Now I'm nervous," I said, pulling back.

"You just told me you were a great dancer."

"I was kind of kidding."

"But you like to dance?"

"In my house. Like I like to sing in my car. That doesn't mean I want to do karaoke."

"This place is too crowded for anyone to notice us. We'll just slip in."

He was pulling my hand toward the door. I was pulling back.

"If you don't like it, we'll leave," he said.

I relented, and he pushed me gently through the door.

Then he said, "But you're going to like it."

And then we were in the crowd, and the crowd was moving, a force on our bodies like a current, and we were caught in it, all of us moving in the same rhythm to the same sounds. The steps were simple, and pretty soon Gardner was pushing me out and pulling me in, spinning me around and leaning me back. I just followed him. My red silk skirt twisted and swung, and I could feel it whispering around my legs. I had thought it was cold in there when we walked in, but on the dance floor, it was just right. Sparkly lights hung from the ceiling, and everything seemed infused with magic.

And there, in the center of it all, was Gardner. He was calm and even. I thought about how nice it was that men had such big shoulders. I thought about what a good man he was.

The next song was a bit faster, and I tried to keep up without thinking too hard. His hand was on the small of my back, and I just relaxed into it. He spoke encouragement at every opportunity: "Good! That's right!"

As the song ended, he pulled me off to the side. We were both starting to sweat some now. "Do you want to rest?" he shouted into my ear.

In general, I was tired. There was never enough sleep. But I felt wide-awake at that moment. The next song was starting up, and the crowd was taking off. I shook my head no, and we slid back in.

I don't know how much longer we stayed out there, or what time it was when we stumbled back out to his truck. It couldn't have been too late—the club was still packed. But as we walked out, the music was still so loud in the parking lot that he pulled me to him and dipped me right beside his truck.

"Thanks for getting me out of the house," I said as I came up.

Gardner sent me out to spin, but when I was near the passenger door, I leaned back against it and pulled him to me. He put his hand against the door. He was a little out of breath, and I reached up to his face, thinking at first I was going to touch his hair. Instead, my hand found a place against his jaw, then settled against his neck. He was looking at my mouth, and I could feel his breath on my face. Then he looked up from my mouth to my eyes.

"I'm not drunk," I said. "Are you?"

"I'm not drunk," he said.

And then he leaned down to put his mouth on mine. He had one arm against the truck and one arm around my waist. I'd been pressed up against him all night, and with this kiss, this amazing kiss, I was awash.

Then, too soon, it was over. He pulled back. “We should be getting you home, I guess,” he said.

There was a pause.

I wanted to pull him back to me, but I didn’t. I just let him turn me toward the car, unlock the door, and position me inside. He even clicked my seat belt. I leaned my head back. Soon he was in the seat next to me, and then we were speeding along the highway. I closed my eyes. The motor hummed.

And then we were in his driveway.

He got out on his side and came around to get me. I didn’t move from my seat. I didn’t even unsnap my seat belt.

“You’re too good,” I said. “There’s got to be something wrong with you. Tell me something that’s wrong with you.”

“This is like that job-interview question,” he said. “ ‘What’s your greatest flaw?’ ”

I nodded. “And you have to say ‘I work too hard.’ ”

“I once got that question in an interview,” Gardner said.

“And how did you answer?”

“I said, ‘I work too hard.’ ”

I nodded. “There’s nothing else you can say.”

He touched the seat belt where it crossed my collarbone.

“So what is it?” I asked. “Your greatest flaw?”

He kept his eyes on the seat belt, and then finally said, “I give up on things too easily.”

“What kind of things?” I asked.

He thought about it a minute. “People.”

“That’s a terrific flaw,” I said. “I’d love to have a greatest flaw like that.”

He helped me out, and we walked arm in arm down to my house. At the door, on the porch, he put his lips against my forehead, breathing in a little as he lingered there. “Put yourself in bed,” he said.

"Not a problem," I said.

"Maybe you and Maxie could come by tomorrow."

"To your house? You're going to let me see it? Are you done?"

"Not quite," he said, "but there's something I want to show you."

And then, as if he was trying to resist but couldn't, he brought his mouth to my neck and kissed me there. It made me feel tipsy all over again. And even after the kiss, he rested his forehead against my shoulder, lingering there like he didn't want to go, like he'd give anything at all to be able to stay in that one place.

Then he pulled back just enough to look into my eyes. "See you tomorrow, Jenny."

And he was gone.

I wasn't quite ready to face my mother. For one, I was late. And for another, I was totally smitten. And she'd be able to tell, and she'd tease me and then I'd give her all the details and then somehow this night would be more of a story than a memory. I didn't want to have to fit it into words just yet. Tomorrow, while I was wrestling Maxie into the car seat, I wanted to be able to go back in my mind and replay it all as if I were almost still there.

I leaned against the door for a minute. I took a deep breath. Something good was happening. My life was rising from the ashes, and the sight of it left me feeling something like hopeful. Gardner could really kiss. And even better than that, something in me was starting to stir.

And then, out of the corner of my eye, I saw a funny thing. In my driveway, mostly blocked from view by the house, was the back end of a Ford Explorer. A navy-blue Explorer. I moved one step at a time to the edge of the porch and leaned out for a better look. And there it was. In the driveway. On this night, of all possible nights, Dean had come home.

27

I almost didn't go into the house. I spent a few minutes with my key in my hand trying to come up with another option. But Maxie was inside, so there was nothing else I could do. I thought about staying on the porch for a while. But I had to go in. If for no other reason than I needed the sleep.

I put my key in the lock and pushed open the door to find my mother sitting, arms folded, across from Dean, who was playing with his keys.

"Look what the cat dragged in," my mother said, gesturing at him.

"How was she?" I asked. First things first.

"She did great," she said. "She woke up twice, and I went in and patted her each time, and that was that. Easy."

"You patted her?" Maxie would never have let me get away with that.

I wanted the blow-by-blow, but it appeared now that I wouldn't get it. My mother was itching to leave. Literally.

"Well," I said, "I guess I can't keep you."

"I'll call you in the morning," she said, gathering her things.

And then she closed the door. I was alone with Dean, whose first coy and slightly flirtatious words were "Damn, your mother is mean." As if I were going to say, "Isn't she?" and pop him open a beer to kick off a late-night bitch session. As if starting off like nothing had happened would make it true that nothing had actually happened. As if there were any degree of meanness that he didn't deserve.

He looked scruffier than I'd ever seen him. His hair was longer, and he had a very unfortunate wispy goatee. It was so strange to see him there, in the flesh. There was this body that I'd spent so much time with, and touched so often, and I could see his chest just under his shirt, a chest I'd put my head on a thousand times. It could have been on the other side of a razor-wire fence.

His approach to the situation was clearly to act perky and cute. It had worked with me many times before—with little things. I marveled at the fact that he was doing it now. It wasn't like he'd forgotten to pick up butter at the store. Could he really think this approach would work? Could he be that dumb?

I didn't say anything. I went to the kitchen and started doing the dishes.

Dean followed me. "Where you been? On a date?"

I just kept washing. I didn't even know how to start talking to him. I put the dishes on a clean towel to dry.

"You look great, by the way," he said.

I brushed past him.

"Last time I saw you, you were pretty big."

I bent over to take off my shoes.

"You really look great," he said again. "You look like the old you."

I stood up. "I'm not the old me. I'm not anything like the old me." I walked into my bedroom.

"Can you hold still?" he said, and then tried to touch my hand.

I jerked it away. "You're not staying here. Go find a motel."

Dean gave me a hurt look.

I started taking off my earrings.

"I gave you those," Dean said.

"You're not staying here," I said.

"Give me one night," he said. "I'll sleep on the sofa and see the baby in the morning and be gone the minute you give the word."

"I have to get to bed," I said.

I walked around the bed that I now slept in the middle of, and I found some blankets in the closet, along with a sheet and a pillow. I threw them at him.

"She'll wake up at least one more time tonight, and I'll go in to nurse her. Do not come in or bother us in any way. Also, don't use the toilet, because it's against the wall her crib is on. If you need to pee, go outside."

"What if I need to, you know, do more than pee?"

This is what we had come to. "Do you?" I asked.

"No. I mean hypothetically."

"Figure it out," I said. "Dig a hole in the yard if you have to." I looked at him. "A deep hole."

"Maybe a neighbor's yard," he said, nodding, as if we were collaborating.

"Whatever you do, don't make any noise. If you wake up the baby, you'll be sleeping in your car."

It was time to go to bed. It was one in the morning. She'd be up at six. Best-case scenario, I'd get four and a half hours.

"Good night," he said as he left the room.

If I could have slammed my door without waking Maxie, I would have.

My mother had been wondering where my rage was. Where was the indignation? The anger? The furious loathing? Well, it must have been with Dean on his travels, because the minute he stepped inside my house, I knew exactly where it was. It was everywhere. How dare he come into my house with bad facial hair and act like he had any right to be there? Tomorrow, I was changing the locks.

Maxie woke two more times that night. None of the other mommies in our group had babies who slept through. Some woke only once. Others slept in their parents' bed and spent most of the night on the boob. Maxie was the wake-up record holder, and when we compared notes, the other moms were impressed with her average. I'd shrug and say, "She's an overachiever." When the next morning came, as was often the case, I felt more tired than when I'd gone to bed.

And then there was Dean to face. Except not really. Maxie and I were up before dawn, and even though we went all through the house doing our usual morning things, Dean slept right on through. I couldn't imagine sleeping like that. Since Maxie, everything woke me up—rain, lawn mowers, folks talking out on the street. Even a strong gust of wind could do it. Every sound was an alarm clock for me. Sometimes I'd find myself standing beside the bed before I knew why I'd gotten up. Only a dog barking. Only a car door slamming. Back to bed.

Dean did not have the same problem. He slept on my sofa—through Maxie crying, through Herman's bird-in-the-magnolia-tree barking frenzy, through my opening and closing the front door on numerous occasions—until eleven in the morning. And he woke at eleven only because I poked him with my shoe. Okay, maybe I kicked him. Maxie was asleep, and it seemed like a good time to get rid of him.

He rolled over and buried his head in the sofa pillows. Then, I suppose, he remembered where he was. He lifted his head and said, "Hey."

"You aren't welcome here anymore," I said.

"Good morning to you, too."

"You need to pack up your stuff and go."

"Can't we talk?"

"No."

"I need to talk to you."

"Write it in a letter, chief."

He hadn't had any coffee, something he always did before trying to think or talk. He was in his boxers, his undressed self exactly the way I remembered it.

"Just give me a couple of minutes to wake up."

"You get two minutes. Maxie's taking a nap, and if you leave soon enough, I might get a nap, too." God, I'd have given anything for a nap.

"You named the baby 'Maxie'?"

"How can you not know that?"

"I know I've been out of touch."

"You have been nonexistent."

"I've just been having a hard time lately."

"Are we going to compare suffering now?"

"Could we just get some time to talk?"

"There is no time, Dean. Not anymore. There is the baby, and there is far too little sleep. And there is nothing in between."

"Except dates. Looks like you've got a few of those."

"Are you trying to guilt-trip me? I've had three hours of downtime in the past seven months. How many have you had?"

"I'm not. I'm not trying to guilt-trip you."

I put my head in my hands. If he'd come home even five minutes before Gardner kissed me in that parking lot, I might have been something almost like happy. But now all I wanted was for him to leave.

"Can I just talk to you for a minute?"

I sighed loudly and walked into the kitchen.

"Where are you going?"

"I'm getting something to eat."

Dean got up and followed me, eager, I'm sure, to root through the fridge for leftovers. We used to have very high-caliber leftovers. What I had now, of course, was orange juice, old pizza still in the box, jars of baby food. The fridge was mostly empty.

Dean pulled out the pizza box, looking ready to reheat the slices.

"I wouldn't eat those," I said. "They're from last week."

"Where is all the food?" he said.

"I've got nuts, seeds, and crackers in the cupboard. I'm having cereal."

"I've never seen your fridge like this."

"You've never seen me as a single mother."

"You're not eating?"

"I'm not doing anything." He had no idea. And why should he? His life had barely changed at all. "If I say it slowly, will you get it? All I do is the baby."

"You don't cook?"

He was standing in the kitchen in just his boxers. As if he lived here. As if we were on those terms. I closed my eyes and pointed back toward the living room. "Go put some clothes on," I said.

And he went. And I was alone in the kitchen. *I should kick him out,* I thought. *Any sane person would kick him out.* But I was waiting for his apology. I was sure it was coming. Every time he opened his mouth, I expected to hear him beg for forgiveness. And I just simply had to hear it. It was like watching a horror movie on TV through your fingers. You should just turn it off, you know—but you just have to see what's going to happen.

When he returned, he had on a T-shirt and ripped jeans. "Had to go out to the car to get these," he said, as if that had been some kind of accomplishment.

I was almost done with my cereal by then. I took a last bite, clanked the bowl down in the sink, and said, "Okay. Why are you here?"

He was standing across the table from me, a place he had stood a hundred times before. We had lived in this house for a year before we'd gotten engaged, then for another year after that. I'd bought the house myself, but I'd never lived here without him until he left me. Now he was back, and as wrong as it felt, it looked kind of right. Since he'd been gone, the house had felt like a photograph with a person cut out of it.

He took a deep breath. "I want to get to know the baby," he said. "I want to come home."

I was going to say, "This isn't your home anymore." The words were right in front of me, and the decision was as easy as saying them. I didn't feel conflicted or troubled. This was just how it was. But in the tiny moment before I could speak, as I was drawing in the breath I needed, a car alarm went off on the street, and Maxie started to cry.

It was my cue to get moving, so I moved. I was in Maxie's room in a flash. I always ran to her when she woke up from sleeping. I felt a need to reassure her that I'd always come quickly when called. She was in the crib, on her back, red-faced and pissed, and I gathered her up and said little things like "Hey, Maxie girl. It's okay. It's okay now." I sat in the rocker, and we started to nurse. Only then did Dean show up in the room.

"That was your car alarm, wasn't it?" I asked.

He nodded.

"Do they serve any purpose besides waking babies?"

But he was lost. He was staring at Maxie. She was nursing away, doing her thing. And he was transfixed.

She was a sight to see. She was seven months now, and she'd turned into a Gerber baby. Her little head was covered in fine yellow hair. She could sit up, and eat handfuls of spaghetti, and she was just starting to work on crawling—all kinds of amazing baby tricks. I was in awe of her. She'd more than doubled in size since she was born. And she was a big flirt. I kept waiting for her to stop nursing to smile at Dean, but she didn't.

"She looks just like you," he said, and came a little closer. "She doesn't look anything at all like me." Then he gave me a big smile and said, "Lucky for her."

I didn't say anything.

After a while, he said, "The whole breast-feeding thing's pretty cool."

If he meant "cool" to mean "Isn't human biology amazing?" I had grappled with that concept and already moved on. If he meant "cool" to mean that he found the whole thing titillating, I did not want to know.

"Don't talk to me about breast-feeding," I said.

He had lots of questions about Maxie. Was she healthy? Was she a good eater? Did she take after me or him? How much did she weigh? How tall was she? Did she have any teeth? Did we nurse in public?

Most of his questions were ones that only a person who knew nothing about babies would ask. He wanted to know if she was walking yet, if she ever ate junk food, if she called me "Mama." I found it hard not to answer him in an increasingly irritated tone of voice. If he had been here, he would know all this. And about an encyclopedia's worth more.

Dean wanted to hold her, but I made him sit on the sofa first. He suddenly seemed like the kind of person who might actually drop her. I put a blanket down on his lap, mostly because his jeans looked like they hadn't been washed since before he left, and I set her down in his arms. We all waited to see what would happen, Maxie included. I had an impulse to get my camera but decided against it. How would I put a picture like that in an album? *"Here is a photo of you just born. This is you eating your first solid food. And this is the first time your daddy ever set eyes on you."* Of all the moments in Maxie's life to capture on film, this one, I decided, might actually rank dead last. And then the matter was truly settled because she decided to cry. She could always tell when she was in the care of someone who had no skills. I snatched her away from him and started on the bobbling moves I'd perfected over the months.

"You really know what you're doing," Dean said.

"It's not hard to know more than you," I said.

"Can I skip out on the insults? Can I come back later?"

"Yes, it appears that you can," I said.

"I'm trying to be nice, here," he said.

It was almost impossible for me to make even neutral comments sound anything other than acidly sarcastic. I said, "I just don't see what nice has to do with anything."

Dean threw up his hands as if to say, *I give up*. Then he asked if he could take a shower. I wanted to tell him he didn't get one until I got one—and make him take Maxie until I had soaked in the tub for an hour, shaved every errant hair on my body, read *Country Home,* and painted my toenails. If he was going to show up here, he could make himself useful. But there was no way I was leaving Maxie with him unsupervised. She might survive, but she'd sure be miserable. And there was no reason to make her suffer just to punish him.

He went off to run the water, but turned back at the door.

"Oh," he said. "I saw a neighbor of yours when I went out to my car and he said to tell you hello."

I froze. "What neighbor?"

"A guy. I don't know. He was walking his dog."

And then I had to know: "Was it the first time you went out to your car, or the second time?"

Dean thought about it for a minute. Finally, he decided. "The first time."

"So you chatted with him in your boxers?"

He nodded as if that hadn't occurred to him before. He watched my face for a second. "Do I know him?"

"No," I said. "You don't know him. But he knows you."

It was all I could do not to drop the baby and sprint down the street to explain. But I held still. I didn't want to do anything that would invite any questions from Dean. I wanted a bit of privacy on that subject.

Dean went to shower, and I snuck over to Gardner's, but there was no answer. I stood on the porch for a long time, hoping he might come to the door or possibly drive up in his truck, but I gave up when Maxie started to get antsy. It would have been a great time to call Meredith, but I didn't have my cell phone with me, and she never answered anymore, anyway. I decided to walk to Claudia's. I needed somewhere to go that was not my house.

"He's not still there, is he?" Claudia said when I told her.

"He is. He's there, and he's probably smoking on my porch by now."

"Well, you have to get rid of him."

"I was going to."

"But?"

"But then he said this thing about wanting to spend time with his daughter. And I started to worry. Is it wrong of me to deprive Maxie of time with her own father just because I am mad at him?"

"Maxie doesn't care."

"She doesn't care now, but she'll care when she's older."

"So he can visit when she's older."

"What I mean is, if he's in the mood to bond, shouldn't I let him bond?"

That one stumped her. Usually, Claudia was a great source for unequivocal opinions. But this time, I made a good case for confusion. On the one hand, he was her father. But it appeared that he was going to be a substandard father. And the standard wasn't even that great.

"Does he seem apologetic?" she asked.

"No," I said. "Not really. He seems to be acting like nothing happened. Like yesterday I was pregnant, and today I have a seven-month-old baby. It makes me want to light him on fire."

"Don't let him stay at your house," Claudia advised.

"I'll try not to," I said.

But I did let him stay. He played the "daughter" card. He wanted to see her. He couldn't afford a hotel. He would sleep on the couch and do all the dishes. He missed me. He wanted to help out. I meant to say no, but I said, "Fine. Don't get comfortable."

The truth is, once people have been in your heart, it's hard to keep them out. It was like he had a key. Even though I hated him, I couldn't seem to treat him like other people. It made me worry for my mother, who had her date with my father tonight.

I had stopped by Gardner's house on the way home from Claudia's, but still no answer. I thought I might try again later, but once I'd agreed to let Dean stay, I wasn't quite sure how I'd explain that to Gardner. Later came and went, and I didn't wind up going over.

And that's how it happened. That's how Dean and I started living together again. I had pictured him coming home at least a thousand times. I had pictured it with me angry and him sorry, with me crying and him crying, with me pouting and him begging, with me silent and him hysterical. But in every scenario, there was always a great release—a dramatic fight that climaxed in some kind of understanding about what we were all about.

What we were doing now was the opposite of every scene I'd come up with. There was no great fight. I was angrier than I'd ever imagined. And that anger never seemed to go away. It just buzzed around me, through every conversation. In my fantasies of his return, I always imagined he would find something to say to me that would really work—that would explain the whole thing so well that it would put everything to rest. But he not only didn't have a perfect explanation, he had no explanation. Even one night, after he'd been back for three days, when I asked him point-blank, all he could come up with was a shrug.

"I panicked," he said.

When I used to want him to come home, I had thought it would be a relief to have things back to "normal." I had thought our little family would feel finally complete, but instead, now, three days in, it felt like Maxie and I had a houseguest. I had thought Dean would help me with the baby, as a partner, and that I'd get some relief. Instead, my mother stopped visiting, because, first, she thought I should put him to work, and, second, she couldn't stand to see him. He wasn't working. He had quit his job when he left town, and now he was back with his band, so he just lounged around all day, strumming his guitar. He did do some dishes a couple of times, so that was something. But none of his cleaning outweighed the mess he made.

And I would never, even for a second, leave him with Maxie. He didn't trust himself, and I trusted him even less. My mother could do babies. She had raised three, and even if her skills were a little rusty, they came back pretty quickly.

"Just like riding a bicycle," she'd said proudly after she got her first newborn diaper on Maxie.

"Without the wheels or the bell," I'd added.

And I, who had never even done any babysitting, had just finished seven months of a total-immersion baby course. Like a language class, but with screaming.

But then here was Dean, showing up, thinking he could pass the test without having studied. Without having read the books or even having come to class. It was like he skipped an entire semester, showed up for the final, and expected an A.

Well, he wasn't getting an A from me. He'd be lucky to pass. I watched him. He'd hold Maxie out in front of him and stare at her blankly while she cried. Or he'd set her down on the sofa with some pillows around her, as if there were anything safe about doing that. All of it made me even angrier. He had no skills and, worse than that, he had no intuition.

Was this how he'd been parented? Had he never been held? Even if his mother had been the type to leave a baby crying in a crib, surely his gaggle of nannies had found some way to compensate. I couldn't believe that he really had no instinct to pick Maxie up. I could only come to the conclusion that he wasn't trying. That he was communicating to me, in some important way, that he not only wasn't trained for the job but didn't want it, either.

Maybe Maxie was picking up on my feelings. They say babies are very intuitive. She didn't seem to like him much. When I'd hand her to him, most often she'd cry. Sometimes she'd stay quiet for a few minutes. But then she'd make a decision: *Nope. Not working.* It was as if Dean had missed a crucial window. If we'd both been bumbling idiots together, she'd have been patient with us. What choice would she have had? But now she had a choice. And she chose me. Or my mother. Or even our mail lady, who stopped to chat occasionally while we were out on the porch swing. Anybody but Dean.

28

Somehow, on the fourth day after he'd come home, which was coincidentally Halloween night, Dean climbed into bed with me. He must have used every ounce of stealth he possessed, because I slept as lightly as a hummingbird, and I didn't even know he was there. When I woke, he said, "Boo," and started kissing my neck, in the darkness, in our bed, the very bed where Maxie had been conceived, the very bed where he'd done the very same thing a hundred times before. He kissed me until, against my better judgment, I started kissing him back. It was like listening to an old song that I'd heard over and over. It took me back. It was dark, and Dean was here, and Maxie was asleep. With the exception of his new whiskers, it was like my old life again, before everything changed.

Then he was pressing up against me, and then he was taking off my shirt, and his shirt, and then we were there all tangled up. And even though I was convinced for weeks and weeks after Maxie was born that I would never, ever have sex with anyone again, and even though my poor nipples had been to hell and back, and even though I wasn't sure that there was anything at all I even liked about Dean, and even though it seemed clear that I was neglecting the possibility of a much better man just a few houses down, we slept together.

And it was good. I was so reluctant, and it took him so long to change my mind, that by the time he did, I was melted. It also had the added allure of being something slightly against the rules. I was barely speaking to him, so getting naked and rolling around was definitely a little naughty. But what can I say? He talked me into it.

My poor body had been so neglected. My whole existence, in fact, had been so devoid of any kind of pleasure—even the basic ones like a good meal or a long hot shower or a good night's sleep, not to mention something as fancy as an orgasm—that I was an easy mark. My brain said no, but my body said *yes, please,* and the next thing I knew, it was five in the morning, Maxie was up, and I was throwing him out of the bed.

"Out," I said, pushing him, still asleep, toward the edge with my feet.

I went in to nurse Maxie back down, and as I sat in the rocker, I decided many things: One, I felt like I was cheating on Gardner. Two, it was crazy that I felt that way, given that Dean had been The One up until not so long ago. And, three, sex with Dean was not going to happen again.

But it did happen again. Even though I told him not to, he climbed into my bed the next night and the next. And I was too wounded and too lonesome and too hungry for any kind of tenderness to say no. Every morning, I told Dean it wasn't going to happen again, and every night, it did. He'd barely been back a week, and we'd already established the pattern of the nighttime booty call.

But I stayed mad. Those quiet moments in the darkness of our old bed had almost nothing to do with what happened in the house during the day. I stayed furious, and he stayed stupidly nonchalant, and that was our new life.

I wondered if this was what it meant to have sex like a man—or like a bad man. My emotions and my actions were not running parallel. I was also too mad to worry about whether or not he was having a good time. It felt strangely powerful, though somehow I figured it probably wasn't.

I never did talk to Gardner about Dean coming back. Once I'd slept with Dean, I didn't even know what I would say to Gardner. And that night of dancing faded from my memory very quickly. In a matter of days, it became almost like something I'd seen on TV. So I started checking for him out the window before I set out with Maxie, making sure the coast was clear. I never walked in the direction of his house. I went a little bit into hiding.

I even lied about it to my mother, who had not been by my house since the night Dean showed up. She claimed she'd been very busy.

"Do not let him near your bedroom," she told me on a call from her cell phone.

"Mother!" I said.

"You know that saying 'Why buy the cow when you can have the milk for free?' "

"You don't want him to buy me!" I said. "Even I don't want him to buy me!"

"I just don't want him using you for sex."

"What if I use *him* for sex?"

"Women never use men for sex, sweetheart," she said, as if she were having to explain to me, at this late date, that the Earth revolved around the Sun.

"The point is," she continued, "that you should keep your milk for yourself."

"Let's not talk about this," I said.

"Fine," she said.

She not only didn't want Dean in my bed, she didn't want him in my house. She said he had shown his true colors. "Don't try to pretend like nothing happened," she told me. "Because it did."

"I'm not sure that you're one to lecture about getting back involved with exes," I said. It was too mean, but it was true.

"Your father and I had one meal. He is not living in my house."

She had a point, but he'd also told me on the phone the day after that she'd stuck out her hand at the end of the night, but he'd taken it and kissed it instead. "She liked it," he said. "I can always tell when she likes things."

My mother was pulling up to the St. Regis, so she had to go. I was left wondering if she had been so absent because she didn't like what I was doing with Dean or because she didn't want to have to talk about what she was doing with my father.

It begged the question of what, in fact, I *was* doing with Dean. And the answer was pretty simple: Playing house. Giving myself all the things I'd wanted and then had taken away. We had the baby, and the house, and the sex. I wasn't sure I still wanted those things, but it just felt good to have them. And feeling good was hard to resist.

And then one day, when he'd been back in my life barely over a week, he told me he had some news. His mother was coming to visit. And he was picking her up at the airport in two hours.

"She's coming here?" I said.

"She wants to meet Maxie," he said.

"She's coming today?" I said.

"I meant to tell you earlier," he said.

"But?"

"But I forgot."

"Your terrifying mother is coming here, and you forgot to tell me?"

"It's not a big deal," he said. "She just wants to see Maxie."

It was a big deal. And Dean knew it was. Which is why he hadn't told me. Things were bad enough for him, having to be contrite all day and accept his position as the Bad Man, deserving of every hostile comment I could toss his way. I'm sure he didn't want to make it worse by saying he'd allowed, or, God forbid, even invited his mother to come down here.

I decided not to clean the house for her this time. But then, with two hours left till impact, I panicked and changed my mind. I spent the next 118 minutes in a fit of adrenaline. I wore Maxie in the carrier and swept, vacuumed, wiped down surfaces, carried out recycling, sprayed the bathroom with nontoxic cleaner, folded the laundry (which included several pairs of Dean's boxers), and made the bed. Maxie was fussy and wanted me to take her out, but I just kept cleaning, and eventually, she fell in step with the project. I was sweeping the front porch when Dean and his mother drove up.

As Dean's mother strode up the front walk in a tan Chanel pantsuit, I felt like a cornered animal. I had planned to change, and to get Maxie changed, but there wasn't enough time to do everything, and it seemed that a messy house was worse than a messy me. In retrospect, that might have been the wrong call. Or there might not have been a right call.

"Jenny," Dean's mother said as she took in my sweaty face and my tangly hair. "Motherhood seems to be tuckering you out."

"Yes, ma'am," I said.

"Don't call me that, dear," she said. "I'm not your grandmother."

I looked at Dean while his mother moved on to Maxie.

"Hello, baby," she said. And then to me, "What happened to her face?"

It took me a minute to understand. Then I got it. The birthmark. It was so faint, I hadn't thought about it since the hospital. And not one person had ever mentioned it. "It's a birthmark," I said.

"It looks like she was kicked by a mule."

"The doctor says it will be gone by kindergarten."

"Kindergarten!" she shouted, startling Maxie and not even noticing. And then to Dean, as if he were her personal assistant, "Remind me to talk to Sloane Wilcox's cosmetic surgeon when I get back to the City."

I looked at Dean again. She had to be joking.

But Dean just had a look on his face like he was actually making a mental note about Sloane Wilcox's cosmetic surgeon.

"It's going to disappear on its own," I said again.

"She can't spend the first five years of her life with a face like that," she said. And then she leaned in to Maxie, "Can you, Elizabeth?"

I looked over at Dean again for some kind of reality check. Nothing. He might as well have been her personal assistant.

"It's Maxie," I said. "We call her Maxie."

"Dean's father and I don't care for the name Maxie," she said. "We are calling her Elizabeth."

I thought about saying to Dean's mother, "That's not for you to decide," but then I thought better of it. I had already lost this battle. I had already lost every battle I would ever have with Dean's mother.

Dean's mother cooed at Maxie a little longer, and then she was ready to hold her. I unsnapped her from the carrier and we made the transfer. Maxie instantly started to cry.

"How old is she now?" Dean's mother asked, over the crying.

"Seven months," I said. Maxie was wailing, and her face was so red and scrunched up, she looked like a completely different baby.

"She's an emotional little thing, isn't she?" Dean's mother said.

She was holding her sideways, and Maxie's arm was kind of twisted behind her. "She likes to be a bit more vertical," I said, but Mrs. Murphy didn't seem to hear me. She didn't seem to hear Maxie, either, and she started talking to Dean about her plans for the weekend, all the while shaking Maxie as if she'd never once held a baby. Maxie continued to protest, and her cries got more insistent, and I actually had to hook my arms behind my back to keep from snatching her away.

And then Dean's mother was ready to go. She handed Maxie

back, straightened her pantsuit, blew us both a kiss, and headed down the walk to wait for Dean to take her to the hotel. I gave him a look that said *That's it?* He shrugged and trailed after her. She hadn't even stepped inside the house.

Over the next two days, she spent about an hour a day with Maxie. The rest of the time, according to Dean, she was shopping and making conference calls about a charity auction she was co-chairing. She took some pictures, and she brought Maxie all kinds of gifts. A hooded towel in the shape of an elephant, a sparkly toy cell phone, a rug for her room with butterflies on it, pink-check overalls, tiny barrettes with bows, a doll with blinking eyes, a stuffed bunny rabbit, a *Curious George* book, a veritable closet of smocked lace dresses that Maxie would never wear, and a tiny pair of infant-size roller skates.

"They're decorative," she said about the skates, as if I might try to put Maxie in them and set her sailing down the driveway.

On her last day, she sat, knees together, on the couch while I held Maxie and Dean unwrapped yet another stack of gifts. "Pick up all this wrapping," she said to Dean. "And then take the baby for a walk. Jenny and I want to have girl talk."

Dean looked terrified at the prospect of being alone with Maxie. He had never taken her anywhere. I didn't even let him be alone with her inside the house. But there was no way out. He would endure fifteen minutes with Maxie, and I would stay and endure girl talk.

As we strapped Maxie in, I imagined her telepathically pleading for me not to let him take her. I said to Dean, "Stick to the sidewalk. Don't go beyond this block. Look both ways before crossing the street. Sing anything by Ella Fitzgerald if she starts to fuss. And if you lose control, come back."

He stared at me with wide eyes, as if he were trying to memorize my list. He said, "Sidewalk. Both ways. Ella Fitzgerald."

And then I was alone with his mother. "You've done a wonderful job with her," she said, touching my hand. "She seems very healthy and happy."

"Thank you," I said.

"Just don't let her get fat," she said.

"I'll try not to," I said.

"Because nobody likes a fat child," she said.

"Right," I said.

"Now, let me share something with you." She leaned toward me. "Dean is going to propose."

"Again?" I said. The first time he'd proposed, we'd been in love. Now we were more like housemates. Who didn't like each other. But who had sex. And a child. At this point, it was more like a collage than a picture. Lots of little pieces and some glue.

"Again." She watched for my reaction. "And I hope you'll accept his offer."

"Marriage?" I said.

She gave a quick sigh, as if to urge me to catch up. Yes. Marriage. Hadn't she just said that? "I believe he has a new ring. For a new start."

"Oh," I said.

"I can imagine you may still be feeling hurt from"—she hesitated—"how things have been in recent months. But let me help you with your decision. Dean's father and I are not comfortable with the current arrangement. We want our granddaughter to grow up in a normal household. If you marry Dean, his father and I will continue to support your little family financially. You won't have to work. Elizabeth will go to private school. You'll have family vacations every year and her college tuition will be paid for." She looked around the room, letting her eyes rest, at last, on a paint-by-numbers scene of a little Japanese bridge in a forest of dogwoods. "If you choose not to marry him," she continued, "we will not."

And that was our girl talk. She'd offered to pay me to marry her son, and we were done. It must have been unpalatable for their son to run around fathering children out of wedlock. I could see why she might like to make things more legal. Dean came back minutes later with a screaming Maxie. I nursed her while his mother averted her gaze as if I were picking my nose. And then we were standing next to Dean's car saying our good-byes.

"It was lovely to see you," Dean's mother said as she air-kissed me. And then to Maxie, "Be a good girl, Elizabeth." She sat herself in the passenger seat of Dean's car, and he drove her off toward the airport.

I stood by the road for a while, waving Maxie's hand. Then Maxie and I decided to go to the grocery store. We needed something to do. She fussed on the drive over, and the store itself was a zoo—people knocking over displays, kids running everywhere, a cashier repeating, "Frank, can I get the master key?" on the loudspeaker, over and over—and after a half hour or so there, I felt like we were a ticking bomb.

And then we ran into Gardner. He was holding the Sunday paper. I, in contrast, was laden with Maxie in the baby carrier and a cart piled high with eggs, bacon, Cheerios, yogurt, bags of nuts, organic milk, several different kinds of chocolate, and everything else that had struck my fancy as we'd snaked through the store. He came up while I was waiting in a checkout line that was so long it curved into the floral section, and he touched my arm and then backed away a little, looking shy.

"Hey," he said.

"Hey!" I said with great enthusiasm. "How are you?"

It was awkward. We'd had such a great date just a week and a half ago. Normal people would be at least scheduling another one by now. Normal people would be riding a pleasant escalator of anticipation. The two of us had a spark, even in line at the grocery store.

But we also had Dean. In my house. On my sofa.

"I saw your boyfriend came back," he said.

"Dean," I offered.

He nodded. "Dean."

"He's sleeping on the sofa," I said, which was not untrue.

"Oh," he said.

"He says he wants to get to know Maxie."

"Sure," he said.

"I was going to kick him out," I said, "but then I wasn't sure it was the right thing."

He nodded. There was a pause.

The grocery line had been inching forward. Gardner had been lingering near me, but Maxie and I were now getting funneled between the magazine racks, and Gardner, who would have been cutting in line, had to hang back.

When Maxie and I made it to the register, I turned to greet the checker, and when I turned back, Gardner was gone.

And just then, Maxie hit her breaking point. She started to wail, loudly enough that people in other aisles turned to look at us. I pulled her out of the carrier and held her in my arms. I waited while the checker rang up item after item: black bean soup, apples, bread, chocolate bars. One slow scan after another. And the bagging guy had disappeared just as we got there, so all the food was just piling up in an eddy at the end of the counter. I started trying to bag the stuff one-handed with Maxie crying on my shoulder. The man in line behind us gave me the hairy eyeball, as if to say *Why can't you shut that baby up?*

I started to think about leaving all the groceries and just walking out of the store, but then, as I dropped a can of tomatoes, Gardner came back, stepped in, and took care of everything for me with ease. He'd gone through the express lane and come back around. I paid and let him put the bags in our cart. Then I followed him out of the store, all the while trying to come up with something to say, sing about, or do to calm my crying Maxie.

The minute we stepped out the sliding door, she quieted right down. It was breezy and cloudy out, and the air even felt soothing to me. I pointed Gardner toward the car. He loaded everything in for me, and I held Maxie and watched.

He shut the back door and turned to me. He was done. It was time for him to go.

This was the moment when I could have said something to encourage him to wait for me. But a current was drifting me back to my old life, and it felt so strong that all I could do at that moment was float, watching my possibilities recede on the shore. I didn't say anything. Not even "Thank you."

And then he was leaning in, pressing his face up against my cheek. I guess he hadn't shaved, because he felt sandpapery, and then I felt his mouth against my neck right below my ear. He pulled back and touched Maxie's cheek with the backs of his fingers. Then he left. And I knew that I wouldn't have to work so hard to avoid seeing him after that.

29

On the drive home, I panicked at the idea that I'd just let him walk away. I took a few deep breaths and tried to talk myself down.

Because life with Dean was my life. It was the life I'd had for five years. It was easy and familiar. And though Gardner was tempting, he was undoubtedly—as everyone is—better in theory than in practice. It was true that Gardner was thoughtful and helpful and very, very—frighteningly—good with babies. It was true that Gardner was taller and better-looking and better-adjusted than Dean. It was true that Gardner always made me feel, whether it was the case or not, that I was his favorite person—while Dean often had the opposite effect. Gardner had great taste in houses and architecture. Gardner was actually good at his chosen profession. Gardner could banter. He was nurturing. He seemed stable.

But. I had no guarantee that Gardner truly was all these things. He was courting me, that much was clear, and men can be very different when they're courting than when they're in the thick of things. Dean and I were certainly not still courting. It wasn't fair to compare.

Dean and I had had a lot of good times. I tried now to see his abandoning me as no big deal. He'd panicked. It had been too much, and now he was sorry. There was no need to punish him forever. Or myself, for that matter. Or Maxie.

And Maxie figured heavily in my thoughts. Because it seemed wrong to deprive her of her father if he was ready to make a commitment and be with us. Would it be fair of me to throw away a man with a biological connection to Maxie? He wasn't here when he should have been, but he was here now. And he said he wanted to be. So he didn't have a way with kids. He'd get it eventually.

"You're disappointed in love," Claudia said in the reptile house one afternoon. "It's easier to be with Dean and have low expectations than to have high expectations of your neighbor and be let down."

"You're calling me a chicken?"

"It's understandable. At least you know what Dean's flaws are."

I nodded. That was right. I could recite Dean's flaws backward and forward, list them in Spanish, set them to music. Gardner's were a little harder to spot. Did I want to gamble the future on a set of flaws I'd never even seen?

"So Dean won't disappoint you," she said. "But he probably won't make you very happy, either."

"Actually," I said, "he'll find a way to disappoint me."

But with Dean in my bed every night for over a week, I wasn't entirely sure that Claudia was right. Dean and Maxie and I fell into a nice little rhythm. We were, after all, a family. And I started to wonder if this could be the way things were supposed to be.

Until Maxie decided she had something to say about that. She started waking up more at night. She'd been waking up some before, of course, but those earlier wake-ups were just appetizers for the full meal of sleep deprivation she was about to serve up. Within two weeks of Dean moving back into my house, Maxie was waking up every single hour, all night long.

I was hell-bent against letting her cry. She was too sweet to be left alone in a dark crib crying. It just wasn't going to happen. So I had no choice. Each time she woke up, I went in and nursed her back to sleep. I put her to bed at 7:00. She woke at 7:30. I went in, nursed her, and had her back in the crib asleep by 8:00. Then she woke at 8:30. I went in, nursed her, and had her back down by 9:00. Each time, I thought she'd be down for at least a couple of hours. But she wasn't. She woke, roughly, at 9:30, 10:30, 11:30, 12:30, 1:30, 2:30, 3:30, 4:30, and 5:30, and was up for the day at 6:30. And each time, when I heard her cry, I trudged in and nursed her. Somewhere in the middle of the night, I decided she was teething. I gave her some infants' Tylenol, but it had no effect.

Needless to say, I did not find time for sex with Dean in between. Wisely, he stayed on the couch and did not even try to find me.

The next morning, I was so tired, my eyes felt like they had been sandblasted.

"I'm going to need you to take her," I said to Dean.

"How about," he countered, "I make you a big pot of coffee?"

"No coffee," I said. "I'm nursing."

He glanced around, stalling for time.

"Just take her on a walk or something. You know how to walk, don't you?"

"I'm not sure."

I thawed out a four-ounce bottle of pumped milk from the freezer. I gave him a bag of Cheerios and some rattle toys. He clutched them while I carried Maxie and pulled the stroller out the front door. Outside, I showed him how to strap her into the stroller. I brought the diaper bag, though I told him not to worry about changing her unless it was a real avalanche.

"What do I do then?" he said.

"Just wipe her up," I said, using cheerfulness to convey how self-explanatory it all was. Then I remembered. "But only front to back. Okay? Only one direction: front to back. And use a clean wipe for each wipe. You don't want to give her a urinary tract infection."

"Right," he said. "That would be bad."

I gave them a push down the sidewalk and then turned and headed to bed. Nothing short of fatigue this extreme could have prompted me to entrust Maxie to him. But I told myself this was good. He'd never become a competent caretaker if I didn't give him a chance.

In bed, I closed my eyes. Ten minutes later, he was back, and Maxie was crying. I hauled myself out of bed. At least he had tried. We'd try again tomorrow, unless Maxie slept well.

But she didn't sleep well. She woke every hour, all night long, for days and days, with no end in sight. I called the nurse at our pediatrician's, who suggested early teething, maybe, and then infants' Tylenol.

"I tried Tylenol," I said, my voice a little too loud. "I tried it, and it didn't help."

"Maybe," the nurse offered, "she's just wakeful."

It was all I could do not to shout, "You think?" Instead, I thanked her and resolved to wait Maxie out. Eventually she'd get so tired, she'd have to sleep.

But not before I turned into a sleep junkie. Sleep became all I thought about. It was the only thing in the world, besides maybe Maxie, that mattered.

But I still had to do all the things I had to do. I had to nurse, rock, love, and amuse Maxie during the day. I had to feed us all somehow and get things like laundry done. I had to stay awake. Every night, I felt amazed that I'd made it through the day.

And then a series of things happened.

Gardner decided to stop in to say hello. Dean was at band practice, and then he had a gig, and I'd had Maxie, who was in a foul mood, since 5:30 in the morning. It was almost noon, and she did not want to nap. She wanted to stay awake and cry. After a while, I started to cry, too.

And that's how Gardner found us: in a living room piled high with Dean's dirty clothes, rumpled blankets, copies of *Rolling Stone,* and bowls of dried mac 'n' cheese. Maxie wailing, and me sunken-eyed and hunched over, listlessly doing a shuffle dance, though I'd lost all hope awhile back that it might soothe her.

He was not expecting to see us this way. "What's going on?" he said, taking Maxie, who settled as soon as she hit his arms.

I told him—how she wouldn't sleep, how Dean couldn't take care of her, how my mother was practicing a policy of tough love and insisting that Dean learn how to take responsibility. He listened, and rocked Maxie back and forth.

"How long has it been since you've had more than two consecutive hours of sleep?" he said, frowning over me like a doctor—or like an ex-doctor.

"I can't remember," I said.

"Okay," he said. He nudged me down onto the couch and set Maxie on my lap. I started nursing her and watched him move around the room. He gathered up toys, the diaper bag, some of Maxie's clothes off the top of a clean laundry pile, several bags of my milk from the freezer. He filled up some grocery sacks with all the stuff and left with them.

When he got back, Maxie was looking sleepy.

"I'm taking her to my house," he said. "And you are going to bed." He told me he would come get me when it was time to get up.

I didn't resist. I didn't even put up a pretense. I just stood up, handed Maxie to him like a bag of sand, and shuffled off to the bedroom. I closed the door and set the clock radio to a static station. There, with white noise cushioning my ears, I slept and slept.

When I woke up, it was nighttime. I charged out into the living room with one eye squinted like Popeye's. There, on the sofa, in a room that had been radically tidied, was my mother, sitting with Maxie in her arms.

"What are you doing here?"

"Your sweet neighbor called me. He thought you might need some help."

"I thought you were practicing tough love with me."

"He was too charming to resist."

It turned out he had watched Maxie at his place while my mom came over to my house and did dishes and cleaned up. Then Gardner had needed to leave, so my mother took over with Maxie.

"He sure is cute," my mother said.

She stayed with me while I ate canned soup and then put Maxie down. Then we sat on the sofa together while she stroked my hair.

"I'm sinking," I told her.

"I'm not going to let you sink, baby," she said.

"Can we call an end to tough love now?"

"We can," she said, "if you'll admit I'm right."

"About what?"

"About Dean."

"I admit you're right," I said. And then, "What am I admitting?"

"That he's not helpful," she said.

Maxie woke up again before my mother left, and she waited for me while I put her back down. When I came out, I clipped the monitor to my sweatpants and followed her out to the car.

"Where is he, anyway?" she asked of Dean.

"They have a gig tonight."

"You know what I think of him," she said.

"Mom," I said. "It's complicated."

"I'm sure it is, sweetheart," she said. "But please trust me when I tell you that no man at all is better than a bad man like that."

I gave her a sweet kiss. "Spoken like a woman who is dating her ex-husband."

30

The next morning, when I heard a knock at the door, I hoped it would be Gardner. Maxie and I tiptoed past a motionless Dean on the sofa and turned the knob. But it wasn't Gardner—it was my dad.

"Hey, sunshine," he said. "I found that picture."

I stepped out onto the porch and closed the door behind me, careful not to let him see Dean. I hadn't told my dad that he was back. I didn't think he would be pleased. Maxie was in her carrier, pleasant and a bit sleepy. I ushered my dad over to the porch swing, and the three of us sat and swung.

"What picture?" I said.

"Our crabbing picture," he said. "Don't you remember me telling your boyfriend about it?"

"He's not my boyfriend," I said as my father handed the picture over.

"I had to go through seven shoe boxes to find that baby," my father said, hovering over my shoulder as I looked.

And there we were. The two of us holding a gallon bucket of blue crabs. My dad in red swim trunks and a wrinkled fishing hat, me in a green one-piece and sneakers. I had zinc oxide on my nose. I must have been about seven. I was missing a tooth. And my father, God bless him, looked young and dashing and just as proud as he'd described.

"I told you I had it somewhere!" he said.

"That's quite a picture," I said.

"Keep it," he said. "It's yours. Pull it out next time you can't remember any good times with your dear old dad."

I pretended to punch him in the arm. "Okay," I said.

I had been concealing from my dad the fact that Dean was back, for some time. I had actually pretended to be sick so he wouldn't stop by the house. I didn't want to see his reaction to the news. But after all that trouble, I'd been found out.

"I hear the bum who knocked you up has returned," he said.

"Mom told you?"

He nodded. "Last night. Just before she told me not to call her anymore."

I winced for him. "Ouch."

"She feels we're not a good match," he said. "Actually, she feels we never were."

"I'm sorry," I said.

"I'm amazed she said yes even once," he said.

"You're very charming," I said.

"And handsome," he added.

"And she really loved you," I said.

He nodded and looked down at his hands. "She really did."

"How are you doing?" I asked.

"Well," he said, "there are some wrong things you'll do in your life that you'll never get to make right."

"Is that what you were trying to do?"

"I was just trying to spend some time with her."

"She's quite a lady," I said.

He nodded. "I didn't deserve her."

We swung for a bit. Maxie was in a porch-swing trance, and my dad seemed lulled by the motion, too. But after a little while, he stood and pulled a folded-up envelope out of his pocket.

"I have something else for you," he said, handing me the envelope.

"What's this?" I said.

"It's just something I thought you could use," he said. I started to rip it open, but he told me to wait until he was gone. Then he said not to return it to him, because he'd give it right back to me. "Stick it in a drawer," he said, "if you don't want it."

"Okay," I said.

He blew a kiss to Maxie and then kissed me on the forehead. "Hey, kiddo," he said. "Here's the best advice I'll ever give you: Lose the idiot on the sofa."

When he drove away, I waved Maxie's hand after him.

And it was there, standing at the curb and waving after my dad, saying, "Bye, bye," in my baby falsetto, that I noticed a yellow sign out in front of Gardner's house. A sign that said FOR SALE.

I walked over and took a look, as if it might say something different upon closer inspection. But there it was. He had listed it with a realtor named Randy, who had his picture on the sign with a cartoon bubble coming from his mouth that said CALL ME! I knocked on Gardner's door, but there was no answer.

"You should make an appointment to see it," Claudia said that afternoon as I paced the neighborhood on my cell phone, Maxie napping in the carrier.

"I'm not going to do that," I said.

"Why not?"

"Because I've never been inside his house," I said. "It would be weird to see it without him."

"You've never been inside his house?"

"He didn't want me to see it until it was finished," I said.

"And now he's gone and you'll never get the chance."

"He's not gone," I said. "He's just not here."

"Important distinction," Claudia said.

That evening, Dean came home from band practice and said, "Your mother has agreed to babysit tonight and I'm taking you out to dinner to celebrate."

"Celebrate what?"

"The fact that we have a babysitter."

I was reluctant to leave Maxie, but my mother showed up a few minutes after he said it and practically shoved me out the door. I put my cell phone on vibrate, tucked it into my jeans pocket, and made her promise to call me at Maxie's slightest discomfort.

"Dean wants to talk," she said. "So go, have a good talk, and I'll be here when you get back."

Dean took me to the restaurant where we'd first met. The candlelight, the wine, it all pointed in one direction. And Dean seemed a bit nervous. He delivered a monologue from appetizers to dessert.

"I haven't been nearly as good to you as I should have. I know it must have really hurt you for me to leave the way I did. I want to be a better person and I believe that I can be. I think you must still love me, deep down, or you wouldn't have let me stay with you and Maxie. And what about Maxie? I mean, she's six months old now—"

"Eight," I said. "She's eight months old."

"Eight," he went on. "And we're great in bed, aren't we? I mean, we are really good together in bed. And though you're angry, and though you've been pretty mean to me lately, I want to stick it out. Because I believe in us."

I took a big slug of wine. The table where we'd first met was across the room. I tried to picture the two of us sitting there, him in that crazy leather jacket he used to wear, me lighting up at the thought that it was me he'd come to find. There we were. Younger, sweeter, far less tired, just starting up this whole story.

"Jenny," Dean said, pulling me back. "I've really changed."

"People don't change, Dean," I said.

He was the flip side of the letter he'd written me all those months ago. One proclamation after another about love and commitment and family. And though I knew what he was working up to asking me, I wasn't sure what I was going to say. I had no clear feelings to point me in a direction. My insides were foggy. I waited for some kind of sign.

At one point, I interrupted him to ask, "What about the girl from your office?"

It was the first mention of her in a long time, and Dean gave me a look like I was really spoiling the moment. Then he shrugged and said, "Well. She's dead."

I nodded, and he revved up again.

And then, after the desserts were gone and a waiter had scraped the crumbs off our table, the ring came out. I'd been waiting for it all night, curious to see how he'd do it, curious to see what this new one would look like. What does an "I'm sorry I left you just before you gave birth to our baby" re-engagement ring look like? His parents must have paid for it. It had to be something fancy, to impress me, to wield whatever kind of persuasive power expensive jewelry was supposed to have. I expected some kind of huge, blinding diamond.

So when he put his closed hand on the table and said, "I have something I want to ask you," I felt a little jolt. I was being proposed to! He was giving me a ring. A new ring, a new start. I reached out and touched his fingers, resolved to get him a clipper for those hangnails, and opened his hand. And there in his palm was the ring he gave me the last time.

"What's this?" I said.

"It's an engagement ring," he said.

"It's the ring you gave me last time!"

"You loved this ring!" he said.

"Did you take it out of my jewelry box?"

Dean shrugged like it was no big deal.

The ring was still lying there in his hand. I didn't touch it.

"What happened to the other ring?" I demanded.

"What other ring?"

"The new ring you got me. 'For a new start.' "

"My mother told you about that."

"Where is that ring?"

He looked down and started pushing the old ring around on the tablecloth with his pointer finger.

I asked again.

He said, "I won't tell you, because I don't think you'll understand."

"I can guarantee you I won't understand."

We stared at each other.

And then he didn't even have to say it. "Band equipment," I said.

He looked away, and I knew I was right. I stood up, picked up my ring, and walked out of the restaurant with it in my fist.

Dean threw some money on the table and scrambled after me. "It was an emergency!" he said. "Like ten things broke all at once! I was going to get it back! I'm sorry! Everybody was counting on me!"

I was outside on the sidewalk, striding so fast he had to bob behind me like a dog to keep up. "Jenny!" he was pleading. "It wasn't about you! I'm sorry! I didn't use it all! I put the rest in a savings account. For Maxie! Jenny, please!"

After a few more steps, I stopped and faced him. "Dean," I said steadily. "I don't believe in you anymore."

I started walking again and left him behind on the sidewalk.

I made it a few more blocks by myself before I faltered and admitted that it was somewhat scary to be a woman alone in midtown at this hour. I started making my way back to the restaurant, figuring I'd call a cab.

When I got there, Dean was waiting for me outside, smoking. We didn't say anything to each other, but I walked with him to his car and got in. We drove toward home, listening to something rattle in the way-back. Maybe a tambourine.

My eyes rested on the FOR SALE sign at Gardner's as we pulled up to my house. "You might want to back into the driveway," I said to Dean, "so you can load up your stuff."

"I'll just park in the street," he said.

We sat in silence a minute after the engine cut out. This was it. This was the end. Then a question came to my mind that I had to ask.

"Dean," I said. "Did you come back because your parents threatened to stop giving you money?"

Dean didn't say anything, just fingered the steering wheel. It was answer enough for me.

"Dean," I said. "You are never going to be happy."

Those could have been my last words to Dean. Inside, I sat with my mother at the dinette and had a cup of tea while Dean carried loads of his stuff out to his car. He could hear everything we were saying, but what he heard or thought didn't really matter anymore.

"I didn't know he was going to propose!" my mother yelped. "I thought he was going to break up with you. He sounded so morose when he called me."

"Nope," I said. "He proposed."

"Well," she said. "I never would have agreed to babysit if I'd known he was going to do that."

When I told her he'd offered me the ring that I already had, she said, "You should have sold it the day he left." When I told her about the other ring, she guessed it right away: "Band equipment!" And when I told her about his parents cutting him off, she offered to paint the word *bastard* on the door of his car with some fingernail polish she had in her purse.

Just as she said that, Dean dropped a pair of maracas, which hit the ground with an amazing clatter. And it was that noise that inspired the last words that I actually ever said to Dean, which were as follows: "If you wake up the baby, I will skin you alive."

He let himself out after that. When my mother got up to pour us each a second cup of tea, she stood at the counter and said, "Sugar, did your daddy come by and give you something recently?"

"Yes," I said, and told her about the crabbing photo.

"Did he give you anything else?"

And then I remembered. "Yes! An envelope."

"Have you opened it?"

"Not yet."

"Do you know where it is?"

I thought it might be in the pocket of the pants I was wearing earlier. "Although," I said, "I may have put them in the washer."

My mother touched my arm in a gesture of urgency. "With the envelope in the pocket?"

I tried to think. "Maybe?"

"Do you know what's in that envelope, sweetie?"

I shook my head.

"It's a check for more money than the down payment on your house."

I raced over to the washer and pawed through the wet laundry. Then I went into my room and found those pants on my bed. And in them, a check for more money than I'd ever seen. And a note that said "There's more where this came from. Love from your grouchy old dad." My mother followed me into my room and saw me staring at it.

I looked up. "You knew about this?"

She nodded. "He asked me if I thought it was a good idea."

"What about his bootstraps?" I asked, more to myself than anything.

"He's just always had a soft spot for you."

At that moment, I couldn't fathom why my mother wouldn't want to be with him.

I imagined my dad as a nine-year-old, already too tall for his grade, standing by the side of the road in his button-down shirt as his father took off down the highway. I could see the way he'd set his book bag down against his Buster Browns and stick his thumb out, the way he'd refuse to watch his father go. I could see the wind blowing his home-cut hair, the morning sunlight on his freckles, the way he'd make eye contact with every driver who passed him by to make sure they knew he saw them. When someone finally stopped, he'd sit politely in the passenger seat and focus his eyes out the window. Plenty of mornings, though, he wound up walking to school and being punished for tardiness.

I felt tears in my eyes. "Were you even tempted at all to start seeing him again?" I asked.

She shook her head.

"Why not?" I asked.

"He just didn't turn out to be the person I'd hoped for," she said. She came over and hugged me as those tears spilled over. "But he did turn out to be a good daddy to you."

31

The next morning, I called Randy the realtor and made an appointment to see Gardner's house.

"How is that going to help you?" my mother asked. "He's gone."

"He's not gone," I said. "We just don't know where he is."

She crossed her arms.

"I just want to see it," I said.

She said she wanted to see it, too, and asked if she could come.

I told her no.

Randy the realtor had a lot of energy. I hadn't told him that I was just a neighbor, and he was ready to sell, sell, sell that house. "This one's a heartbreaker," he said as he rattled his key in the front door. "It's too good to be true."

Randy talked a blue streak as I walked through the sunny rooms. "The owner rewired and replumbed everything. He refinished the floors, retiled the kitchen and bath, and installed new fixtures."

"He sounds pretty handy," I said.

"Oh," he said, "you wouldn't believe it." Then he winked and added, "And gorgeous!"

I was pleased to see that Gardner's taste in furniture was entirely acceptable: mission-style, with a slightly Asian influence. It didn't look decorator-y. It just looked like he had some nice things. And it was very clean.

"If I have questions about the house," I said, "can I contact the owner directly?"

Randy laughed at that one. "No, dear. That's not how it's done."

The kitchen had brushed stainless fixtures, white cabinets, and muted-yellow walls. A window over the sink opened out onto a bougainvillea bush blooming bright pink. I gasped when I saw it.

"Yep," Randy said. "This baby's not going to stay on the market long."

We'd covered the inside, and as we headed out the back door, Randy said, "Now, this can be torn down."

We stepped out onto a back porch. A huge back porch the size of two rooms. On one side, there was a long dining table, and on the other, there were wicker sofas and chairs around a coffee table. Ceiling fans up top, painted gray floor. It was just like my grandparents' porch. I put my hand up to my mouth.

"It's brand-new," Randy went on, watching my expression. "And the craftsmanship is top-notch." He rapped on the screen frame with his knuckles. "But most people would rather have the yard space."

At the end of our tour, Randy gave me the hard sell. "I don't want to rush you. But if you like it, I'd move on it. This house has been shown eleven times in two days. It's going to go fast."

"I am very interested in the house," I said. "But I'd like you to ask the owner a question for me."

Randy got out a pen.

But I couldn't think of anything. I had hoped to come up with a coded message about old houses that would sound like a real estate question to Randy but sound like "I've kicked Dean out! Please call me!" to Gardner. And at that point, I'd wasted so much of Randy's time, and he'd worked so hard to get me to buy the house, that I couldn't bring myself to come clean and just ask him for Gardner's contact information. In the end, I just waved after Randy as he drove off, and then I walked back home, where my mother was watching Maxie.

"I can't believe you didn't let me come," she said as I walked in the door.

I took Maxie from her.

"How was it?" she asked.

"It was a heartbreaker," I said.

That night, after Maxie was down, I wrote Gardner a letter. Actually, I wrote him about ten letters, throwing them away and starting over almost as soon as I'd finished. But a letter seemed like the right idea. He'd have to go through his mail eventually.

In the end, I had a draft I was pretty pleased with:

Dear Gardner,

I want to let you know that I asked Dean to leave, mostly because I realized that after everything, amazingly, I didn't like his personality.

Now Maxie and I are back to our real life, which has a hole in it with you gone.

We miss you. I miss you.

Love,
Jenny

P.S. I went to see your house with your realtor. I really liked it. Especially the porch. That is one hell of a porch.

I called Claudia and read it to her. It had taken her an hour to put Nikki to bed. Now she was detoxing with a half-empty carton of Häagen-Dazs.

"Where's the part that says, 'It turns out I'm in love with you'?" she asked.

"Come on," I said.

"Because that might be a good thing to add."

"It's there," I said. "It's between the lines."

"You're trying to be subtle?"

"The point is," I said, "what if he doesn't like me?"

"It's not possible that he doesn't like you," Claudia said. "A man does not build a porch for a woman he doesn't like."

"But his feelings could have changed."

"Why?"

"Because of Dean. Because I disappointed him."

"You didn't tell him you slept with Dean, did you?"

"No," I said.

"Then, if anything," she said, "not being able to have you made him want you all the more."

"And then he went to Dallas."

"To lick his wounded heart."

"Or because he had no reason to stay."

"Look," Claudia said. "This is a time to be brave! Send him a long letter! Let him know how you feel! Lay it all out!"

Inspired, I started again and wrote unrestricted confessions of love for four pages.

But then I sent the short letter. Largely because I got the two envelopes mixed up.

"He builds you a porch and all you can muster for him is two paragraphs?" Claudia wanted to know.

"It was an accident!"

She was caught up in the details. "But why did you mail it, anyway, when you could just walk over and drop it through his slot?"

"In case he's forwarding his mail."

She nodded. She liked my thinking. "We won't let him get away," she said.

"Right," I said. I was just going to have to watch and wait. The house already had a SOLD sign. He'd have to come back eventually—if for no other reason than to get his stuff. And Maxie and I would be at the window, waiting.

But he didn't come back. Not his truck, not a moving truck, not even the folks who were buying the house. The SOLD sign stayed up, and nothing happened down there. I watched from the window, and the porch swing, and the front yard. Maxie and I walked the block and watched. I peered in his windows whenever Maxie and I went by. Nothing.

And in the meantime, I got on with things. I cleaned up the house and removed all evidence of Dean, including a coffee can of cigarette butts I found on the back steps.

I wrote a long letter of thanks to my father, accepting his check and telling him that I would wait to deposit it until my funds had truly run out. I told him I thought I could stretch that money out for a year. I told him that, because of him, I could stay home with Maxie, and that it was the best, kindest thing he'd ever done for me. I told him I was grateful.

Maxie started sleeping through the night a few days after Dean left. Maybe she hadn't liked the disruption of having him around. Or maybe she hadn't liked Dean himself. But with him out of the house, she was giving me five hours a night of uninterrupted sleep. I would have taken eight, or ten, or fifteen, but five would do just fine.

I didn't go out to the garage after Gardner was gone, and I didn't do much about starting the shop. It suddenly seemed like too much. I didn't have time to run a shop, not really. The idea of a shop was one thing, but the reality of running a business was quite another. I wasn't sure what I had been thinking.

And then I got a phone call from Meredith. She wanted to bring me my motherhood gift.

"What motherhood gift?" I asked.

"The one I have for you," she said, as if I should be on top of it. "When are you free?" she asked.

"I'm always free," I said, trying not to sound bitter. "Just hangin' out with Maxie."

It had been months since I'd seen Meredith. And even though I knew that most women dropped all their friends for a while when they fell in love, and even though I was guilty myself of having done it to Meredith when I first met Dean, I was still feeling very injured. The part of me that wanted to defend her said that she couldn't have done things differently. She'd never really been in love before. It was bound to hit her like a Mack truck. But the part that wanted to defend me couldn't deny that her timing had been very bad.

We arranged for her to meet me the next day at my house during one of Maxie's naps. That way, we could talk a little and catch up before I was back on duty and distracted.

When she showed up, she was carrying flowers and a red box with a white ribbon. She looked prettier than I remembered, and she burst into tears as soon as I opened the door.

"I'm sorry!" she said, and wouldn't let go of our hug.

"No big deal," I said.

"I'm a bad friend," she said.

"You fell in love," I said. "It happens."

We sat down on the sofa.

"How is your Dr. Blandon, anyway?" I asked.

"How is *your* Dr. Blandon?" she countered.

I glanced over at him, belly-up on a dining room chair. "Still handsome," I said.

"Mine, too," she said, looking a little flushed.

"You guys are still happy?"

"Still happy," she said.

"I thought maybe you called because you'd dumped him."

"No," she said, straightening a little. "I called because I missed you."

"Okay," I said.

"Actually," she said, "we're getting married."

And then it was hard for me to be mad. She told me that after he asked her, the only person she wanted to call was me, but she wasn't sure if we were even on speaking terms anymore, she'd been so neglectful. She wanted me to be her maid of honor.

"Who are the other bridesmaids?" I asked.

"Just you," she said. And then she started to cry again.

I shushed her and made her give me all the details of everything. I insisted on feeling nothing but happiness for her, and did not let myself think, even for a minute, about my own crappy, loveless situation.

We hadn't yet exhausted the wedding topic when Meredith checked her watch and said, "How long before Maxie wakes up?"

I said, "Maybe half an hour, if we're lucky."

"Let's do the present, then," Meredith said. "I just want you to be able to concentrate." She handed the box to me.

Inside was a sterling-silver charm bracelet laden with charms. "Wow," I said as I lifted it up and started to examine them.

"They're vintage," Meredith said. "I've been collecting them ever since you got pregnant."

Some of them were baby charms: a little carriage with moving wheels, a baby bootie, a bottle, a rattle, a teddy bear, a pacifier, a stork with a bundle dangling from its beak. Lots were about love: a box of candy that said YOU'RE SWEET, a fan with blades that said I LUV U, a letter that said SEALED WITH A KISS, and a lock in the shape of a heart. Others were charms Meredith knew I would just like: a sombrero, a boot spur, a seal with a ball on its nose, a little perfume bottle with a removable top, an hourglass with sand inside, a dragonfly.

I flipped through the charms again and again, feeling the weight of them. Meredith looked very proud. "They're mostly from the forties and fifties," she said. "I thought Maxie might like playing with it. And I also thought, when she grew up, you might give it to her to wear when she has her own kids."

We put it on my arm, and I shook it a little. It made a great rattle. "Maxie's going to love it," I said.

"I'm really sorry I disappeared," Meredith said.

"It's okay," I said.

After Maxie woke up, we sat out in the backyard on a blanket. Maxie found a spot in the grass and tried to eat every fallen pecan she could get her hands on. Meredith tried to bond, poking at her and saying things like "Hey there, little person." Meredith told me she'd quit her job at the antiques shop because our boss had refused to hire anyone to replace me, and Meredith was starting to lose her hair under the strain of doing two jobs at once.

"Literally," Meredith said. "You should have seen the shower drain."

"Why wouldn't she hire anybody?"

Meredith just looked at the sky and shook her head.

"What are you going to do now?" I asked.

"I have an offer from the guy at that place on Nineteenth Street."

"Do you want to work for him?"

"No," Meredith said. "But I do want to work."

We brainstormed other people we knew who might be looking for help before I had the idea I should have had months before.

"Come with me," I said, picking Maxie up and heading toward the garage.

Meredith followed me inside. "Oh, my God."

She wanted to know what had happened, so I gave her the whole story of Gardner and how I'd let him get away. That got us off the topic of my idea for a while, and Maxie started to fuss after we'd been in the garage too long, so Meredith came with us on a little stroll around the neighborhood.

"You have to find him!" she said.

"I can't," I said.

"He must have a cell phone," she said.

"But I don't have the number. I never even had the number to his house."

"Can't you call information and find his parents?"

"I tried that," I said. "There are sixty-five John Gardners in the Dallas–Fort Worth area."

"Let's start calling them!" Meredith said.

I shook my head. "I sent him a letter. He knows how I feel. If he wants to see me, he'll find me."

"You're so Zen," she said with admiration.

"I'm just tired," I said, which brought me back to my idea. "Why don't we go into business together?"

I was too tired to run a shop. But I wasn't too tired to help out. We could be partners, fifty-fifty. Meredith could run it and do the books, and I could own and maintain the building. We could both hit estate and garage sales on the weekends. "It's perfect," I said.

Meredith did not hesitate. "We'll need a sign," she said, and she knew just the guy to make one. And we were in business.

The next weekend, we started hitting the estate sales to build up inventory. Maxie came along in her stroller, wearing a fabulous polka-dot wool cap and mouthing frozen sticks of organic yogurt. We found great stuff right off the bat: a red rotary telephone (that worked!), a box of random old family snapshots, a rocking chair, a collection of paint-by-numbers art, an old fish crate, a red tricycle.

Meredith kept strict records of everything, and we marked it all up to ridiculous prices. Meredith believed that boutique prices made things seem more valuable. She believed in the power of display. She said you had to create an atmosphere of swankiness. And so she did just that. She played swing music around the clock. She put zinnias in antique planters out front. She made curtains out of bark-cloth tropicals. She kept the doors open and fresh air breezing through—winter in Houston, unlike summer, is a great time for fresh air. Everything felt bright and clean and fabulous. Even my mother walked in and said, "Adorable."

Christmas came and went. Maxie wore a little Santa suit on the big day, and she got a set of books from my mother, a little cart to push around from me, and a burnt-orange T-shirt with the University of Texas longhorn on it from my dad. "That's Bevo," he said to Maxie, who grinned her four new teeth at him. He tried again. "Say Be-vo."

"Mih-meh," Maxie said.

"Be-vo," my dad said. "Bevo."

The shop opened for business the first week in January, and three weeks after that, the local paper sent a reporter and photographer to do a piece on us. We were a little bit of a phenomenon.

And in all that time, I didn't hear from Gardner. But it was okay. Sort of.

32

I kept busy. My dad took to coming by on Sunday evenings for a little visit with Maxie. My mom still came by at least once a day. I saw Claudia every Saturday at the zoo, and also many evenings for walks around the neighborhood. We still had our once-a-week mommy group. I signed Maxie up for a baby gymnastics class and made some new mommy friends that way.

Meredith worked at the shop all day, and Maxie and I helped out when we could. It was great to see so much of Meredith. Dr. Blandon, who followed Meredith around like paparazzi, became the shop cat and took to sleeping near her by the register in a leopard-fur-lined kitty basket with the word PURR-FECTION written on it in rhinestones. Meredith was so pleased to have him back in her life that she couldn't resist buying him gifts. He even had a rhinestone collar to match his bed.

"He's the Liberace of cats," I said.

"Yeah," Meredith admitted.

Meredith also had trouble resisting gifts for Maxie. Sunglasses. Mittens. Tiny flip-flops.

"You turned out to be a big softy," I said.

"No," Meredith said. "Just a shopaholic."

I met the people who'd bought Gardner's house. Their names were David and Irma, and they tore down the screen porch before they moved in because they really preferred the yard space.

Claudia started dating someone—a contractor who had done some work on her house. He was ten years younger than she was, and had lots of nieces and nephews. He was wanting to start a family, and Claudia wasn't sure if he was coming on too strong. But he'd brought her lemonade one night, and they'd sipped it on the porch. Things, she said, were looking up.

We didn't talk about Gardner much. Then, one day at the zoo, near the porcupine hut, I said, "I think there's really no hope." Maxie was asleep in the stroller, and that fact was suddenly seeming clear to me.

"There has to be some hope," she said.

"It's been over two months," I said. "If he were going to call me, he'd have done it by now."

"Maybe he didn't get your letter," she said. "He seems to be bad with mail."

"No one's that bad with mail," I said.

"Maybe he's just waiting for the right moment."

Some kids were throwing popcorn at the porcupines, hoping they might come a little closer for a snack.

"The right moment," I said, my voice rising a little, "came and went. And I'm getting tired of spending my whole life waiting for men to come back to me."

"You're not saying he's anything like Dean."

"I'm just saying I wish I didn't care."

"Then stop caring."

"I'm trying!" I almost shouted.

Claudia shielded her face with her hands. "Okay," she said.

"You're too cheerful about love to talk to," I said. "You're not heartbroken."

"Are you heartbroken?" she asked.

"You know what I am?" I said. "I'm stupid."

We were at the elephants now. One of the babies had a bandage on its leg.

"Clearly, he's moved on," I said. "So I'll just have to move on, too."

"Okay," Claudia said.

And so it was decided. I was moving on. Again. Just as soon as I got home from the zoo.

The truth was, I felt a little ashamed for fixating on Gardner. Happily Ever After seemed like a lot to expect out of life. I was lucky in about a thousand ways, and it seemed adolescent and a little selfish to think that I would never be happy without this one thing, this one person. I thought about all the people in the world who had it way worse than I did. I thought, in particular, about the girl from the plane crash, the one who had set all these changes in motion. I couldn't even remember her name anymore. But I kept thinking about her face on my refrigerator, and how she had watched me for weeks before Dean took her with him the night he left. If she could talk to me now, I felt sure she'd tell me to be more grateful. For Maxie. For my shop. For good things like ice cream and hot showers and sunlight, but also even for things like traffic and mosquitoes and heartbreak. I knew if she were back on my fridge, gazing at me like she used to, she'd be telling me not to let one wrong thing ruin everything else.

And then, one night, very late, there was a knock at my door. I went to the window in my pajamas to see who it was, hoping that it might be Gardner in the same way, when I was in sixth grade, I used to hope to bump into Patrick Swayze at the mall. In that impossible, crazy, expectant way that girls sometimes hope for love.

And it turns out it was Gardner.

I paused for a minute behind the door, trying to decide if I should go fix my hair or put on some lipstick. And just as I had decided that, yes, it was worth the extra time to go to my room and get a little gussied, my hand put itself on the doorknob.

I opened the door. He was leaning into the doorframe, as if he might have tried to push through if I hadn't answered. The collar on his blue oxford wasn't buttoned, and he hadn't shaved that day. My eyes lingered for a second on his neck, and his Adam's apple, and the way the edge of that shirt collar was slightly frayed from rubbing against his five o'clock shadow.

"Were you asleep?" he asked.

I remembered that mouth. "No," I said.

He had an envelope in his hand. He held it out to me. It was my letter. "I just found this," he said. Things seemed to move in slow motion. A moth batted itself against the porch light.

And at that moment, Maxie woke up and started to cry.

I took hold of his shirt and pulled him over the threshold, then let go to move toward Maxie's room. "I'm sorry," I said, nodding him toward the sofa.

He waved me toward her room. "I'll just hang out here."

It took about half an hour to get her back down, but given how badly I wanted to get back out to the living room, it should have taken far longer. When I came back out, Gardner had Dr. Blandon in his lap. The letter was on the coffee table.

"How is it possible you just found that letter now?" I said. "It's been months."

"It's kind of a long story," he said.

I sat down across from him in a chair, crossed my arms over my chest, and said, "Let's hear it."

"It got stuck in a catalog," he said. "And then it wound up in a stack of mail that I forgot to bring back from my folks' house when I left Dallas."

"When did you leave Dallas?" I asked.

"A while back," he said. "I sold this house, and then flipped the money to buy another one I had my eye on. So I came back and got to work."

"You've been in Houston all this time?"

"Yep," he said. "About six blocks away, actually."

"Why didn't you come to see me?" I said.

"I thought your old boyfriend was here."

"But he wasn't!" I said.

"But I didn't know that."

"And you weren't going to bother to find out?"

Gardner looked around the room. "I just had the feeling he wasn't going anywhere."

"You gave up on me too easily," I said.

"It looks like I did."

We stared at each other.

"So." Gardner continued with his story. "My dad has a knack for woodworking, and he came down last weekend to help me with some built-in bookshelves. And my mom sent down this stack of junk mail I'd forgotten up at their place—which I teased her about, because who saves junk mail?"

I nodded.

Gardner nodded. "And just now, I was about to throw the whole bag in the paper bin at the recycling center, when I dropped it, and everything fell out, and your letter landed on my shoe."

"My letter landed on your shoe?"

"It did."

"Okay," I said.

"And so I read it," he said.

"Okay," I said.

"And then I left that pile of recycling on the sidewalk and drove straight here," he said.

"From the recycling center?"

He nodded. "I think I ran four stop signs, but it may have been five."

I moved over to sit next to him on the sofa. Dr. Blandon moved from Gardner's lap to mine.

"You ran stop signs to come find me?"

"I did," he said.

"I didn't think you were coming back," I said.

"I didn't, either," he said.

"But here you are."

"Here I am."

And that's when he put his hand in my hair and pulled me into the kind of kiss you can only get from a man who's run at least four stop signs to see you. And I was grateful. For all the things that had brought me to this moment, and for every single thing that would follow.

Acknowledgments

At St. John's School in Houston, where I spent kindergarten through twelfth grade, Juliet Emery, Shirley Greene, Peggy Paulus, Jane Eiffler, Dwight Raulston, Tony Sirignano, and John Zammito stand out in my memory for their encouragement.

At Vassar College, Leslie Dick, Eamon Grennan, and Karen Robertson were all terrific mentors. And Beverly Coyle: my dear friend and champion. I will never forget the day she said, "Whatever it is that writers have, you have it."

At the University of Houston's Creative Writing Program, I was lucky to work with Rosellen Brown, Daniel Stern, Ellen Currie, Kathleen Cambor, and Mary Gaitskill, and to spend a weekend hanging out with Rick Moody.

I am also grateful to the good friends and family who have helped me, encouraged me, and made me feel proud of myself: Nicole Holbert, Sam Nichols, Mike Maggart, Marion Carter, Philip Alter, Elizabeth Hughes-Salazar, Rebecca Wolff, Jebbie Scoggins, Faye Robeson, Herman and Mimi Detering, Edward Davis, Ingrid and Al Center, and Yetta Center. Thanks to Tom Gould for being a great reader, to Allison Schapker for her writing encouragement, to Lucy Chambers for her Cliffs Notes on the publishing industry, to Hillary Harmon for her publicity help, and to Emily Kemper for laughing so hard while she was reading the manuscript that at first I thought she was crying. I also want to thank Kathleen Woodberry for my fantastic website.

Many thanks also to friends who helped me with child care, child rearing, and generally surviving motherhood: Donna Holloran, Dr. Caroline Long, and Mary and Jeff Harper. Special thanks to Katherine Weber for taking countless baby-advice phone calls. I am grateful to my mommy group, as well—in particular, Jenny Nelson, Andrea Campbell, and Erika Locke, for many hours of Deep Thoughts about motherhood. I also owe a debt of gratitude to Helen T. Vietor.

And I don't even know how to start to thank the folks who made this book happen. Fellow novelist Vanessa Del Fabbro so graciously offered to read this novel, and then passed it along. Helen Breitwieser, my agent, has completely turned my writing life around by representing me, and I am in absolute awe of her savvy in every possible realm. She is also so sharp and funny that I get at least one belly laugh every time I talk to her. Laura Ford, my editor, is the kind of miracle reader whose comments make you want to sprint to the manuscript and get back to work, and whose patience, cheerfulness, and smarts made this experience nothing short of blissful. Many thanks also to Brian McLendon, Kate Blum, and all the folks in publicity who have given this book such amazing support. I am so grateful to Libby McGuire, Kim Hovey, Gina Centrello, Amy Edelman, Janet Wygal, Jennifer Hershey, Lynn Buckley, Dana Blanchette, and everybody at Random House/Ballantine. They have brought a level of enthusiasm and support to this book that I never even dared to hope for. I may well be the luckiest person ever.

And a special shout-out to my family. My sister Shelley Stein has been encouraging me to write since we were kids. In fact, she dared me to write this book. She is my most dogged supporter, and she waded through many drafts of this novel with mind-boggling tenacity and energy. Shelley's husband, Matt Stein, has also been a great source of encouragement. My other sister, Lizzie Pannill, is my go-to girl for romantic comedies of every sort, and I am so grateful to her for her sharp editing eye, general enthusiasm, and style tips. My mother, Deborah Detering, has always had far more confidence in me than I've had in myself, and is the person I must call first thing every morning to get my sea legs for the day. And my dad, William Pannill, is a riveting storyteller and a great connoisseur of the written word as well as a fountain of inspirational stories about writers who triumphed over rejection.

And last, I want to blow kisses to my own little family. My daughter, Anna, is the funniest, feistiest little three-year-old I know, and my baby son, Thomas, is a total dreamboat-in-the-making. They have both taught me more than I ever thought possible about love and how it works and why it matters. As has their daddy, Gordon. What can I say about you, Gordy? You're a wonder. And I do thank my lucky stars for you—every single day.

About the Author

KATHERINE CENTER graduated from Vassar College, where she won the Vassar College Fiction Prize, and the University of Houston, where she received the Delores Welder Mitchell fellowship and earned an M.A. in fiction. A former fiction co-editor for the literary journal *Gulf Coast,* she has also worked as a freelance writer and a writing teacher. She lives with her husband and two young children in Houston.